AN
OXFORD
ANOMALY

NORMAN RUSSELL

ROBERT HALE

First published in 2016 by
Robert Hale, an imprint of
The Crowood Press Ltd,
Ramsbury, Marlborough
Wiltshire SN8 2HR

www. crowood.com

www.halebooks.com

British Library Cataloguing-in-Publication Data
A catalogue record for this book is available from the
British Library.

ISBN 978 0 7198 1985 8

Typeset by Catherine

Printed and bound in India by Replika Press Pvt Ltd

CONTENTS

1

A MADWOMAN CURED

As THE COACHMAN urged on the horses through the driving rain, a vivid flash of lightning rent the sky. It was gone in a moment, but not before the occupant of the closed carriage had seen for the first time the square white bulk of Frampton Asylum, surrounded by its cloak of swirling, storm-tossed trees. The pitch dark of the countryside returned, and as they left the muddy track to rumble over a brick causeway, the expected crash of thunder seemed to shake the very foundations of the earth.

The coachman drew the horses to a halt in front of the house, and at the same moment a door opened, and two servants emerged, carrying umbrellas. They hurriedly opened the carriage door, and helped its occupant to alight.

'Can you bring the coachman inside, and give him something to eat and drink? He's soaked through to the skin.'

One of the servants motioned to the man to get down from the box, and all four hurried into the candle-lit hall of Frampton Asylum.

A gentleman in evening dress stood waiting for them. The servants ushered the coachman down a dim passageway towards the kitchen quarters of the house.

'Dr Oakshott?' asked the gentleman. 'I am Dr Samuel Critchley, the Chief Physician here. What a night you have chosen to come out this far from town! Come into my office. There's a good fire burning there.'

Critchley thought, so this is old Ambrose Littlemore's nephew. A nice enough fellow, quite smartly dressed, but rather nondescript. A beard or moustache would have improved his appearance, and taken people's eyes away from the bald patch developing on the crown of his head. In Critchley's view, not to make the best of one's appearance was a rather perverse form of affectation.

The office was a large, cheerful place, which to the man called Oakshott seemed part drawing room and part laboratory. The flickering firelight threw moving shadows on the glazed cabinets lining the walls, and glinted from a number of glass vessels and medical instruments laid out on a long table. There was also a phrenologist's model of the human head; Oakshott hoped that this was a relic of the past, not something that was used in the enlightened years of the late nineteenth century.

A desk calendar standing among the instruments showed the date: Monday, 6th August, 1894. It would surely be remembered as a particularly important day in the annals of the Littlemore family.

'We have not met before, Dr Oakshott,' said Dr Critchley, motioning his visitor to an armchair placed on one side of the fireplace.

He sat down opposite him, placed the tips of his fingers together, and regarded him with what seemed professional interest. To Oakshott he looked like a man very much at ease with himself, a man hovering between fifty and sixty, red-faced and clean shaven, with a shock of abundant greying hair.

'So you are a doctor?' he said. 'I expect, then, that you will be well acquainted with Miss Arabella Cathcart's mental condition on admission here in 1879—'

'Excuse me, sir,' said Oakshott. 'I am a Doctor of Civil Law.'

'I beg your pardon. Well, this establishment offers asylum and treatment for certain persons who have been declared clinically insane. We have manic depressives, mentally impaired epileptics, and some people who are criminally insane, but declared not responsible for their own actions, and so placed with us. These criminal lunatics are by law kept under restraint. And then we have a few sad cases of septic insanity—'

'Most interesting, Doctor,' said Oakshott. He desired to hear no more. His imagination conjured up visions of ropes, manacles and straightjackets. 'And what can you tell me about Miss Arabella Cathcart's history? Although I am here at the behest of my uncle, I am myself distantly related to that lady.'

'Miss Cathcart was brought here in 1879. To all outward appearances, she was sane, but in fact she was a victim of delusional spasm. She was then in her forties – much the same age, I should think, as you are now, Dr Oakshott. Miss Cathcart had become jealous of a neighbour's young daughter, a girl of twenty-two. She envied the girl's prettiness and liveliness, and also her intellectual ability. One day, while this girl was telling her about the latest book that she was reading, Miss Cathcart stabbed her in the back with a pair of scissors.'

Oakshott listened to the rain driving against the windows. He glanced at a painting above the fireplace, which showed Frampton House, a four-square, white stucco mansion raised in the last century. He imagined its unseen rooms and cells, and some of the demented people confined there. Had Uncle Ambrose's sister-in-law been a murderess?

'The young girl died?' Oakshott asked.

'Yes, she did. Arabella Cathcart ran away, and the girl bled to death. Murder, you see. Miss Cathcart at first could not see that what she had done was wrong,' Dr Critchley continued, 'and that, of course, is one of the hallmarks of criminal insanity. She was arrested, but found unfit to plead, and so the authorities ordered that she be brought here.'

'And she was confined to a cell?'

'Only for six months. After that, we deemed her ready for a course of treatment involving psychiatric counselling, drug therapy, and regular sessions of electrical stimulus to certain areas of the brain.'

Oakshott shuddered. He would be relieved to get Aunt Arabella, as he called her, out of this asylum and back to Hazelmere Castle. How had she survived being incarcerated in this sinister place for fifteen years?

'Well, Dr Oakshott, I am delighted to say that we effected a complete cure! Miss Cathcart is now able to take her place once more in society. It was a protracted business, but it was worth all those long years of perseverance. After you've taken some refreshment, I'll bring you the necessary certificates of discharge for you to deliver to Mr Ambrose Littlemore, your uncle. By then, Miss Cathcart will be ready to accompany you back to the bosom of her family.'

'These words that we use, physician and layman alike,' Oakshott asked, 'what do they really mean? Madness, insanity – what would you say, Doctor, were the hallmarks of the madman or madwoman? To me, they seem to be an acceptance of violence, even murder, as something justifiable. But not all insane persons are what one calls "raving mad".'

'No; no, indeed,' Dr Critchley replied. 'There are many clinically insane people who outwardly seem as normal as you or I. Let me give you an example. A colleague of mine at Bethlem Hospital in London had a patient who was convinced that he was the richest man in the world. He claimed that all the banks on earth belonged to him, so that his wealth ran into countless billions of pounds.'

'And what did he do?'

'Do? He did nothing. He was a highly respectable, educated man, a good conversationist, and a very able player of the violin. Visitors to Bethlem often mistook him for one of the doctors. But because of that single mental flaw – belief that he was the richest man in the world – he had to be confined for life.'

'Why? Surely he was merely an eccentric?'

'Oh no, Dr Oakshott. A man like that could, at any moment, decide to believe something else equally insane. He might take it into his head that all red-headed men, for instance, were instruments of the devil, and set out to rid the world of them. That kindly, educated gentleman could in theory become a mass murderer if he were ever to be released from the confines of an asylum. People like Miss Cathcart betray their madness through acts of violence, and so can be treated early, and in many cases are able to return to society fully cured, like your aunt.'

Dr Critchley permitted himself a little giggle. He was a man not at all averse to the occasional joke.

'When you return to Oxford, Dr Oakshott,' he said, 'keep a wary eye on some of your colleagues, especially those who seem most sane and sober. You never know!'

The rain gave no sign of abating on the journey back from the asylum. Oakshott lit the carriage lamp fixed to the doorjamb, blew out the wax vesta, and carefully returned it to the match box. By the dim light of the flickering candle, he covertly studied the woman sitting opposite him.

She had a long face, deeply etched with lines of suffering. Heavy eyelids all but veiled her dark eyes. Her hair, which he had seen when Dr Critchley had brought her down to the study, was steely grey; it was now hidden beneath the hood of her travelling cloak. She sat upright on the carriage seat, her hands folded in her lap.

The carriage toiled through the dark country lanes, the driver, now clad in borrowed oilskins, urging the horses on through the night. They clattered through a hamlet, and Oakshott heard a church clock striking. He slipped his watch from its fob-pocket, and by the light of the carriage lamp saw that it was ten o'clock.

Insanity … People had often remarked glibly that there was

insanity in the Littlemore family. It was not a pleasant thought, because the Oakshotts were closely related to the Littlemores. Dr Critchley, presumably, considered himself to be eminently sane and sober, but who knew what strange proclivities lurked dormant in the mind of a man who spent his time inserting electrodes into the exposed brains of his wretched patients?

Aunt Arabella seemed to have fallen asleep. Oakshott withdrew a wallet from an inner pocket of his coat, and extracted two photographs, which he studied by the feeble glimmer of the carriage lamp. One was a faded *carte-de-visite*, showing a beautiful auburn-haired girl of eighteen or so, her eyes fixed nervously on the camera lens. Oakshott's eyes brimmed with tears. Vivien … It had not been scissors in her case.

The second photograph was modern, taken only a few months previously. Here was a woman in her forties, handsome, assured of herself and of her position in society, looking fearlessly at the photographer, her face animated by a slightly sardonic smile. They had met several times at various meetings and seminars, and she had given him the photograph when it had apparently dawned upon her that she was in the process of attracting not only a kindred spirit, but a potential lover. He and Celia Lestrange were destined to be soul mates.

Oakshott had visited Vivien's grave earlier that year. The stone had begun to sink, and the glass dome placed over the white marble flowers had been shattered. All that beauty, all that vivacity, all that promise … No, it had not been scissors in Vivien's case. The visit had been quite unbearable. He would never go again.

'I don't think that I have had the pleasure of your acquaintance.'

The quiet tones of Miss Cathcart, who had not spoken to him since his arrival at Frampton Asylum, made Oakshott jump with shock. The voice was that of an educated lady, but even in those few words it seemed that she was mocking him. He hastily returned the photographs to his wallet, and slipped it back into his pocket.

'I am Jeremy Oakshott, the nephew of your brother-in-law, Mr Ambrose Littlemore,' he said.

'Hmm … And what do you do for a living, Mr Oakshott?'

'I am a Fellow of Jerusalem Hall, in Oxford.'

'A Fellow? Not much money there, then.'

Miss Cathcart closed her eyes, and seemed to go to sleep again. Jeremy Oakshott thought, either she really does not remember me, or she is pretending, for some odd purpose of her own. This woman, with her hand luggage on the seat beside her, had murdered a young girl. She had escaped with her life, but had paid in part for her crime by long years of confinement in a lunatic asylum. He would be glad to be rid of her, so that he could return to his familiar set of rooms in Jerusalem Hall. The revelation of what she had done awakened disturbing memories in his own past, memories that he had long striven to banish from his waking thoughts.

Did madness run in some families? Perhaps so. It was an unpleasant thought.

At last! They were entering familiar territory. Here was the village of Hadleigh, where his friends David and Mary McArthur lived. Another half hour, and they would enter the grounds of Hazelmere Castle.

'I'm unwilling to bring her from one confinement to another, Jeremy,' said Jeremy's Uncle Ambrose, 'but I shan't produce her when I'm having company here, until I think she's ready to face that ordeal. I've prepared a suite of rooms for her on the first floor, and engaged both a maid and a nurse to see to her wants. Your friend David McArthur will be in constant attendance.'

'Does Dr McArthur know about – about Aunt Arabella's past? You realize, of course, that *I* knew nothing about it?'

'Oh, yes. McArthur knows all. As the family physician, it was imperative that he was *au fait* with the whole matter. As for you

– well, I didn't think you needed to know about it. I told you that Arabella was suffering from "nervous affliction", and you seemed contented with that.'

Uncle Ambrose was sitting in his favourite chair in the castle dining chamber. Cadaverous? Was that the right word to describe him? Oakshott looked at his skull-like face, with its prominent cheekbones and sunken eyes, and decided that skeletal was a more apt description.

'Did Dr Critchley—'

'Yes, Uncle. He told me all about it. He volunteered the information, you know. I didn't ask for it.'

'You're a good fellow, Jeremy, and I think you know how highly I regard you. I wish you had embarked on a career that would have paid you a stipend – the Church, or the Army, you know. But there. You chose to be a scholar. Well, never mind.' He waved his hand around the room. 'One day, Jeremy, all this will be yours.'

Jeremy Oakshott dined and slept at the castle, and was relieved when the next morning proved to be warm and sunny. His uncle's coachman was ready with the second coach and fresh horses to convey him the five brisk miles back to Oxford. He marvelled at his own ability to behave quite normally in close proximity to a gentlewoman who had murdered a young girl by stabbing her in the back with a pair of scissors.

'Have you everything you want, Mr Sanders?'

The question was a mere formality, requiring the briefest of answers, so Mrs Tench was startled when her paying guest paused in the business of trimming his sparse, greying moustache to give her his full attention.

'If I had everything I wanted, Mrs Tench,' he said, 'I don't suppose I'd be staying here in Hadleigh. I'd be dining up at the castle with Mr Littlemore. If I had everything that I wanted, I'd be living in style at the Savoy…. Who knows? One of these days I may well be doing just that. As the old Romans used to say, Mrs

Tench, *Audentes fortuna iuvat*, which, as you may know, means, "Fortune favours the brave." So … There, I've lost track of what I was saying. What did you ask me?'

'I was just asking, sir, if you'd everything you wanted on that breakfast tray. There's bacon and eggs under that china cover, and the tea's fresh-brewed.'

Her guest managed a rather shamefaced smile.

'There, now, I've been wasting your time with my idle chat. I'll eat my breakfast straight away, before I get dressed. And then I'll – I'll go for a stroll down to the Bull, for a pick-me-up.'

Mrs Tench surveyed her paying guest as he moved away from the mirror over the mantelpiece and made his way to the little table standing in the bay window. Poor Mr Sanders! He couldn't be more than forty or so, but he moved like an old man. He'd been handsome once, no doubt of that; but his cheeks had fallen in, and his shoulders sagged like those of someone defeated by life. Still, he'd kept his fine shock of black hair. Later, he'd plaster it down with one of the creams or pomades that he kept on the dressing table.

There were little healed scars on his cheeks, where he'd obviously cut himself shaving. His right hand trembled, but it wasn't the onset of palsy. The room smelt of drink. It was drink that had loosened his tongue that morning. When he'd gone down to the Bull, she'd open the windows and air the place.

'He's been at the bottle again,' said Mrs Tench to her husband. 'He'll not last long if he goes on like that.'

Mr Tench bit into his bacon sandwich, and chewed silently for a minute. A wiry, sun-bronzed man in his sixties, he spent his days out of doors on his extensive smallholding. With another couple of acres, he could have called himself a farmer.

'They're all the same, Doris, these commercial travellers,' he said at last. 'They meet together in alehouses to listen to each other's stories, and then they get addicted to spirits, and beer, and such like. But he's no trouble, is he? Very polite, and quiet, like. Pays up on the nail every Friday.'

'I wonder why he mentioned Mr Littlemore, up at the castle. Do you think he knows him? Or maybe he's heard about Miss Cathcart being brought home. One of the other commercial travellers may have mentioned her. She's settled in well, from what I hear.'

'Very like,' said her husband.

'He tries to take care of himself,' Doris continued, 'but his clothes are getting threadbare. I offered to darn his socks, but he said he was going into Oxford tomorrow to – what did he say? To "replenish his wardrobe". But I don't think he will, Joe.'

'He's been more cheerful of late, Doris,' said Joe, 'so maybe there's some good fortune coming his way. I hope so. He won't make much money trying to sell cravats and waistcoats to little village tailors. Not round here, he won't.'

'The trouble is, he's not used to that kind of work. You can see that. Poor he may be, but he's obviously a gentleman.'

Joe Tench stood up, and wiped his mouth on his sleeve.

'It's ten past eight,' he said, 'time I was out in the fields. I'll be in at twelve. And don't worry about Mr Sanders. You know what they say: a creaking gate lasts longest. He'll be all right. And he pays up regular.'

Mr Sanders cupped his chin in his hands and looked in the mirror on his dressing table. With an almost violent act of imagination he could see his younger self staring back at him. But the younger self didn't have bloodshot eyes, or a feeble man's tremors about the temples. God! He was a wreck. Wrecked and ruined.

But he would go ahead with what he had sworn to do. Jeremy Oakshott was a clever man, who would be able to tease out the meaning that would lie unspoken behind the words that he would utter when they met. For Jeremy had, rather to his surprise, responded to the brief note that he had sent him. Perhaps for old times' sake?

He completed the trimming of his moustache, and dressed carefully in the dark blue town suit that he favoured. A tear on the left shoulder, that had revealed the lining, he had treated with black ink, so that the white didn't show. His shoes, though down-at-heel, he had polished to a brilliant shine. He would not have to stay here at Mrs Tench's much longer. He had £10 in half-sovereigns left. That should see him through to the end of his project.

It was time to subdue his recalcitrant hair. He picked up a jar of Hollerith's Citronella Pomade, and unscrewed the cap.

The village of Hadleigh, where the Tenches lived, lay in a wooded valley near Forest Hill, some five miles out of Oxford. It was a working village, with a smithy, an oil shop, a number of work-shops, and a livery stable. Most of the men were agricultural labourers, though a few, like Joe Tench, augmented their living from their own smallholdings. A public house, the Bull, lodged in two whitewashed cottages knocked into one, formed the social nucleus of the village.

The Tenches' boarding house looked on to the main street, at the end of which, situated discreetly behind high thorn hedges, was a huddle of detached stone-built houses known as Hob's Lane. One of these houses belonged to Hadleigh's physician, Dr David McArthur. He and his wife were early risers, who liked to take breakfast on a little wooden veranda overlooking the back garden.

'Those lilac bushes, Mary,' said Dr McArthur, 'are starting to exert themselves in a way I don't like. I'll root them up at the end of autumn, and plant something else.'

His wife, who was sitting opposite him at the cast-iron table, had finished her breakfast, and had turned her attention to the previous Friday's edition of *Jackson's Journal*, Oxford's daily paper.

'I agree about the lilacs,' said Mary McArthur, 'but everything else is very nice – those alliums, the foxglove (you could poison the whole village with those!) and the gypsophila – "baby's breath", they call it – which is charming in its way.'

Dr McArthur looked at his wife, and thought how lucky he had been to win her affection all those years ago in Edinburgh. He had entered the School of Medicine in 1869, and had been walking the wards at the old cramped and crowded Royal Infirmary, before it moved to the new building in Lauriston Place. Mary had been a nurse there.

'It's Monday today,' said Dr McArthur. 'So in two days' time—'

'It will be Wednesday.'

'Precisely. And I've contrived to leave the whole day free for our visit to Oxford. I've always wanted to hear Mrs Herbert Lestrange ever since you came back from visiting your sister in London in June last year, and told me about her lecture at the Queen's Hall. Did you meet her? Speak to her, I mean. I forget what you said she lectured on.'

'No, I didn't speak to her,' said Mary McArthur, 'but I was content merely to listen. I admire her for all that she has achieved since her husband's tragic death. By the way, Jeremy Oakshott was there. At the Queen's Hall, I mean. I gather that they've met more than once. I think he's falling for the lady!'

'Well, that wouldn't be a bad idea. Although he's unmarried, he's not really what I'd describe as an "old bachelor". And of course they're both experts on the Middle East, in their own particular fields.'

'That's what she lectured about, David. Her archaeological discoveries in Syria, among the old Crusader castles. She showed us some lantern slides that she had made of her work. She's been out there again, and apparently she's made some spectacular discoveries that will set academia in an uproar. That's the rumour, anyway.'

Dr McArthur took a card from his pocket, and read what was written on it aloud.

The Principal and Fellows of Jesus College, Oxford,
cordially invite you to a lecture entitled
'New Discoveries at Krak des Chevaliers'
to be given by
The Honourable Mrs Herbert Lestrange
In the college hall at 2.00 pm
On Wednesday, 5 September, 1894
RSVP

'Hugo Harper, the Principal of Jesus,' said Dr McArthur, 'is a man of very wide interests, though mathematics is his *forte*. He's in very poor health, and is not entirely loved by the Fellows, I'm afraid.'

'Why is that?'

'Well, Jesus is a Welsh college, and Harper wants to widen its remit, so to speak. But look! It's nearly nine. I must open the surgery. There's plenty for both of us to do before Wednesday.'

2

AT JERUSALEM HALL

JEREMY OAKSHOTT STEPPED out of the prison cell, and stood in the stone passage while the warder slammed the iron door shut, and locked it with one of the keys hanging in a bunch from his belt. The passage echoed with the savage noise: this particular warder believed in reminding the wretched inmates of HM Prison Oxford that they were not locked up there for the good of their health. They were an affront to him, to the good citizens of Oxford, and to society in general.

'You'll do no good with John Smith, Dr Oakshott,' said the warder. 'He's a bad 'un through and through. He's due out on the fifth, and I don't doubt that he'll be back here again in a week or two.'

'Well, Warder, you may be right. You *are* right. I don't suppose he ever reads the tracts I bring him. But we have to try, you know. Being a prison visitor can be rewarding occasionally. I expect I'll see you again towards the end of the month.'

The warder escorted his companion to the gate, and watched him as he walked away from the prison in the direction of Queen Street, which would take him back to Carfax and civilization. A nicely dressed gentleman, with thinning hair, and a slightly defeated way about him, but always pleasant and soft-spoken.

How old was he? No more than forty-five, though he somehow contrived to look older. He'd sometimes ask the most peculiar questions. 'What's it all about, Warder?' he'd say. Well, what was the answer to that?

Dr Oakshott was a good man – far too good to be wasting his time on riffraff like Smith. Robbery with violence was Smith's speciality. He'd left behind him a string of terrified shopkeepers and householders, all to a lesser or greater extent bludgeoned and battered into permanent ill health. Twice he had got away with murder by threatening witnesses. One day he'd go too far, and find himself on the gallows.

Jeremy Oakshott turned into Leper's Lane, a winding alley lying behind the great chapel of New College. Jerusalem Hall lay ahead of him, its crumbling ivy-covered gatehouse still supported by massive wooden buttresses erected after the collapse of its foundations in 1879. There was talk of rebuilding it, but nothing had come of it. Jerusalem Hall had been founded after the Second Crusade in 1153 by Sir Guy de Bolingbroke, in thanksgiving for the preservation of his life during the attack on Damascus.

Jerusalem Hall was a poor relative among the family of Oxford Colleges. The *bijou* hall and chapel were noted for their beauty, though later buildings, raised in the seventeenth and eighteenth centuries, were plain and nondescript. There was a Rector, ten Fellows, and an undergraduate body of forty young men. The Fellows received no stipend, and were expected to support themselves. It was a fulfilling but beggarly existence for a man like Oakshott, a man of what his friends politely called 'slender means'.

His companions in the senior common room openly sympathized with him over his poverty – all the dons knew each other too well for him to take offence – and one or two of them consoled him by bidding him remember that his enormously wealthy uncle, much advanced in years, and ailing, had no doubt left him all, and that one day he would be a very rich man.

Oakshott knew all about the Crusades, as he was a Reader in Mediaeval History, but that morning his mind was elsewhere. Could that man John Smith be redeemed from his life of violent crime long enough to be given employment of quite a different kind? Despite the warder's views – based, admittedly, on long and bitter experience of recidivists – Oakshott thought that something could be done with John Smith.

Tonson, the porter, emerged from the small lodge to greet him, and the man's cheerful 'Good afternoon, sir!' brought him out of his reverie. 'There's a letter for you, Dr Oakshott. It came just after you left for the gaol this morning.'

Oakshott took the letter, and crossed the quadrangle. It was small by Oxford College standards, no bigger than Mob Quad at Merton, and the great gothic windows of the hall and chapel seemed to have huddled together, as though jostling for position in the confined space.

Oakshott lived in a suite of rooms on the first landing of stair-case V. The book-lined walls of his study enclosed him in their welcome embrace. On his desk, placed in front of a window which gave him a view of an ancient flint wall above which rose the north side of New College Chapel, lay the as yet unfinished manu-script of the second volume of his great work on the Crusades.

Dr Jeremy Oakshott sat down at his desk, and opened the letter that Tonson had handed him. It was from Michael Sanders, confirming that he would call upon Dr Oakshott as agreed, on Tuesday morning at ten o'clock. Oakshott thought, he doesn't say what he wants. Money, certainly; but I've a feeling that there'll be more than that.

Michael Sanders…. Oakshott's mind took a regretful leave of the present, and visited a past world that he had long tried to forget. He was a boy again, enjoying a carefree childhood in Henning St Mary, where, as the son of the schoolmaster, he felt quite special and important. In his mind's eye he could see Wellington Lodge, where Michael had lived with his parents, and across the upper ward of the Herefordshire village, facing Ford Lane, he saw Priory House, an imposing villa set in spacious walled gardens. Vivien had lived there.

How happy they had been! He and Michael, both sent to Uppingham School, a place of learning which they had both enjoyed, and where they had both acquitted themselves well; and Vivien, educated at home by governesses, always there in the vacations to delight them both with her beauty and vivacity. Was Critchley right? Did madness really run in families? Oh, what a blight had fallen on them all, and on their families!

With a conscious effort Oakshott jerked himself back to the present. He laid the letter aside, and dipped his pen into the ink well. Soon, his mind had expelled any thoughts that were not relevant to the treacherous activities of the Byzantine Emperor Manuel I during the Second Crusade.

That night, Oakshott had a dream. He was sitting at one end of the long table in the dining chamber of Hazelmere Castle, his Uncle Ambrose's preposterous sham-gothic mansion hidden in a wooded estate some miles from Oxford. Uncle Ambrose sat in his great oak throne at the other end of the table. His head, with its skin tightly drawn across the cheekbones and its sparse hair, seemed more skull-like than ever.

'One day, Jeremy,' said his uncle, waving a hand vaguely in the air, 'all this will be yours.'

Even in the dream-world, a part of Jeremy Oakshott's mind thought of the hundreds of thousands of pounds that Ambrose Littlemore's father had amassed in the heady and dangerous days of the railway mania. It was wealth of that kind that had enabled him to build his fantastic dwelling, part castle, part cathedral, where every turn on every stair startled the visitor with a grotesque, writhing and often morbid corbel in the form of a tormented spirit in Hades. A friend of Oakshott's, an architect, told him that the whole place was poorly and cheaply built on questionable foundations, as Uncle Ambrose's father had been fond of a good bargain.

Then, hovering behind his uncle's chair, Oakshott made out another figure, a tall, spare woman in her fifties, who laid a thin hand on his uncle's shoulder. A ghost of a smile played about the woman's lips.

This was a recurrent dream, but the woman – it was his Aunt Arabella – was not always present. Whenever she appeared Oakshott felt a sudden alarm, which often jolted him awake. But this night, a new figure emerged from the dormant part of his mind to take form and shape. The light from the many candles in the dining chamber dimmed, and an unseen door opened to admit a young woman in a white dress, a woman with long auburn hair falling loose over her shoulders.

'Vivien!'

Jeremy Oakshott woke with a start, his heart pounding. Had he cried out? He felt for the box of vestas on his night table and lit the candle. No, all was quiet in the old college. He rose from bed, and pulled open the curtain. He looked up beyond the black bulk of New College chapel to the star-lit sky. Vivien did not belong to that dream. He asked himself why she had appeared, and immediately made a little exclamation of vexation. Why pretend? He knew very well why Vivien West had walked into his uncle's phantom chamber that night. He also knew that the white dress that she wore was, in fact, a shroud.

'It was good of you to invite me here, Oakshott,' said Sanders. 'I thought you'd be disgusted at my reminding you that we were at school together—'

'They were happy days, Sanders, and you did well to recall them. The carefree sixties! Uppingham was a wonderful place in retrospect. With the passing of the years, one forgets the beatings!'

Sanders had arrived punctually at Jerusalem Hall, and the old clock above the gatehouse was striking ten as the genial Tonson brought him upstairs to the door of Oakshott's rooms. He had ordered tea to be brought before his visitor arrived, otherwise he would have felt compelled to offer his guest something stronger, which would not have been wise.

'This is a quaint old place,' said Sanders, glancing round the ancient room. 'But it's a haven, isn't it? I believe you live here, in the college, with service and all found? It's very – very satisfying, isn't it?'

Oakshott laughed.

'Yes, old fellow, it's very satisfying – all found, including coal and candles! But come, now, what can I do for you?'

How wretched Sanders looked! He had become one of the shabby-genteel, hovering perilously near the workhouse. He had employment of sorts, but first opium, and then drink, had made him a shadow of his earlier self. He had been such an attractive, outgoing boy at school.

Sanders did not meet his eye. He sipped his tea, and looked thoughtfully at the carpet. His hands were trembling, and a vein was pulsing at his temple.

'I've been thinking a lot about old times, Jeremy,' said Sanders. 'What times you and I had in our youthful days. I think of the jolly girls we knew, and particularly of … well, you'll know who I mean. Such a tragedy. It ruined me, you know. They brought in a verdict of "murder by a person or persons unknown", but a lot of people wondered…. Half a lifetime has passed since then, and with time, old hidden secrets rise to the surface. People begin to remember things, and tell others …'

'Look here, Sanders,' said Jeremy Oakshott, 'I know you're too proud to ask for help, so I'll save us both embarrassment by assuring you that I am only too happy to assist you, if only for old times' sake. Yesterday I sent you a cheque for £100 – no, please don't thank me; you're more than welcome. I expect you'll find it waiting for you when you get back today. It's made out to 'Bearer', so you'll be able to cash it over the counter at any bank.

Meanwhile, here's a five pound note to tide you over.'

Sanders got up from his chair, and took the note that Oakshott offered.

'I'm so very much obliged to you, Oakshott,' he said. 'Perhaps I shall see more of you now that we've met again after all these years. There was so much, you know, that bound us both together. As you may recall, I approached you ten years ago, hoping to renew our friendship, but you were very distant, as I remember, and nothing came of it. Is your Uncle Ambrose any better? It's so sad that wealth and health don't often go hand in hand!'

Sanders rose, and walked towards the door. He paused on the threshold, and said, 'Yes, they declared that it was a mystery, but you and I know the truth of the matter. I can't put it into words, because it's too frightful for anyone to hear. But I can imagine a time when I, for one, may feel obliged to speak out.'

When Sanders had gone, Oakshott sat for a while in thought. A hundred pounds had been about right; any lesser sum would have created the wrong impression. Poor, wretched man! The two of them were inextricably linked by events in the past, and it had been almost inevitable that one day he would have to take care of him. Ten years ago he had made it clear to Sanders that his applications for relief were not welcome. It was too late to maintain that approach now.

He rummaged among the many papers on his desk and found the invitation that Hugo Harper had sent him to attend Mrs Herbert Lestrange's lecture at Jesus College. Nothing would be allowed to interfere with that. Perhaps, when the lecture was over, he would be able to have a word with her? His own knowledge of the Crusades was universally recognized as little short of phenomenal, but Celia Lestrange had actually been on those ancient fields of battle, and in the very fortresses which the Crusaders had manned. They had corresponded for some time. It would be a wonderful privilege to meet her again.

*

Jeremy Oakshott and his friend Jonathan Grigg, college lecturer in Chemistry, emerged from New College Lane, and made their way past the Sheldonian Theatre into Broad Street. Wednesday had proved to be one of those delightful days that looked backward to summer rather than forward to an uncertain autumn. It was warm, with a gusty breeze billowing their masters' gowns behind them as they walked.

'She was one of the Clive-Newtons of Bellpath, you know,' said Jonathan Grigg, a red-faced man with bulging eyes and an ample greying moustache, 'and she was very young when she married Lestrange. They were both fascinated by the East, and had planned an expedition to Syria with Sir Breedon Harcourt in '82. And then the riots broke out in Alexandria. Captain Lestrange went out there with his regiment, and was killed in the riots. He was only thirty-two.'

'How do you know all this, Grigg? You hardly ever leave Oxford.'

Grigg laughed. It was a humorous, self-deprecating sound.

'It was in the London papers for weeks,' he replied. 'And besides, I had a girl cousin who was married to one of the Clive-Newtons. Anyway, when it was all over, young Mrs Lestrange went out to Syria with Harcourt, and discovered her vocation in life. She's only forty now, but she never remarried. She's devoted herself to archaeology, with resounding success. By the way, is it true that you and she are special friends? I've heard rumours—'

'Oh, stow it, will you, Grigg! Here we are at Turl Street. We've ten minutes before the lecture starts.'

A tall, distinguished man in a black morning suit and silk hat brushed past them as they neared the gate of Jesus College. A man of swarthy complexion, he wore little round tinted glasses.

'Look,' said Grigg, 'that fellow's going into Jesus College. I wonder if he's a Syrian?'

'He could be,' Oakshott replied. 'Why don't you ask him?'

Grigg laughed, and the two dons made their way through the

first quadrangle and into Jesus College hall.

In Oakshott's view, the hall of Jesus College was one of Oxford's finest, with a grace and elegance that he found unique to it. In the early eighteenth century, the original hammer-beam roof had been hidden by a fine rococo plaster ceiling. On the north wall, above the high table, an exuberant plaster cartouche contained the college arms: *Vert, three stags trippant argent attired or.*

The hall was already packed with guests when the two dons from Jerusalem Hall arrived. Most were sitting on either side of the tables running the length of the hall; others were occupying a diverse array of folding chairs brought in for the occasion. Oakshott and Grigg took their seats, and waited for the proceedings to begin.

On the high table, beneath the great portrait of Queen Elizabeth, the Founder, a large screen had been erected, and at the rear of the hall, a powerful modern slide lantern stood on a kind of metal plinth, attended by a young man in a very stiff collar, who was obliged to work with his back pressed against the hall door.

Somebody walked out of the large window embrasure and called for silence. Then somebody else – was it Wallace Lindsay? – told them that they were all very pleased to welcome the Honourable Mrs Herbert Lestrange that afternoon, and that they would all be very interested and instructed by the subject of her lecture – Krak des Chevaliers.

Jonathan Grigg had had further business in town, so Oakshott walked back to Jerusalem Hall alone. The lecture had been fascinating, and the lantern slides, made from Mrs Lestrange's own photographs, had brought much of her subject to life. An impressive, handsome woman of forty or so, she had been dressed in a business-like green tweed skirt and jacket. When she consulted her notes, she donned gold pince-nez attached to a slender chain around her neck.

It was when the lecture ended that she had approached him directly, greeting him by name. She told him that she had taken volume one of his work on the Crusades with her to Syria, and had frequently consulted it during the excavations that she had supervised at Krak. Then she had taken him into the window embrasure and told him something that set his pulses racing.

'In the course of my excavations,' she said, 'I uncovered a hidden chamber containing a number of ancient manuscripts, written in Arabic. Their contents revealed that our ideas of what happened in 1271 need to be seriously revised. You recall that Sultan Baibars was said to have forged a letter, ostensibly from the Grand Master of the Knights Hospitaller, ordering them to surrender Krak. Well, Dr Oakshott, it was not a mere rumour. I found that letter among the cache. And that was not all. There were other letters, showing that King Otakar II of Bohemia was also involved in a sort of unholy conspiracy ...'

When she had finished her account of her findings, she made the invitation that he was both expecting and dreading.

'I am making a further expedition to Krak in March,' she said, 'and I think it's imperative that you accompany me. The French authorities have been fully cooperative, and will lend me one of their expert translators to look thoroughly at all those manuscripts, which I have removed to a secret place. They now need a specialist historian, someone of your distinction, to interpret them. I will give you free use of your findings for inclusion in volume two of your great work.'

Oakshott walked down Leper's Lane, thinking about the invitation, which he had instantly accepted.

'We're funding this expedition ourselves,' she had told him. 'The Royal Albert Trust think that they've given us enough, and are turning their attention to quite different fields of study. So it will cost us each £6,000. Listen, we must meet for tea somewhere in town. There's something I want to show you.' She had smiled then, and walked away to talk to the earnest young man in the very stiff collar.

He had caught sight of David and Mary McArthur in the throng, and had made a point of greeting them. They were old friends, and also well known to his uncle, but all the time that he was talking to them he was thinking of Mrs Lestrange's invitation.

Six thousand pounds! He had never amassed a sum of that immensity in the whole of his professional career. His annual income, from a sum invested for him by his late father in government stock, was £340. So it was impossible for him to go to Syria. In God's name, what had made him accept the invitation?

Oakshott suddenly felt that he was being followed. He turned, and saw the tall, bearded man with tinted glasses standing halfway along Leper's Lane. He was writing rapidly in a note book. Presently, he put the note book in his pocket and hurried away.

Jeremy Oakshott dismissed the man from his mind. He was so preoccupied with his own folly that he did not reply to Tonson's cheery greeting as he entered the lodge of Jerusalem Hall.

At half past eight on Friday morning, 7 September, Doris Tench loaded her tray with the breakfast things for Mr Sanders, and knocked on his bedroom door. Mr Sanders usually responded by opening the door to her. Drink or no drink, he was an early riser. Evidently, he'd decided to sleep in that morning. They'd not heard him come in, but earlier in the day he'd been in high spirits, and had told Joe that for once in his life he had something to celebrate!

The door was slightly ajar, and Mrs Tench pushed it open with her knee. The curtains had not been opened. She put the tray down on the table, and turned to the bed.

3

A CUT-THROAT BUSINESS

INSPECTOR JAMES ANTROBUS stood beside the bed, and looked down at the man who lay there dead. He must have been quite handsome in his youth, but his face bore the signs of a man ravaged by drink. His moustache, though, was well trimmed, and his black hair had been slicked down with pomade. He was fully clothed in a threadbare but well-cut suit, and his feet were shod with well-polished boots.

His throat had been cut from ear to ear, and he lay in a congealing pool of his own blood.

Antrobus looked at the police constable standing deferentially near the door. He had identified himself as PC Mark Roberts, warrant number 476. Roberts seemed to confirm the popular belief that the older one got, the younger the policemen seemed to be. He was probably in his early twenties, but he looked no more than eighteen.

'You did right to send for me, Constable,' said Antrobus. 'Just tell me in your own words how you came to be summoned here to this house, and what you did when you saw the body.'

'Sir,' said PC Roberts, opening his notebook, 'I was sent for today, Friday, 7 September, 1894, at a quarter to nine o'clock, by Mr and Mrs Tench, who sent a boy to tell me that their paying guest,

Mr Michael Sanders, had been found lying dead in his bed, with his throat cut. I sent for Dr McArthur, who came straight away, and as neither of us could see any weapon in the room, we concluded that Mr Sanders had been murdered. I went immediately and told my friend Seth Bolt, the blacksmith's brother, who rode over to Forest Hill, and telegraphed to Oxford Police Station from there.'

Constable Roberts put away his notebook and watched the inspector as he made his own examination of the body. Mr Antrobus had a reputation for getting to the root of things. It was only last month that he had solved that tragic business at St Michael's College.[1]

Inspector Antrobus was an alarming man to look at, or so Constable Roberts thought. He was tall and gaunt, with a face as white as parchment. He had deep hollows around his eyes. He wore a light beard and moustache, which looked as though he'd grown them because the business of shaving had become too much of a chore. He'd been very ill, so he'd heard, but illness hadn't dulled his wits.

He'd brought a detective sergeant with him. There he was now, skulking around the back garden, and darting in and out of the bushes, a thickset little man with a straggly moustache, wearing a bowler hat and a drab overcoat. For a little man he had a very loud voice. But then, little men were often bumptious. What was the inspector doing now?

Antrobus had stooped over the body, and was examining the wound in its throat. Constable Roberts shuddered as the inspector delicately inserted the little finger of his right hand into the wound, and then examined the tip of it through a jeweller's lens which he had produced from a pocket.

'He's been dead about six hours, Constable,' he said. 'Six to eight hours. That's what the congealing of the blood in the wound tells me.'

---

1. *An Oxford Tragedy*

He turned the head carefully to one side, and looked closely at the scalp. There was a contusion there, the result of a blow that had broken the skin, but not cracked the skull.

'Yes,' said Antrobus, 'the state of congealment suggests that this unfortunate man was killed at about one o'clock this morning. He'd been knocked unconscious before his throat was cut. Did anything strike you as unusual about this business, Constable?'

Constable Roberts ran a finger round the inside of his collar. It was a hot day for September, and he was sweating profusely in his heavy serge uniform. It was time that they moved the body. Very soon, it would start to make its presence known. A number of curious flies had started to take an interest in poor Mr Sanders who, meaning no disrespect, was on the turn.

'Well, sir,' said Roberts, 'I did wonder why he was lying there fully dressed. It's usually drunks who collapse on their bed with their boots on. But before you arrived, sir, I made enquiries at the Bull, and the landlord told me that Mr Sanders had been a little merry, but certainly not drunk. He'd not seen him leave, as the bar was very busy, but it would have been some time after twelve.'

'You went to the Bull, did you? That was very clever of you, Constable. Now, if Mr Sanders wasn't drunk, why did he lie down on his bed fully clothed? He could at least have taken his boots off. No, I don't want an answer; I'm just thinking aloud. Was that window open when you arrived here?'

'It was, sir. Wide open, as you see. It was quite warm last night, sir. Perhaps that's why he opened the window wide, and lay on the top of the bed.'

Inspector Antrobus had crossed the room, and was looking at the window sill. He bent down, and examined the oil cloth covering the floor.

'There are drag-marks here, Constable,' he said. 'And there are traces of soil on the window sill – soil from someone's boots. I'm beginning to think—'

The door of the room opened, and Sergeant Maxwell came into the room.

'Sir,' he said, 'there's a dense shrubbery separating these premises from those of the neighbouring cottage. I conducted an examination, and saw at once that two of the bushes had been disturbed. I also found long tracks, left by the heels of boots or shoes when their owner had been dragged along, unconscious or dead, sir, by the shoulders.'

'Constable Roberts,' said Antrobus, 'this is Detective Sergeant Maxwell. As you can see, his investigations in the garden complement my own observations by the window sill. Mr Sanders must have been attacked out there, in the shrubbery – waylaid, on his return from the Bull – and then dragged across the grass, hauled up over the window sill, and into the bedroom. Then his killer laid him down on the bed.

'Now, Constable, where do you think his throat was cut? Be careful.'

'He'd have had his throat cut in the shrubbery, sir, away from prying eyes. Maybe the murderer threw his knife away among those bushes. Shall I go and have a look?'

'That won't be necessary, Constable,' said Sergeant Maxwell with a kind of smirk. 'I've already searched the garden, and the road beyond. There's no sign of any weapon.'

'PC Roberts,' Antrobus continued, ignoring his sergeant's interruption, 'if he was attacked out there, then the grass, and the floor of this room, would have been covered in blood spurting from a wound of that nature. No; he was stunned out there in the bushes, dragged into the bedroom, and his throat was cut here, which is why the bed, and the floor beneath it, are soaked in blood. That's what happened here.'

He turned to look at the body.

'Constable,' he said, 'ask your friend the blacksmith's brother to ride over to Forest Hill again, and telegraph to the Oxford City Mortuary. They're to send a closed van here as soon as possible to convey the body away. We don't want him to start emulating Polonius behind the arras. Sergeant, go with him, and find some men to help him carry the body to a stable or outhouse. Incidentally, where are Mr and Mrs Tench? I've not seen either of them since I arrived.'

'They're in the kitchen, sir, consoling each other, and supping tea. Come on, PC Roberts, let's find some men to move that body.'

'Who was that Polonius, Sergeant?' asked the constable, as the two men made their way across the cottage garden. 'The one that Mr Antrobus was talking about?'

'Never you mind about him, Constable,' said Maxwell. 'There are all kinds of crimes that he and I are investigating at the moment. Polonius was one of them. It's all very secret, you see.'

It would never do to lose face before a junior officer. Sometimes, he'd no idea what the guvnor was talking about. The trouble with Mr Antrobus was that he read too many books.

Once the body of Michael Sanders had been removed, the two detectives set to work examining the dead man's effects. A travelling salesman's sample case stood in an alcove beside the fireplace. It contained a number of cravats in cardboard display boxes, and half a dozen fancy waistcoats arrayed on folding hangers. There was a printed catalogue, and an order book, which showed that he had been successful in securing orders in four tailor's shops, all in the Oxford area, and during the last fortnight. Not a fortune, but he'd receive enough commission for him to pay his rent, and have a bit left over.

'Joe,' said Antrobus, 'go into the kitchen, and find out from Mr and Mrs Tench what kind of a man this Sanders was. I'll carry on looking through his things. Get them to give you a cup of tea, try to look sympathetic, and take them into your confidence. *Festina lente.*'

'*Festina....* Yes, sir.'

Muttering under his breath, Sergeant Maxwell left the room.

A chest of drawers yielded some underclothes, neatly mended, a spare shirt, and a box of starched collars. They were arranged neatly in the drawers, and folded with some care. In another drawer a zip-up pigskin purse held a pipe, and a pack of Ogden's pipe tobacco. A pair of rolled-up socks concealed ten gold half-sovereigns.

Ah! Here was an old leather wallet. Antrobus took it across to the table in the window alcove, and sat down to examine its contents. No banknotes. Perhaps there were some in the pockets of his coat, but he had chosen not to disturb the body more than had been necessary until he saw it in the city mortuary.

Here was a trade card, saying that Mr Michael Sanders was a representative of Samuel & Company, Clothiers, of Banbury. And here – hello! A cheque for £100, made payable to 'Bearer', and drawn on Hodge's Bank, 31a Queen Street, Oxford. It was signed by a J. Oakshott. Whoever he was, he must have been a good friend to poor Michael Sanders. Or so it would seem. To a man who had clearly been in straitened circumstances, £100 was a great deal of money.

And here was a letter, still in its envelope. It was headed Jerusalem Hall, Oxford, and dated 28 August.

My dear Sanders (it ran),

How pleasant it was to hear from you after all these years! Do please come here, to Jerusalem Hall, next Tuesday, 4 September, about mid-morning. We can chat about old times. I am sorry to hear that all has not been well with you, and will be only too happy to do what I can to help.
With best wishes,
Jeremy Oakshott

There was no mention of the cheque for £100 in the letter, so the benevolent Mr Oakshott had probably sent it to Sanders under separate cover.

The door was pushed open, and Sergeant Maxwell came into the room. He was dabbing his untidy moustache with a spotted handkerchief.

'The body's been laid in the barn of a farmer called Robinson, sir,' he said. 'The closed van will arrive from Oxford in about half an hour's time. I've sent Constable Roberts home. He's a smart lad, to my way of thinking.'

'Did you see how the Tenches are?'

'I did, sir. They gave me a cup of tea – very good it was, too. They liked Mr Sanders a lot, because he paid them regularly, and was polite in his way of speaking. In their view, he was a gentleman. He used to use foreign words occasionally, Latin, French, that kind of thing. He wouldn't be the only one to bewilder honest folk with foreign words. That's another reason that they thought he was a gentleman. He'd been boarding with them for a month – he came to stay on 6 August. He told them that he worked for a firm in Banbury, but from the way he spoke – his accent, I mean – they didn't think he was an Oxfordshire man.'

'Hmm…. What do you think of that letter, Sergeant, and the cheque for £100?'

Sergeant Maxwell held the letter close to his eyes, and mumbled to himself, as though he was quietly reading it aloud. Then he threw it down on the table.

'It looks as though it's in reply to a cadging letter from the late Sanders, sir, tapping an old friend for money. He certainly chose the right friend. A hundred pounds!'

'Jerusalem Hall…. I've heard the name, but I don't think I've ever seen it. Do you know it?'

'Yes, sir, it's a tumble-down sort of place in that maze of lanes behind New College. It's near the Archangel public house, where I occasionally partake of a glass of their special porter.'

'You're a positive cornucopia of information, Joe. We'll have to pay a visit to this Jeremy Oakshott in the very near future. I've searched this room, and so far, I've found some clothes, all neatly darned and folded, a pipe, that cheque, and that letter. Now, here's a little leather satchel – it was in the bottom drawer of the dresser. I haven't opened it yet. Let's see what's in it.'

Antrobus removed two books from the satchel. One was a copy of Ovid's *Metamorphoses*, bound in cracked and stained vellum. It was well thumbed, and there were pencilled annotations in some of the margins.

'Ah!' said Antrobus. 'Ovid! This book takes me back to my schooldays. Oh yes, look: *Omnia mutantur, nihil interit*. What do you think of that?'

'I think, sir, that as well as being a sponger, our Mr Sanders was also a learned man. A scholar and a gentleman, as you might say, despite that fact that he was as poor as a church mouse. Mr Tench said he drank too much.'

Sergeant Maxwell's face suddenly flushed with vexation. He eyed his superior with something approaching malevolence.

'Sir,' he said, his voice growing louder as he spoke, 'I've temporarily forgotten what that bit of Latin that you quoted meant. Would you oblige me by refreshing my memory?'

Inspector Antrobus laughed. Sergeant Maxwell didn't approve of his occasional shows of learning. When he quoted bits of poetry, or some Latin, Maxwell evidently thought that he was aiming above his station.

'Of course, Joe,' he said. 'It means, "Everything changes, nothing perishes". Now, let's see what this second book can tell us about its owner.'

It was a copy of *The Book of Common Prayer*, bound in white goatskin, and with little brass clasps to hold it closed. Antrobus opened it, and saw that the end-papers had been inscribed very elegantly in copperplate script.

Vivien West, Priory House, Henning St Mary, near Hereford.
May, 1872.
A betrothal gift from Jeremy.

Sergeant Maxwell was standing at the window, commenting on the arrival of the mortuary van from Oxford, but Antrobus scarcely heard him. For some reason, the prayer book was beginning to exert a disturbing influence on him. Jeremy…. Was that Jeremy Oakshott, the benefactor of Michael Sanders, lying dead in Robinson's barn? And was Vivien West Sanders's wife? If so, she must be traced. But it was early days yet.

A stiff card of some sort had been inserted some way into the book. When Antrobus turned to the place that it was marking, he saw that it was the marriage service. The opening page, and the page preceding it, were splashed with blood, long dried to a sullen brown. Splashed? Or sprayed? Had the bride had a sudden nose bleed as the service commenced? Even as he framed the thought, he dismissed it. It was too banal, too like an excuse for not contemplating more disturbing possibilities. He began to experience a kind of depression, in which the very light seemed to fade from the room. *The Form of Solemnization of Matrimony….* But this wedding, he felt convinced, had never taken place.

He examined the book mark. It was printed in black on a white card, and showed a veiled woman kneeling at the base of a grave-monument, upon which was written the single word RESURGAM – I will arise. There were things here crying out for interpretation. He looked through the remaining pages, noting that many sections of text had been underlined in pencil.

Why had Michael Sanders brought this book with him on his journey as a commercial traveller? The book of Ovid's poetry was evidently an old favourite, brought along to pass some idle moments when they offered themselves. But the prayer book was surely a precious relic, something very personal and private. Had he brought it with him to show to the man called Oakshott, who had sent him a cheque for £100? The man called simply Jeremy in Vivien West's inscription?

Antrobus suddenly began to cough, a harsh, hacking convulsion, accompanied by stertorous breathing. Maxwell turned to look at him, and then resumed his watch at the window, whistling what sounded like *The British Grenadiers*. Joe always behaved like that when he had one of his coughing fits. He brought out his handkerchief and delicately wiped his lips. When he put it back in his pocket, it was stained with fresh blood.

He had suffered from consumption of the lungs for over five years, and had dutifully submitted himself to the various treatments available. He had endured spells in hospital, lying in beds on open balconies. He had received intensive courses of the creosote treatment, and injections of tuberculin. His left lung was virtually useless, and he had been told that one day it would have to be removed. Well, life had to go on. He took a small paper sachet from his pocket. A pulmonic wafer always gave him relief.

'Sergeant,' he said, 'I think our investigation lies elsewhere. If anything of significance happens here, Constable Roberts will keep us informed. On the way back to town, I'll tell you about this old prayer book, and some of the things that I found in it. And tomorrow, if all goes well, we'll pay a call on Mr Jeremy Oakshott, of Jerusalem Hall.'

Inspector Antrobus and Sergeant Maxwell arrived at Jerusalem Hall just after nine o'clock on the Saturday morning. The porter in the lodge, who told them that his name was Tonson, informed them that Dr Oakshott was closeted with the Rector, and would not be available until ten. Would they care to see some of the college buildings while they waited?

They were shown the college hall, a rather gloomy chamber smelling of stale food. Its panelled walls were hung with faded old portraits, and there were three gothic windows dark with stained glass blazons of ancient benefactors. The long tables held lines of battered candle sticks containing unlit guttered candles. It was so dim that they could not quite make out the ceiling, but Tonson informed them that it was constructed of open beams. The whole place reminded Antrobus of the fanciful illustrations by George Cruikshank in Dickens's early novels.

'We're rather out of the way here, Mr Antrobus,' Tonson said, 'and I'm told that there's not much money in the college coffers. It's by way of falling down, is Jerusalem Hall. Very sad, really. Now let me show you the chapel.'

The chapel was lighter than the hall, and contained some very fine carved stalls. It had evidently escaped the wholesale restorations that had taken place elsewhere in the mid-years of the century. The altar was a Jacobean table covered with a carpet in the old style. Like the rest of the college, the chapel was lit by candles.

'It's not much of a place, is it?' said Maxwell loudly, clutching his black bowler hat to his chest, and looking round the chapel with distaste.

'Well, no, Sergeant,' said Tonson, 'you could never compare it with our grand neighbour, New College. There's some that rather unkindly refer to us as New College's Coal-hole. Not very nice, really.'

'Joe,' whispered Antrobus, 'when this Dr Oakshott finally appears, go back to the lodge with Tonson, and find out all you can about him. Oakshott, I mean, not Tonson. You know the kind of thing. When we're done here, we'll adjourn to that public house you mentioned – the Archangel – and compare notes over a glass of something reviving.'

As they emerged from the chapel, a man in academic dress appeared from the entrance to one of the staircases.

'Here he is, gentlemen,' said Tonson. 'Dr Oakshott, sir, you have two visitors. From the police.'

'Inspector, I'm devastated. Shocked beyond words. Poor Sanders! Was it robbery? If so, these villains will get nothing. Michael Sanders had no money and few possessions. You say he was murdered. How – how was it done?'

'His throat was cut, Dr Oakshott—'

'What?'

Jeremy Oakshott had sprung up from his chair behind the cluttered desk of his study. To Antrobus, it was as though the man had suffered a physical blow. His shock seemed natural enough, but then, some of the deepest-dyed villains could bring tears to your eyes with their tales of woe.

'His throat was cut? Just like … Have you found out who did it?'

'Dr Oakshott,' said Antrobus, 'just now you began to make a comparison between the manner of Mr Sanders's death, and something else, which you didn't specify. "Just like", you said. Just like what, sir?'

'Did I say that? I can't recall what I could have meant.'

Antrobus let the matter drop. He delved into one of the pockets in his greatcoat, and brought out the bloodstained prayer book. He saw the other man's eyes widen with something like fear.

'Dear God! Is that … is that Vivien's prayer book? Where did you get it? Of course, poor Michael Sanders must have had it with him. I expect he took it with him everywhere. Poor man! Poor fool! Oh God! May I see it?'

His hands trembled as he opened the book, and Antrobus saw him mouth the words of the inscription silently. Tears welled up unbidden in his eyes. He opened the book at the cardboard marker, and turned as white as marble when he saw the dried bloodstains. Antrobus waited in silence. In a few moments' time, this man would be compelled to speak.

Oakshott closed the book, and pushed it across the desk to Antrobus.

Jeremy Oakshott sighed deeply, and sat back in his chair. He seemed to have regained his equanimity, and the inspector saw that he was composing himself to tell a story. The man was too intelligent to pretend that the prayer book – and its history – were unknown to him.

'Inspector,' said Oakshott, 'there is a deep and terrible mystery here, and I must not make it any more obscure by keeping silent. I cannot begin to imagine why anyone should have wanted to harm Michael Sanders.... He was a poor, friendless man, with a very sad history.'

For a while Oakshott remained silent, evidently reliving the past. Then he spoke again.

'There were three of us, Mr Antrobus, three friends from child-hood, and we all lived with our respective families in a little town called Henning St Mary, near Hereford. My father was headmaster of the grammar school there, and we were quite comfortably off – he had a small annuity of £30 from a family trust. Michael – Michael Sanders – was the only child of Mr Bertram Sanders, Assistant Vice-Chancellor of the Diocese of Hereford. And Vivien....

'She was a beautiful, vivacious girl, Mr Antrobus, the daughter of a local landowner, and we three were true friends. Michael and I were sent to Uppingham School, in Rutland. Michael and I both loved her, and continued as friendly rivals for her affection until 1870, when she was eighteen. It was then that she declared her love for Michael. He was a very handsome, charming young man, you know, in those days. Her parents raised no objection to their betrothal, and their wedding was planned to take place in Hereford Cathedral on 20 May, 1872. She and I were just twenty, Michael a couple of years older. I was to be the best man.'

'You have a very good memory, sir.'

'I am a professional scholar, Mr Antrobus, accustomed to committing many facts to memory. But every day and date in that year is etched on my memory. Those memories usually lie dormant, but now, as you will realize, they have come into the forefront of my recollection.

'On the Friday before the wedding, Vivien was sitting in the garden of her family's house, a pleasant villa in a place called Ford's Lane. It was a lovely sunny day, and she had arranged herself in a basket chair, placed in a grassy arbour at the rear of the garden. I had given her that prayer book as a present at the time of her engagement, and she was to carry it with her to the altar on her wedding day. She had taken it with her into the garden, to read over the marriage service. When she was found—'

Oakshott suddenly broke off, and hid his face in his hands. Antrobus waited. It was over a minute before he resumed his story.

'When she was found, Inspector, she was sitting dead in the chair, with her throat cut from behind. The prayer book, still open, was stained with her blood. It was Michael who discovered her body. There was, of course, a full police investigation, but no culprit was ever found. The years passed, and Michael and I went our separate ways. I studied for a while in London, and then came here. I have been here ever since.

'Michael never recovered from losing his fiancée. He took to drink, and fell into the opium habit. His late father placed him as a clerk in a number of legal establishments, but he was always dismissed for poor time-keeping and drunkenness. Eventually, he found work as a commercial traveller, and it was in that capacity that he approached me only days ago, ostensibly to chat about old times, but really, I knew, to apply to me for help. And there it is. I am shocked and saddened by poor Sanders's murder, and I trust that you will do your utmost to bring the killer to justice.'

4

MR TONSON REMEMBERS

'THIS LODGE IS a snug little place, Mr Tonson,' said Sergeant Maxwell. 'A man can be king of his castle in here.'

'True enough, Sergeant. I see everyone that comes and goes. Not that there's much going on out of term time. Mind you, it's not a place I'd like to live in. Its foundations are weak, and they're always saying that it'll fall down one of these days, so I'm glad that I live out. Mrs Tonson and me have a nice little cottage in Waynefleet Lane, just a stone's throw away.'

The porter's lodge was very small, but an ingenious use of shelves and cupboards allowed it to hold rows of box files, ledgers, sand buckets, storm lanterns, and a long letter rack, divided into pigeonholes. A sort of glazed hatch could be opened into the gatehouse vestibule when visitors wanted to make enquiries. Fixed to the wall facing the hatch was an electric telephone.

'Looking at you, Mr Tonson,' said Sergeant Maxwell, 'I can see that you're an observant man, the kind of man we'd like to have in the detective police. Now, here's a question for you. Did you happen to see a visitor who came here last Tuesday morning? He came to see Dr Oakshott.'

'Oh yes, I remember him. He came through here, and asked me how to get to Dr Oakshott's rooms. He wanted to show me a letter, to vouch for who he was, but I said that wouldn't be necessary. A Mr Sanders. He came by appointment. A polite gentleman, he was, well-spoken, though I think he'd fallen on bad times. He was smart enough, but a bit threadbare, if you know what I mean. He was wearing a frock coat with a felt hat. It set me wondering whether he couldn't afford a topper, which would have been the correct thing to wear. Sitting here, by this hatch, you come to be an observer of people and their little ways.'

'Did he bring anything with him? A case, perhaps?'

'No, he just came by himself.'

'How long did he stay?'

'About an hour, I think. But see here, Sergeant, what's all this about? Why are you asking me all these questions?' There was an edge of truculence in the normally equable porter's voice.

'Well, the fact is, Mr Tonson, that this Mr Sanders has just been murdered – yes, terrible, isn't it? Somebody cut his throat. The inspector's come today to ask Dr Oakshott if he noticed anything unusual about Mr Sanders when they had their meeting, and to tell us something of his history. At the moment, of course, we don't know anything about him.'

'Murdered! Well, you do surprise me, Sergeant. He didn't look at all like a man who was going to be murdered. When did it happen?'

'Friday night, in the early hours.' The time had come to try a little cunning. This Mr Tonson seemed a nice chap, but he wasn't among the brightest of God's creatures.

'It makes you thankful, Mr Tonson,' he said, 'that your Mr Oakshott came back safely, seeing as there was a killer at large. The murder took place at Hadleigh, about five miles from here. Somebody told us that he'd been out in those very parts on Thursday or Friday.'

It was nothing more than a wild surmise, but it achieved its purpose.

'Dear me, is that so? Mr Oakshott *did* go out to visit somebody at Hadleigh. He went up Thursday night, and came back Friday morning, about eleven. Yes, he could have been murdered, too!'

Maxwell saw Inspector Antrobus emerging from an arched doorway into the quadrangle. Evidently his interview with Dr Oakshott was over.

'I've enjoyed this little chat with you, Mr Tonson,' he said. 'Here's my guvnor now. I'll tell him what you said about Dr Oakshott going out to Hadleigh last Thursday, though, now I come to think of it, he's probably told him already.'

'Yes,' said Tonson, opening the lodge door. 'It was Thursday, the sixth. "Oh, Tonson," he said to me that morning, "I'm going out to Hadleigh this evening, and will be staying the night. I'll be back Friday morning." He's very courteous in that way, you know. He lets you know his whereabouts, in case he's needed. Not that he ever is, but it's a kind thought. He's a kind man altogether.'

Inspector Antrobus and Sergeant Maxwell sat at a well-scrubbed wooden table in the deserted back bar of the Archangel, an ancient hostelry not far from Jerusalem Hall.

They had each drunk a pint of Morrell's best bitter. Antrobus had given his sergeant a full account of his interview with Jeremy Oakshott. In return, Maxwell had told him about his conversation with the porter.

'So Oakshott was actually in Hadleigh at the time of the murder,' said Antrobus, 'which puts him immediately under suspicion. And yet he quite openly told the porter that he was going there. A man contemplating committing murder at Hadleigh wouldn't have done that.'

'Maybe he did that because he's clever enough to know that the police would find out in the end, anyway,' said Maxwell. 'Covering his tracks before he'd made them, in a manner of speaking.'

'That could be so. We need to find out who it was that he was visiting that night. We could ask him outright, but I'd prefer us to ask a few questions in Hadleigh. Oakshott would only tell us what he'd want us to hear; others might be more forthcoming. When we judge the time's right, you'd better go out there to Hadleigh, and make some discreet enquiries.'

Antrobus took a packet of cigarettes and a box of vestas from his pocket. Maxwell watched him as he lit up, and inhaled the smoke. He coughed and wheezed for nearly a minute, and then sat back in his chair. The guvnor swore by his Richmond 'Gem' cigarettes. His doctor had told him that they would help to clear the air passages.

'Those two men, Oakshott and Sanders,' said Antrobus, when he had recovered from his coughing fit, 'knew each other since childhood, and were linked together further by that old tragedy – the barbaric murder of a young woman called Vivien West. They were both in love with her. Who knows what festering resentments may have come to the surface this summer, culminating in murder?'

'Do you already suspect this Oakshott of murdering Sanders, sir?'

'Well, it's more than possible, isn't it? Two members of a little coterie of friends, murdered by having their throats cut, two murders, Sergeant, separated by nearly twenty-five years, but with the same *modus operandi*. We need to go back into the past, and look anew at the story of Vivien West, the murdered girl. Part of our investigation is going to take us away from Oxford for a time. But not just yet. First thing Monday morning, we'll go to the city mortuary. Dr Armitage will perform a post mortem on poor Sanders late tonight. On Monday, we'll find out what secrets the dead man – and his clothes – have to reveal.'

The Oxford City Mortuary was situated in a little street called Floyd's Row, in the Oxford suburb of St Ebbe's. The two detectives mounted the steps of the grey stone building, and pulled the bell; they could hear the jingling response from somewhere inside. In a few moments the door was unlocked by an attendant, and they entered the cold, silent mortuary. As they did so, a tall, fair-haired young man wearing a long white laboratory coat came out into the vestibule. To Antrobus he looked tremendously vital, tall and strong, a force for life in the house of the dead.

'Inspector Antrobus? And Sergeant Maxwell? Dr Armitage, the Chief Anatomist, is away from Oxford this week. I'm Dr Hugh Grossmith, from the Radcliffe, and I have the results of Saturday night's autopsy on the late unfortunate Michael Sanders.'

Grossmith ushered them into a chilly office, containing little more than a table, a filing cabinet and a number of Windsor chairs, and motioned to them to sit down.

'Michael Sanders, gentlemen,' he said, 'died as the result of his throat having been cut, thus severing the jugular vein. The fatal cut was made by someone standing behind him, using considerable force. The nature of the wound indicates that a very sharp knife had been used.'

'Would the assailant have been a strong man, Doctor?'

'He would be a man with powerful arms, I should think, Inspector – powerful arms and nerves of steel. I won't play the detective with you, but I'd say there would be little blood on his clothes, as he attacked his victim from behind. The dead man's heart and lungs were in good condition, with no signs of tubercular lesions in the latter. His liver was badly pervaded by yellow atrophy. At some time, long in the past, he had suffered a broken wrist.'

The young doctor expected to be asked a question, but was startled by its nature when Antrobus spoke.

'Are you a rugby man, Dr Grossmith?' he asked. 'The game, you know, not the school.'

'Yes, Inspector. I played prop forward in the Varsity match in '79. And I still turn out for local teams. Were you a rugby man in your youth?'

Antrobus managed to suppress a smile. To this young man, no doubt, he seemed very old.

'I was only ever one of the seven backs, as you'll no doubt

appreciate, Doctor,' he said. 'I was too slight for the forward line. But I was a good straight runner. I played until I was sixteen, when ill health took me off the field.'

Sergeant Maxwell smoothed his moustache and picked up his bowler hat from the table. He made a great business of clearing his throat.

'Mr Antrobus likes to reminisce, Doctor, when the occasion offers,' he said. 'But at present I'm sure he'd want to examine the late Mr Sanders's effects, by which we mean his clothes and suchlike.'

He glanced briefly at his superior officer, and saw him mouth the words, 'Thank you.' The guvnor bore his afflictions well, but there were some things that he deeply regretted having to give up. Rugby had been one of those things.

Dr Grossmith rang a bell, and the attendant appeared. With Sergeant Maxwell at his side, he preceded Antrobus and the doctor into the vestibule.

'Inspector,' the doctor whispered, 'I can see that you have consumption of the lungs, and suspect that you have fallen into a confirmed phthisis. Was that why you asked me about rugby? I expect you could see from my physique that I probably played the game.'

'That was very perceptive of you, sir. Yes, I suddenly felt envious of your youth and health, and recalled how the delights of the rugby field were suddenly denied me. I contracted typhoid fever, which was said to have weakened my heart. It was very unprofessional of me to ask you those questions. My sergeant, in his own blunt way, warned me to be quiet, and get on with the task in hand. I hope you'll forgive me.'

'I will, Inspector. And you're entitled, I think, to feel that kind of envy. One day, a cure will be found, but not, I fear, until some time very far in the future. I must leave you now. Goodbye, Inspector. Try to get out into the fresh air as much as possible.'

*

The attendant showed them into a windowless room, its un-plastered walls painted with lime wash. A heap of clothes lay on a trestle table. The attendant lit a gas-jet fixed by a bracket to one of the walls, and left the room.

There was a set of clean but heavily darned underwear, and a decent shirt with buttoned cuffs; its matching stiff collar, and the two studs needed to fix it to the shirt had been placed beside it. The trousers yielded a handkerchief, and 3/11d in loose silver and copper.

'This jacket's got the label of an Oxford tailor, Walters & Co., stitched in it, sir,' said Maxwell. 'It's bursting at the seams, and poor Mr Sanders had hidden some of the tears with ink, but it must have been quite costly when new. There's nothing in the main pockets, but – ah! – here's the return half of a train ticket. It's an open third class ticket from Birmingham New Street.'

'Birmingham – well, that doesn't surprise me,' said Antrobus. 'I think we'll find that poor Sanders had lodgings there, as well as in Hadleigh. I expect that he'd lived in lodgings in different towns and villages for years. But he came originally from Henning St Mary, the place where that poor young girl had her throat cut in '72. It's a point worth remembering. Henning St Mary.... I must go there, Joe, and ask some pertinent questions. Two murders. Two throats cut. Surely there must be a connection?'

'There's something sewn into the lining here, sir,' said Maxwell. He ripped the silk lining away from the cloth, and removed an old, stained envelope. It bore a penny stamp, and was franked as coming from Henning St Mary, via Hereford, 1 Oct 1885. Maxwell handed it to the inspector, who removed a single sheet of stained and much-folded paper. It was a brief letter, headed '2, The Cottages, Henning', and written in a spidery hand, the ink faded to a dull brown.

Dear Michael (it ran)
   I never knew anything for certain, and it's years ago now. But

a lot of folk knew that he was very much in love with Vivien, and jealousy can lead to terrible things. Amy is still convinced that he did it, but can produce no evidence of any kind for her belief. We will never know the truth of it. It was Caleb Williams who said he'd spoken to someone who'd actually seen Jeremy do the deed, but Caleb was a demon of a man, bitter, and thinking that the whole world owed him a living. So if you want to take up with Jeremy again, do so, because all these rumours are just talk. No one will ever know for certain who killed poor Vivien West.

Your old friend,

Alison Savernake.

'More names,' said Antrobus. 'I want you to go out to Hadleigh tomorrow, Joe, and find out what Oakshott did while he was there. Try the Bull first – no one there will have seen you, as neither of us wandered very far from the Tenches' house when we went there to view the body last Friday. Oakshott may be entirely innocent – I hope he is, because he seems a very pleasant kind of man. But he may be one of those people who can act with great boldness and ruthless courage when they see themselves threatened. So find out what he did on Thursday night.'

As they left the dreary lime-washed room they were accosted by young Dr Grossmith. He was holding a letter.

'Inspector,' he said, 'I have written a full report on Michael Sanders, and you have now examined his effects. Will it be in order to release the body? I have a letter here from a friend of Sanders, offering to arrange for his burial. He further asks whether he can be given Sanders's effects, as he was a close friend of the deceased since boyhood, and knows that he is entirely without relatives.'

'I suppose this friend is Dr Jeremy Oakshott, of Jerusalem Hall? Well, you can certainly release the body, and entrust poor Sanders's things to Oakshott. There was a sum of £10 in half-sovereigns. That should be held by one of the coroner's officers until after the inquest.'

'When will that take place, Inspector? I have a very busy schedule—'

'It will be a quick affair, Doctor, open and closed on the same day. Its purpose is to announce publicly the cause of death, and the inevitable verdict in this case: murder by a person or persons unknown. You may be called to state your findings, but it's more than likely that your written account will be sufficient.'

The landlord of the Bull public house in Hadleigh placed a tankard of mild in front of the sole occupant of the bar. It was mid-morning, and all the men were out at work. At first, he'd thought that this stranger was a debt collector, or if not that, then some kind of Methodist preacher. He was dressed entirely in black, and had placed his black bowler hat on the trestle table at which he was sitting. A nervy sort of man, for ever sucking at his moustache. But preachers didn't down a pint of mild as this chap did.

'I heard in town that there'd been a dreadful murder here last Friday,' said Sergeant Maxwell. 'A poor old beggar-man, wasn't it? Stabbed to death in a lodging house. It's a hot day today, landlord. Why don't you draw yourself a glass of something, on me?'

The landlord relaxed, and viewed his customer with a smile. Whoever he was, he wasn't going to demand a glance at his books, or preach him a sermon.

'Well, that's very kind of you, mister. I'll have a glass of bitter. Yes, we had an awful murder here last Friday, but it wasn't a tramp. He was a commercial traveller, and he'd come in here most nights, and most mornings, too, for a drink of something. Spirits, mostly. He was all patched and darned, but you could see he'd been a gentleman, once.'

'A drunk, was he?'

'Oh, no, not a drunk. He was too old a hand at drinking to be that. He'd always walk out steady, no matter how much he'd had. It was a crying shame. He spoke well, you know, and he'd come out with bits of poetry and foreign words, but there was no side on him. Mr Sanders, his name was.'

'Sanders? Was it *Michael* Sanders? Well, dear me, isn't that sad? That's why I'm here today, landlord. That Mr Sanders had friends in Oxford, and one of them in particular wondered whether his friend from former days was the man who'd been murdered. He gave me his name, and asked me to find out for certain. And he was stabbed to death?'

'No, his throat was cut, in the garden of Joe Tench's boarding house. Terrible, it was. It was Doris Tench that found him dead on his bed on Friday morning.'

So that's what he is, thought the landlord. He's one of those college servants, or scouts, as they call them.

'Yes,' said Maxwell, 'this friend of his is a Dr Oakshott, who's a Fellow of Jerusalem Hall. He told me that he was actually here, in Hadleigh, on the night of the murder. As you can imagine, he's very upset.'

'Oakshott? Oh yes, he's quite well known here, mister. And he was a friend of poor Mr Sanders? Well, what a coincidence! Dr Oakshott came here last Thursday evening. He'd posted me a note to meet him with the trap at Forest Halt, which I did.'

'And he stayed here, did he?'

'Well, no, not here, at the Bull. He had his valise with him, and I carried it for him as we walked across the village to Hob's Lane. He was staying the night with Dr and Mrs McArthur. As you know Dr Oakshott yourself, you'll realize what those three folk have in common!'

When Sergeant Maxwell arrived at Dr McArthur's house in Hob's Lane, he showed the maid his warrant card, and told her to take him directly to her master. The time for anonymity had passed. He was shown into a pleasant sitting-room, furnished in the light, simple style that Mr Antrobus had told him was called *art nouveau* – English was no longer good enough to describe new fashions. The room opened out on to a veranda, where Dr and Mrs

McArthur were sitting at a cast-iron table, drinking coffee, and reading what appeared to be the London newspapers.

'Sergeant Maxwell?' said Dr McArthur, rising from his chair. 'What can we do for you? Constable Roberts told me about your investigation at Mr Tench's house, and was kind enough to give me the gist of Inspector Antrobus's conclusions.'

A pleasant, friendly man in his forties, thought Maxwell. And his wife must have been a real beauty in her younger days. They seemed to be undisturbed by the presence of a policeman in their house. But appearances could be deceptive.

'Dr McArthur,' said Maxwell, 'did you know that the late unfortunate Michael Sanders and your good self had a mutual friend? I refer to Dr Jeremy Oakshott—'

'Jeremy? Well, you do surprise me. Did you know that, Mary? Sit down here with us, Sergeant. How very odd.... The three of us have been friends for a number of years, but Jeremy – Dr Oakshott – never mentioned this Michael Sanders. I saw him lying dead, you know. PC Roberts called me in as soon as he saw the body, and I gave a provisional description of the cause of death.'

'Not that there was much doubt, Sergeant,' said Mary McArthur. 'The poor man's throat was cut from ear to ear.' She smiled knowingly at Maxwell. 'And I suppose you've come here to find out whether Jeremy had an alibi – that's the word you policemen use, isn't it?'

'Well, ma'am, you're quite right, so I've no need to beat about the bush. Dr Oakshott arrived here in Hadleigh on Thursday evening, and was brought over here by the landlord of the Bull. The landlord told me that you three had some kind of connection. He didn't tell me what it was, and I never asked him.'

Maxwell had allowed his words to be coloured by a faint belligerence. Mrs McArthur's smile had been unforced and without malice; but there was nothing amusing about murder.

'My wife and I, Sergeant,' said Dr McArthur, 'are fiendishly attached to the game of whist. We are both gold medallists of the

Oxford County Whist League. Dr Jeremy Oakshott is the leading whist player in the county. He comes here to dine and sleep every two months or so, and we play far into the night. Sometimes, he'll stay for a few days with his uncle at Hazelmere Castle, which is only a mile from here, and on those occasions we invite other players from the villages round about to join us for a private contest.'

'And Dr Oakshott never left this house during the period spanning the evening of Thursday, 6 September, and the morning of Friday, the seventh?'

'He did not. George Standish – the landlord of the Bull – brought him here, and here he stayed. We dined early, and set up the tables at seven o'clock, when we started play. We played until after one o'clock—'

'Are you quite sure of that time, Doctor? After one o'clock?'

'Yes, in fact, it was nearer half past. I remember looking at that little carriage-clock on the mantelpiece, and remarking that we'd been known to go on as late as two.'

Maxwell had been writing in a notebook for the last few minutes. He wrote very swiftly, and McArthur saw that he was recording the interview in shorthand.

'Sir,' said Maxwell, putting down his pencil, 'it takes four to play whist. Who was the fourth player?'

'It was the vicar, the Reverend Matthew Parkinson. He, too, is a bridge fiend! When he left, the house was locked up, and we all retired to bed. The maid who answered the door to you lives out.'

'When did Dr Oakshott leave?'

'I called him at six – it was too early for our maid to have arrived. My wife brought him a jug of hot water, so that he could wash and shave. He came downstairs at seven, drank a cup of tea and ate a couple of biscuits, and left. George Standish was already waiting outside with the trap, to take him to Forest Halt.'

Dr McArthur stood up, indicating that the interview was over.

'So there you are, Sergeant Maxwell,' he said. 'I can account for Dr Oakshott's entire stay here. When the house is locked up for the night, I place the keys on my bedside table. Of course, you did quite right to seek for an alibi, but Jeremy Oakshott is a kindly, gentle man, who would hurt no one. In your search for the assassin of Michael Sanders, you must look elsewhere.'

5

MISS PROBERT'S TESTIMONY

JAMES ANTROBUS ARRIVED at the Herefordshire village of Henning St Mary at mid-morning. Wednesday had proved to be one of those quiet, sunny, late summer days when few people seemed to be about. Henning was a town of mellow redbrick houses dating from the previous century, some with stuccoed fronts and classical porticoes.

Following the instructions given to him by a porter at the station, Antrobus made his way along the high street until he reached a pair of ornamental iron gates, which took him into the graveyard of an ancient Saxon church, beside which stood an elegant rectory, built, as far as he could judge, in the reign of Queen Anne.

Drawn up in a leafy lane just beyond the rectory he saw a closed coach standing, its driver sitting on a wall, smoking a clay pipe. As he opened the gate into the rectory garden, someone looked out of the coach window. For a moment Antrobus thought it was the figure of a nun.

In response to a ring on the bell, the door was opened by a smiling girl of fifteen or so, clad in a green cotton dress over which she wore an unbleached linen smock. She had just accepted Antrobus's card when two little girls erupted into the hall.

'Annie, Annie!' they cried. 'Who is it? Is it someone to see Daddy?'

'Yes, it is,' said the girl called Annie. 'Now, Beth, take Mary-Jane with you back to the kitchen, and finish your milk and gingerbread. Daddy's going to be busy for a while.'

'I'm sorry, sir,' said Annie, when the little girls had scampered away, 'Beth's very lively today, and whatever she does, Mary-Jane copies. Beth's only five, and Mary-Jane's three, so they can be quite a handful. But let me take you through to the study. The Rector's expecting you.'

Annie led him down the hall and into a spacious room at the rear of the house. It was lit by four tall windows, which looked out on to the sunlit churchyard. Standing by the fireplace was a fair-haired young man in clerical dress, in the process of lighting his pipe. He looked alert and poised, as though most of his time was spent in purposeful activity. Antrobus judged him to be no older than thirty.

'Rector,' said Annie, 'this is Mr Antrobus, the detective from Oxford.'

'Excellent. Pleased to meet you, Inspector. Annie, did I hear those two terrors making loud demands in the hall? I thought they were being fed.'

'They are, sir. I've sent them back to the kitchen.'

'And Miss Probert?'

'She's with me in the kitchen, too, sir. When I've taken the girls away for their morning nap, she and I will have a cup of tea together.'

'Good. I'll ring for her when she's needed. I suppose Mullins is content to sit on the wall? Good. Now, Inspector, let us sit down by the fireplace. It's very hot today for September. Would you care for something cool to drink? Annie, could you bring us each a tankard of cold beer?'

Antrobus attempted to speak, but his host held up a hand to enjoin silence. Not until the beer had been brought in did the inspector venture to break the enforced calm.

'You are the Reverend Hezekiah Daneforth?'

'Yes, indeed I am,' said the young clergyman. 'I've only been Rector here for two years, but that's long enough for a parson to hear a lot about both the innate goodness and the unfathomable wickedness of mankind. I've no doubt, Inspector, that you also think much on those things.'

'I was very taken by your little girls, sir,' said Antrobus. 'They must be a cause of great joy for you and your good wife.'

'Beth and Mary-Jane? Yes, they're my great treasures, as I'm sure you'll understand. Annie is their nurse-maid, and does wonders with them. She's an orphan, you know, not quite fifteen yet. I look upon her as their elder sister, and thus a daughter of my own. Miriam – my wife – is out visiting in the parish. But come, Inspector, I'm intrigued to hear how I can help you.'

Mr Daneforth picked up a letter from a table placed near his right hand.

'This is a letter from the Archdeacon of Warwick, asking me to "afford you every assistance", and so on. Well, I suppose I must do so. Old sins cast long shadows. You've come, I expect, to look back into the past at the appalling murder of a young woman, Vivien West. She was only twenty, I've been told, and about to be married.'

Antrobus took from his pocket the letter that Sergeant Maxwell had found sewn into the lining of Michael Sanders's jacket and handed it to the Rector, who read it and then gave it back to the inspector without immediate comment. He regarded his guest in silence for a while before he continued.

'Inspector,' said Mr Daneforth, 'your name is not unknown to me. Even in this quiet backwater we have heard of your various triumphs of detection. It is only weeks ago that you solved the mystery of Sir Montague Fowler's death in Oxford. But at times, one comes across human tragedies that are impossible to fathom, and the death of Vivien West seems to me to be one such tragedy.

I've heard so many accounts of her tragic story over the last two years. None of those versions are ever quite the same. She, and her terrible death, have become the stuff of legend. To my mind, she's like one of those droopy, dreamy girls in Tennyson's poems, part real, and part myth.'

The Rector paused for a while, and closed his eyes. Perhaps he was in prayer.

Antrobus could hear a gaggle of sparrows chattering somewhere in the churchyard. He glanced at a clock on the mantelpiece, and saw that it was just on twelve. At the same time, the clock in the church tower began to strike the hour. The Rector opened his eyes.

'You know, Mr Antrobus, there's so much saving work to be done in a parish like this. There are people for me to seek and to save, poor, indigent folk to visit and relieve. Sunday schools to establish and run. Nothing that we can do can alter the deeds of the past. Things would be much better to my way of thinking, if people would be content to let the dead rest.'

The young Rector seemed to exude an air of caution, not unmixed with distress. He had received his visitor hospitably, but Antrobus sensed that his quest for the truth of Vivien West's death was not welcome.

'You see, Inspector,' the Rector continued, 'all those people mentioned in that letter you have just shown me – Alison Savernake's letter – are dead. They're all lying out there, in the churchyard. Gossip's an ill-natured thing, born usually of envy and spite. Yes, it was all a very long time ago.

'As for those names in the letter,' he continued, 'an old lady in the parish once told me about Alison Savernake. She was a decayed gentlewoman, one of the three daughters of a man called John Savernake, a landed proprietor who lost everything in one or other of the railway manias. I've been told about Michael Sanders, too. Alison, apparently, was a particular friend of his.'

'That letter,' said Antrobus, 'was a reply to one from Michael

Sanders, who was himself cruelly murdered this Friday gone – murdered by having his throat cut from ear to ear.'

'Yes, we read about it in the *Hereford Times*. That letter was written in 1885, thirteen years after Vivien West's death, and the man whom Michael was hinting may have been her murderer was Jeremy Oakshott. I've made a study of this matter, Mr Antrobus, which is why I'm familiar with all the names and personalities. But I note in that letter that Sanders was simply asking for local opinion, because he wanted to rekindle his old friendship with Jeremy. It appears that Jeremy Oakshott was, indeed, much in love with Vivien West, but it was Michael whom she chose. In the event, of course, she married neither of them. She's out there, too, you know. In the churchyard, I mean.'

James Antrobus was not a superstitious man, but for a moment he imagined that the Rector's study was suddenly peopled by shadowy figures, the ghosts of the past.

'So, Inspector, you suspect that Jeremy Oakshott murdered Michael Sanders? That's why you're resurrecting the case of Vivien West. Those other people named in Alison's letter – I've heard all about them, too, from my old women in the almshouse, and other parish gossips. Amy Phelps, I'm told, was a strong-minded woman, much given to good works, who trusted too much to her defective judgements. She had convinced herself that Jeremy Oakshott had murdered Vivien because she didn't like Jeremy, who was given to mocking her unwelcome and unwanted attempts to improve the minds of the labouring classes. Caleb Williams, I'm told, was a congenital liar, with a genius for hating everyone and everything better off than himself. No credence could be given to anything that he said, apparently.'

'Caleb Williams…. I had hoped to interview him, but from what you said about the folk in the graveyard, I suppose he's dead as well. What happened to him?'

'He died of drink. They say he repented at the end, and had sent for the then Rector, Mr Balantyne, but Williams died before he could see him. It was all gossip, you see, and surmise. Nothing was proved.'

Antrobus drained his tankard, and as no table was near to hand, he put it down on the hearth. It had been a very welcome drink, and it had been a kindly thought of the young clergyman to provide it.

There was an outburst of merriment from the hall. The terrors had evidently escaped from wherever they had been taken. James Antrobus caught the Rector's humorous smile, and suddenly felt that he was wasting valuable time. Whatever the truth was about Sanders's murder, it was not to be found here, making fruitless enquiries about a past tragedy.

Antrobus rose to make his leave, but the Rector motioned to him to remain seated. He rang a hand-bell placed on the table beside his chair, and when the nurse-maid appeared, he said, 'Ask Miss Probert to come here, Annie. I'll take the girls back to their room, and read them a story. Inspector, I want you to listen to the tale that Miss Probert will tell you. After that, perhaps you would come out into the churchyard. There's something there that I want you to see.' He left the room through a door in a far corner, and at the same time the nurse-maid announced Miss Probert, and then withdrew.

Miss Probert was a strongly-built woman of indeterminate age, with steel-grey hair and an immobile face that revealed little of her character. She was wearing a sensible but well-cut costume suit. An impressive, rather forbidding woman, thought Antrobus, who needs no adornments of jewellery or lace to make her stand out from the crowd. She walked with the aid of a stout stick, and leaned forward heavily on her right side. Antrobus wondered whether she had at one time suffered a stroke. He half rose from his chair, but Miss Probert prevented him with a gesture, and sat down opposite him in the Rector's chair.

'Mr Daneforth warned me that you would be coming,' she began without preamble. 'This little town is a precious sort of place, full of kindly people, and a whole host of good neighbours.

It should not be remembered merely for the tragic murder that took place here over twenty years ago. I have no doubt that the Rector has shown you how the mystery of that girl's death is impenetrable. No one – no one, that is, except me – knows the truth of the matter.'

'And you do, madam?'

'Yes, and I am going to tell you that truth now. Others, no doubt, will deny the veracity of what I am going to say, and call me a liar. So be it. It was said that Vivien West was murdered by a jealous lover. Some thought it was Jeremy Oakshott. That, I may say, was the most evil calumny of them all. Jeremy was a gentle and compassionate young man, and at one time a devoted suitor of Vivien West. Some even suggested that Michael Sanders himself had done it, when he discovered that Vivien had turned to another man. That, too, was nonsense, a diabolical suggestion. The Prince of Darkness was abroad here in Henning St Mary on that bright summer's day, poisoning minds and sowing slanders—'

'And the real culprit?'

'Yes, the Devil was abroad that day,' Miss Probert continued, ignoring Antrobus's interruption. 'And unrequited love was at the bottom of it.'

Miss Probert closed her eyes for a while, and her inscrutable face gave no sign of what she might have been thinking. She sat, sphinx-like, until her eyes opened once more.

'In those days, Mr Antrobus,' she continued, 'there was a girl who lived here with her parents, a feeble-minded girl called Margaret Meadows. She was on the verge of insanity, but like many such people, she was cunning enough to conceal her true nature, so that she could remain at liberty. Sometimes a cat would be found stabbed, and for a time there was an outbreak of attacks on sheep in the outlying farms – the poor beasts would be found with their throats cut – stupid, bleating creatures, feeding freely from the fruits of the earth without mind or sensibility – but there, they did not deserve to be treated like that. No, indeed.'

Miss Probert shuddered, and a spasm of fear crossed her normally impassive face.

'This Margaret Meadows – was she in love with Michael Sanders?'

'Yes, she was. It was very shrewd of you to deduce that. Well, after poor Vivien was murdered, the Meadows family left these parts, and went to farm a few acres in Cheshire. It's time now to tell you who I am. I was, for all my working life, a wardress at Prenton Bridge Criminal Lunatic Asylum, a few miles out of Chester.

'In the year 1880 this same Margaret Meadows was admitted to our wards after a warrant had been issued by one of the Masters in Lunacy for her detention. She had— she had committed dreadful mutilations of sheep, and finally murdered a town librarian who had rebuffed her advances with horror. Was that she? Did she kill that man? Yes, of course she did. My mind is getting tired. I must concentrate on what I am saying.'

'And this woman murdered Vivien West?'

'Let me finish, Mr Antrobus. Let me get my memories together, so that we can make an end of this business. On admission, she was placed in one of the constraining cells, because she had become very violent, and dangerously unpredictable. After a few weeks, one of our doctors, Samuel Critchley, proposed administering electric shocks to certain areas of Meadows's brain via electrodes inserted through a trepanned opening in the skull.'

Antrobus shuddered. Miss Probert seemed quite unperturbed.

'The treatment was very successful. Within an hour, all tendencies to violence were seen to have stopped altogether. Unfortunately, Meadows fell into a sudden decline, and the ward physician told us that she would die within six hours.'

So that, thought Antrobus, is what these people accounted as success.

'It was soon after this diagnosis, Inspector, that Meadows sent for me, and confessed that it was she who had murdered Vivien

West eight years earlier. She had been consumed with jealousy, because Michael Sanders had not even deigned to glance at her. She hated Vivien for her beauty and her happiness. On that fateful day, she had crept into the garden of the Wests' house, and into the double hedge where Vivien was sitting, reading the marriage service in her prayer book. "I meant to stab her," she said, "but when I saw she was reading the marriage service, my hatred welled up, and I decided to treat her as I treated those stupid sheep. I leaned through the hedge, and cut her throat from behind. And then I fled."'

'So she confessed? She repented of her deed?'

'Oh no, Inspector. She boasted of it. She was afraid that she would die without anyone knowing what she had done. Her vile crime, you see, was to be her proud epitaph. She died some hours later, with a smile on her face.'

'And I suppose that she, too, is buried with the others out there in the churchyard?'

'Indeed not. She was buried within the confines of the Lunatic Asylum.'

Antrobus glanced around the room. He imagined that the ghosts were still there.

'Why did not the asylum report the matter to the police?'

'The woman was quite unfit to plead. The Law would never have permitted any attempt at arrest or interrogation. And there you have the truth of poor Vivien's death. It's all in the past, Inspector. I am told that you are investigating the murder of Michael Sanders. Well, you are wasting your time here. Go back to Oxfordshire, and look for your killer there.'

Antrobus found the young Rector sitting on a bench in the shadow of the church.

'Come with me, Mr Antrobus,' he said, 'I want to show you something.'

They picked their way through the long grass until they came to a lichen-covered headstone, partly concealed by an overgrown rhododendron bush. Antrobus read the epitaph.

Sacred to the memory
of
Vivien West
Only daughter of Francis and Jane West
Died 17 May 1872
Aged 20 years.
"O LORD, thou hast seen my wrong: judge thou my cause."
Lamentations 3, v 59

'A great tragedy, Mr Antrobus, but a tragedy belonging firmly to the past. Of all the people concerned, I know nothing personally. All I have heard are stories passed on from father to son and from mother to daughter. Miss Probert's testimony is just one among many accounts of what happened. What is the truth of the matter? We shall never know. I firmly believe that we should all leave this poor girl to rest in peace.'

After a few civilities, Antrobus left the rectory. He saw that the closed coach in the lane, with its mysterious occupant, was no longer there.

'So there it is, Sergeant,' said Antrobus, 'the story of Vivien West belongs to the past, and belongs to the dead. She was murdered by a crazed lunatic woman, who is now dead herself. I've wasted a good deal of police time, and need to wrench myself back into the present.'

The two policemen were sitting once more in the back bar of the Archangel. Sergeant Maxwell took a tentative sip of his pint of Morrell's bitter, and pulled a face.

'With all due respect, sir—'

'When you say that, Sergeant, you usually mean the opposite.'

'With all due respect, sir,' said Maxwell, ignoring the

interruption, 'I thought from the start that you were going on a wild goose chase, and what I was told at Hadleigh only confirms my hypothesis. Dr McArthur accounted for every minute of Dr Oakshott's time while he was there. So we need to ask some more questions.'

'It's not a hypothesis, Sergeant, it's merely an opinion. A hypothesis is a supposition posited as a basis for further investigation. Your opinion is that I should cease any further enquiry into the past. Well, you're right. I've wasted too much time.'

Maxwell sat back in his chair and looked at his superior officer. He was pale and drawn, and those hectic spots had appeared again in his cheeks. He'd insisted on walking across town to the Archangel because he liked its quietly forlorn atmosphere: it always seemed to be empty. But he should have gone to the Chequers, in High Street. That would have avoided the coughing fit that he'd had as they'd hurried up New College Lane.

The trouble with Mr Antrobus was that he had no wife to look after him. He had a nice, comfortable billet down at Botley, near the railway station, and his landlady did her best for him. But that wasn't the same as having a wife. He and Mrs Maxwell persuaded him to come for Sunday dinner every couple of months, and the experience always did him good. Mr Antrobus seemed content to remain a widower, and it was not their place to persuade him otherwise.

'You said we needed to ask some more questions, Sergeant. What questions would they be?'

'Well, sir, we need to get Constable Roberts to find out if any strangers had been lurking round Hadleigh that Friday night. He needs to ask the landlord of the Bull if any visitor had been in for a drink, or to ask questions. He could knock on a few doors roundabout, and ask if anyone had seen any strangers in the village acting suspiciously, or in a furtive manner.'

Antrobus nodded, but made no reply. It was time, thought Maxwell, for them to get back to the police station. The guvnor looked depressed and dissatisfied. It was very obvious that he didn't want to let go of Dr Jeremy Oakshott.

'I'll tell you something else, Guvnor,' said Maxwell. 'Just because someone spins you a plausible yarn, there's no need for you to go and believe it. Third-hand evidence is not always to be trusted.'

'Are you referring to something in particular? Or are you just dispensing general wisdom?'

'All I'm saying, Inspector, is that you're not obliged to believe everything that you're told. This Rector – what do you know about him? And the lady he trotted out for you to interview – all very nice and cosy, Guvnor. What do you know about her?'

'So you think this ordained clergyman, and this retired prison wardress were conspiring against me in order to lead me astray?'

'That's as may be,' said Sergeant Maxwell.

6

A DINNER AT THE RANDOLPH

JEREMY OAKSHOTT AND Mrs Herbert Lestrange were having afternoon tea together in one of the quiet lounges of the Clarendon Hotel in Cornmarket. There was a certain faded charm about the Clarendon that had always appealed to Jeremy. Perhaps, he mused wryly, it was because it chimed with his own inner conviction that he was a washed-out, dull sort of fellow.

Mrs Lestrange was pouring tea from a battered silver pot, talking the while of Syria and its mysteries. Outside, the clock in the ancient Saxon tower of St Michael at the North Gate struck four.

'I told you that I had something to show you,' said Mrs Lestrange, when they had disposed of the buttered crumpets and fruit cake. 'It's something that I hope will make you realize that there is a potential world of ground-breaking scholarship waiting to be recorded outside the bounds of Oxford and Cambridge.'

She opened her reticule, and took from it a tin pencil-case, which she opened. Oakshott saw that it contained a slip of parchment, some three inches wide, filled with ancient Arabic writing in what he recognized as Kufic script.

'I found this length of parchment in that cache that I told you about. Let me read it to you.'

They were sitting in an alcove, so that no one else in the room could hear Mrs Lestrange as she read to Oakshott in a low, urgent voice. As he listened, he was conscious of the fact that he was blushing with something approaching shame. For she was speaking in Arabic, the rich sounds punctuated by occasional glottal stops. He looked up and caught her eyes, and she stopped abruptly.

'How thoughtless of me,' she murmured. 'You don't speak Arabic, do you?'

'No. And I don't read it, either,' he added, with a kind of foolish truculence.

Jeremy Oakshott suddenly felt provincial and second-rate. The modern world of exploration and discovery had passed him by, leaving him marooned in a scholastic cul-de-sac. How long was it since he had consulted a primary source for his own work on the Crusades?

'Let me translate it for you, Dr Oakshott. You know that some scholars deny that Sultan Baibars could have forged a letter purporting to have come from the Grand Master of the Knights Hospitaller, ordering the defenders of Krak to surrender the fortress. Well, listen to what is written here, on this slip of parchment.

'"The Commander of the Faithful sent gold secretly to the Frankish King Otakar, who furnished him with a scribe well versed in the Latin and Frankish tongues. He it was who wrote that letter as coming from the Infidel Lord of the Hospitallers. And the men who held Krak were deceived (it was the Will of Allah) and threw open their gates." And so it goes on. And it concludes with a date: "From the Year of the Hijra 649", which in the Gregorian Calendar is 1271. Proof, you see. And it will be you, Jeremy – do you mind my being so familiar? It will be you who will confirm the truth of that old legend in the second volume of your great work.'

'Wonderful,' Oakshott murmured.

'But there is more than that,' said Mrs Lestrange. 'Turn the parchment over, and see what is written there.'

Oakshott did so, and saw an inscription in what he immediately recognized as an ancient form of French called the Langue d'Oïl. *Pro Deo amur, et pro christian poblo et nostro commun salvament....*

Jeremy Oakshott uttered a stifled cry, and half rose from his chair.

'That is the Strasburg Oath,' he said, 'sworn by Louis the German to his brother Charles II, King of France, in 842 AD. Yes, it's there, and at the end is a signature: "Otto, scribe, wrote this out for his lord Louis, to send to the hidden prince in Syria, the fourth day of December, in the year of Our Lord 842." What can it mean?'

Mrs Lestrange held out her hand for the parchment slip, and returned it to its tin box, which she dropped into her reticule.

'Do you know what we archaeologists call a find of that nature?' she asked. 'We call it an "anomalous artefact". That letter about Sultan Baibars belongs securely to the period of the other documents in the cache. But as you see, it has been written on the back of a copy of the Strasburg Oath, penned centuries earlier, in 842. How did it come to Krak? Who was the "hidden prince" in Syria? That slip of parchment was out of its place and out of its time. It didn't belong there, and yet it was there for the Arab scribe to use when he came to write the Baibar letter. And that's what we archaeologists call an anomaly.'

'It could have been Fulke de Barbazon,' said Oakshott. 'Or maybe it was—'

Leaning across the table, Mrs Lestrange took Jeremy's hand in hers, and looked earnestly into his eyes. He felt his heart leap with sudden excitement.

'I knew that you would be stirred by that inscription,' she said. 'Already you are suggesting some kind of solution to the mystery. You *must* come out with me to Krak next season. Our combined skills will make the academic world ring with our discoveries! There are other documents still sealed up in that cache, waiting for your interpretation. As for that anomaly, you may become

renowned as the solver of the puzzle that it presents. If you were
to write a paper on it immediately after your return from Krak,
you will become uniquely associated with it. People will start to
call it "The Oxford Anomaly", because it was the distinguished
Oxford scholar Dr Jeremy Oakshott who gave his interpretation of
it to the academic world.'

Mrs Lestrange sighed, and sat back in her chair. Her companion seemed to be lost in a trance. She had worked hard to bring
him on to her side. It was time to press home her advantage.

'That little college of yours, Jerusalem Hall, is a dead end, a
backwater. Come out with me, and when you return, and publish
your findings, the universities will be clamouring to offer you
professorships! Have you been to America? No? Well, there are
boundless opportunities for a man of your calibre there. I speak
of our combined skills. You are a bachelor. I am a widow. Could
you consider, even for a moment, the possibility of a more intimate
union between us? There, I have made you blush again, and I
apologize for being so forward. Perhaps you have other plans.'

'No! No, I – Mrs Lestrange – Celia – I can see a whole new
world opening for both of us. But I will need time to think, to
assess my current financial position—'

'Will you be at the Randolph tomorrow night? The dinner of
the Richard Hoare Society? I'll see you there, then. Meanwhile,
keep in mind old Horace's adage: *Carpe Diem*. Seize the day!'

As they left the lounge of the Clarendon Hotel, a tall man with
tinted glasses came out of the public bar, and followed them as far
as the cab rank in Broad Street, where Oakshott handed her into
a cab. The man watched Oakshott as he walked off towards New
College Lane. Then he turned on his heel and passed through the
ornamental gates of Trinity College.

Unless you lived in that part of Oxford known as Osney Town,
you would never find Ditch Lane, a kind of alley marooned
behind the old dwellings in Becket Street.

Ditch Lane consisted of a single row of old three-storey brick houses, each approached by a flight of steps. At the end of the lane a blank wall, topped with broken glass, cut off all communication with the rest of the area. Opposite the houses was an engineering shop belonging to the Great Western Railway.

James Antrobus lived at number three, a boarding house kept by Mrs Hardy, the relict of a scout who had worked at Worcester College. He occupied the first floor front, which consisted of a sitting room, bedroom, and a minute kitchen. What Mrs Hardy called 'the usual offices' were at the end of the landing.

It had been a trying day, and he was glad to get away from Sergeant Maxwell and the whole business of police work for the evening. At five o'clock Mrs Hardy would bring him his dinner, which tonight was to be a steak pie with cabbage and potatoes. He sat down in a sagging but very comfortable chair in the window, and looked across at the railway workshops. It was very near the railway here, and at all times of the day you could hear the trains thundering and clanking and letting off steam. You got used to it with time.

His little round table was set for tea, with knife and fork, cruet, and napkin. On top of his well-stocked bookshelf stood a framed photograph of his late wife, wearing a dress that had been fashionable in the early eighties. She was only just into her thirties when she had died of a seizure.

There was a knock at the door, and Mrs Hardy came in, wiping her hands on her apron. She was a rather stout, kindly soul, who mercifully did not fuss over him, which would have made him feel even more of an invalid than he was. It was too early for tea. What did she want?

'Mr Antrobus, sir,' she said, 'You've got a visitor. It's Superintendent Fielding. Shall I show him up?'

Antrobus sprang up from his chair, and glanced in the mirror over the fireplace. Did he look presentable? He straightened the black tie under his wing collar, and pulled his shoulders back.

'Yes, show him up by all means, Mrs Hardy.'

The heavy tread on the stairs heralded the appearance of Antrobus's superior officer. The superintendent wore the black frogged uniform jacket, buttoned to the neck, and pill-box hat that went with his rank. He was a man nearing sixty, with silver grey hair, and luxuriant side whiskers. His voice betrayed the fact that he was a Londoner in origin.

'I hope I don't inconvenience you, Inspector,' he said, standing on the threshold. 'I just want to have a little word with you. How are you? Are you coping well with your sad complaint?'

Antrobus made no reply, knowing from experience that none was expected. He motioned to the superintendent to sit down in the chair opposite his, and waited for him to speak.

'I don't know whether you are aware of the fact, Antrobus,' said Superintendent Fielding, 'but yesterday evening the Vice-Chancellor gave a reception for senior officers in the Oxford City Police, and a number of, er, legal luminaries. Yes, I think that is how best to describe them. It was held in the Sheldonian Theatre.'

Fielding had placed his hat on the table, and was looking out of the window. He seemed curiously constrained.

'And did the Vice-Chancellor minister to the inner man, sir?'

The superintendent smiled, and gave his full attention to Antrobus.

'What? Yes, he did. There were very substantial refreshments, and a commendable quantity of alcohol. And it was there, Antrobus, that I met the Rector of Jerusalem Hall. He told me that you had been investigating the *bona fides* of one of the Fellows, Dr Jeremy Oakshott, the distinguished historian of the Crusades. Apparently, some friends of Oakshott's living in the country had told him – told Oakshott, I mean – that you had been asking questions about him. You had also, it seems, interviewed Oakshott himself at Jerusalem Hall. Not unnaturally, Oakshott is feeling peeved about all this, and had complained to the Rector, who mentioned the matter to me, last night.'

'I did interview him, sir, because—'

'Before I came here, Antrobus, I went to the police station in High Street, and made your Sergeant Maxwell tell me all about it. His air of belligerence cuts no ice with me. Apparently, you've been up in Herefordshire delving into this man Oakshott's antecedents. All this, I gather, is connected to the murder of a certain Michael Sanders out at – what was the place called? Hadleigh. Do you think that Oakshott murdered him?'

'Sir, I felt entitled to regard him as a suspect until I could prove otherwise. I have now done so, and can eliminate Dr Oakshott from my enquiries.'

'Well, see that you do. As you know, I'm a man who shows no favour to anyone merely because of their rank or standing, but I have to maintain the delicate balance of amity between Town and Gown. I want no importunate dons interfering with police work. So tread lightly, Antrobus, will you? I know you too well to be deceived by your verbal blandishments. Keep away from Oakshott, do you hear? Look elsewhere.'

'Today,' said the elderly Catholic priest sitting on Oakshott's right, 'is the Feast of the Exaltation of the Holy Cross.'

Jeremy Oakshott looked out of the window of the private dining room on the first floor of the Randolph Hotel, and saw the elegant spire of the Martyrs' Memorial rising in front of the little cemetery of St Mary Magdalen's. What would those unfortunate polemicists Cranmer, Ridley and Latimer, have thought about a Catholic priest enjoying a five-course dinner so near the spot where they had died for the Protestant religion?

'I mention the fact,' the priest continued, 'because our guest of honour, the Honourable Mrs Herbert Lestrange, was born on that day.'

There were twenty ladies and gentlemen sitting at the long table, which was adorned with silver-gilt epergnes, tall candelabra, and the special set of china belonging to the Richard Hoare

Society. This eighteenth century pioneer of archaeology had taken for his rallying cry the words: 'We speak from facts, not theory.'

Raising his voice above the excited babble of the members, Oakshott asked his neighbour whether he was personally acquainted with Mrs Lestrange.

'I knew her husband, the late Captain Herbert Lestrange, quite well – but I say, we have not been introduced! I know who you are, of course, your fame has preceded you in your magisterial studies of the Crusades. I am Father Cuthbert Linacre of the Society of Jesus, one of the clergy at St Aloysius's church in Woodstock Road.'

Father Linacre was a balding gentleman in his seventies. He wore little gold spectacles that made him look like Mr Pickwick. He sat well back in his chair, savouring the delights brought up from the Randolph's kitchen.

'Yes, I knew Captain Lestrange quite well. He was a dashing sort of fellow, though there was a strain of weakness in his character that didn't quite sit well with his vocation as a soldier. He was only thirty-two when he was killed at Alexandria. That's when *she*' – he waved his fork in the direction of Mrs Lestrange – 'that's when *she* began her career as a lecturer and frequenter of dinner parties, progressing from that to being a practical archaeologist.' He laughed.

'You don't like her?'

'Oh, yes, I like her well enough. But those four books that she published…. The first one, a selection of her husband's letters, was an instant success, and deservedly so. He wrote well, and engaged the reader in his accounts of life in the East. But you know, the other three volumes of letters – well, there are some people who claim that she wrote them herself!'

'And you are one of those people, I take it, Father Linacre?'

The priest suddenly looked vexed. He realizes that he'd said more than he should have done, thought Oakshott. The excellent wines from the Randolph's cellars were apt to loosen tongues at events like this one.

'Dr Oakshott, I was myself an archaeologist working on several of the Vatican digs in Egypt and Palestine in the seventies and eighties. In those three later volumes I have detected inaccuracies, descriptions of sites and objects that are no longer there, accounts of meetings with people who were dead at the times when she claimed to have spoken with them, and recorded their words. I say "she", because I am convinced that it was she, not her husband, who composed those accounts.'

'And why have you come to this dinner, Father?'

'I've come because, like you, I'm a member of the Richard Hoare Society, and because I know they feed you well here. Ah! Here's the roast lamb coming in!'

Oakshott turned his attention to the guest of honour, the Honourable Mrs Herbert Lestrange, who sat at one end of the long table. Dear, enigmatic Celia! She looked very striking in her black silk evening dress. Her corsage was adorned with a deep red rose, and she wore a necklace of flashing diamonds, with matching earrings. She was talking animatedly to a lady sitting on her left, whom Oakshott recognized as a distinguished Fellow of St Hugh's College. And then, for a single moment, Mrs Lestrange threw him a speculative look, a kind of unspoken questioning that made him blush. Already, they were more than friends.

'There's no money there, you know,' said Father Linacre, 'that's why she's for ever holding those fundraising events.' He turned his whole attention once more to the saddle of lamb.

Well, why shouldn't she bestir herself and raise funds for her archaeological expeditions? It was all very well for his Jesuit neighbour to cavil about those published diaries; he had the wealth of the Catholic Church behind his own sallies into the ancient East.

The chairman of the meeting banged on the table, and launched into an interminable speech that held his audience in the grip of a quite desperate boredom. When he had finished, he called upon the guest of honour to address the members of the society, and

Mrs Lestrange rose to speak. She spoke for half an hour, but it seemed like only ten minutes. She held them all, including Father Linacre, spellbound with her descriptions of treasures unearthed, ancient manuscripts found sealed in amphorae, of the opening of tombs lost for centuries, where lanterns caught the gleam of gold, and the painted eyes of mummies regarded them incuriously as they were brought to the light of day after the darkness of millennia.

Oakshott glanced around at the many faces, all holding a look of total absorption in what Mrs Lestrange was telling them. Among those faces was the man with tinted glasses. Perhaps Grigg had been right. He was probably a Syrian academic, visiting Oxford to research in the Bodleian Library or the Indian Institute.

Before sitting down to rapturous applause, the Honourable Mrs Lestrange made a brief appeal for patronage, and told her audience that a list of current patrons could be taken from a tray near the door. The chairman proposed a toast to the evergreen memory of Richard Hoare, followed by the Loyal Toast. Then the company broke up. Carriages were to be at eleven, and it was near that hour now.

In the vaulted passage leading from the dining room, Mrs Lestrange detained Oakshott by placing a hand on his arm. How handsome she looked! How vital!

'Jeremy, have you yet spoken to your uncle about the expedition?' she asked.

'I have. I went out to Hazelmere Castle yesterday. But it's hopeless. He's not dismissive of the project, but he has refused adamantly to advance me the money. It's not as though I'm begging him for charity; I made it clear that I was asking him for a loan.'

'And what did he say to that?'

'He said that to make me a loan would only encourage my improvidence.'

For the second time that evening, Jeremy Oakshott blushed.

Mrs Lestrange withdrew her hand. She looked at him with what seemed suspiciously like haughty contempt.

'Don't let this opportunity pass you by, Jeremy,' she said. 'When you return from Syria – for go you must – you will have become Europe's foremost authority on Krak des Chevaliers. You will have interpreted the whole of the Second Crusade afresh. Find the money! Today is my birthday. Bring the money to me as a birthday present! My dear Jeremy, you are already one of the most distinguished scholars of the history of the Middle East. Now add practical experience to your many academic distinctions. "We speak from facts, not theory." Do all in your power to keep your appointment with Destiny!'

7

UNCERTAINTIES

IT 'WAS RAINING when Oakshott emerged into Beaumont Street. He hurried across the road and into the Broad, where he climbed into one of the many hansom cabs drawn up in the middle of the wide thoroughfare. They clattered past the Sheldonian Theatre, the decaying carved stone heads of the Roman emperors dimly discernible in the light of the gas standards lining the road. They were soon in New College Lane.

Whatever the difficulties, he would go out to Syria with Celia's expedition next year. She was right: his destiny was beckoning him. Already a widely respected authority, the combination of his own academic research and the findings of practical investigation would possibly ensure that he was awarded a university professorship.

'The Oxford Anomaly'.... What wondrous matters lay waiting for discovery in those ancient manuscripts that she had told him about after her lecture at Jesus College? How thrilled he had been to hear the translation of the piece of parchment in the tin box! And what an intriguing mystery was waiting to be solved concerning that ancient French text on its reverse!

Money.... He had little that he could sell, and the prospect of arranging a commercial loan at exorbitant interest filled him with terror. What was he to do?

The cabbie stopped at the entrance to Leper's Lane, and Oakshott alighted. There would have been no space for the cab to be turned round at the Jerusalem Hall end. He gave the cabbie ninepence, and passed into the grateful shelter of the gatehouse. There was no one in the lodge, though it was lit by two spluttering gas mantles. Tonson was probably engaged on what he called 'doing the rounds'.

The old college buildings assumed a mysterious air at night. A few lights burned in one or two windows, and the small quadrangle was dimly illumined by oil lanterns suspended at the entrance to the staircases. Lowering his head against the rain, he hurried along the path that would take him to the common room.

The old oak-panelled chamber was warm and inviting, and a small fire was burning in the grate. All the candles were still lit, though it was very late; even as he entered the room one or other of Oxford's many clocks began to chime a quarter to twelve.

His old friend Jonathan Grigg was sitting spread-eagled in an armchair near the fire, a bottle of port beside him on the hearth. His prominent eyes were comfortably glazed, and his face even redder than usual. He raised a hand in greeting.

'I've been in the Abbot's Kitchen for most of the day. You know that Professor Oddling has given me the corner of a bench to conduct my analyses of deadly poisons? My own laboratory here in college is quite adequate, but they've a lot of new equipment there. I did some very satisfying work today, and I've been celebrating ever since. But sit down, Oakshott, and tell me about the dinner. Did the siren make a dead set at you? Have a cigar: there's some in that box. And there's a couple of glasses of port left in that bottle. The other fellows have retired to bed.'

He's sozzled, to use the latest undergraduate word, thought Oakshott. But then, so am I, to some extent. The 'Abbot's Kitchen' was the name given to the University chemical laboratory out in South Parks Road. It had been designed to resemble the Abbot's

Kitchen at Glastonbury. Despite his fondness for the bottle, Grigg was doing first-class research there.

Oakshott gave Grigg an account of the evening's doings, and then rummaged in a pocket until he found a copy of the subscription list that Celia had provided for the members of the Richard Hoare Society. He handed it to Grigg, who scrutinized it, using an eyeglass to do so.

'It's an impressive list, I grant you,' he said. 'Impressive in its length, I mean. But I don't know many of these fellows, do you? They've all promised £100 or more, so they must be quite well heeled. "George Jones, Esq." – no, I've never heard of him. Comes from Middlesbrough, it says here. Sir Jacob Chantry – I thought he was dead. Sir Philip Margrave – I thought he was dead, too.'

He handed the list back to Oakshott.

'So Mrs Lestrange has been making eyes at you?' said Grigg, laughing. 'What was it that old Sam Weller said to young Sam? "Beware of widders, Samivel."'

'Don't talk such rot, Grigg,' Oakshott replied, laughing in spite of himself. But she *had* given him that special glance across the table, a glance meant for him alone.... And she had all but proposed marriage to him when they had met in the Clarendon Hotel. Marriage!

His eyes filled with tears. *Vivien. Oh, Vivien.*

He looked out of the window, and saw Tonson snuffing out the lanterns in the quad. It was one of the irksome inconveniences of Jerusalem Hall that piped gas, the installation of which had begun in 1880, had never gone further than the porter's lodge. Soon, Tonson would come to turn them out of the common room, extinguish the candles, and make all safe from fire. It was time to go to bed.

When the Honourable Mrs Herbert Lestrange left the Randolph, the chairman of the meeting hailed a cab for her, and told the driver to take her to Dragonfly Lane, Park Town. They set off up

St Giles, and then into the Banbury Road. Within twenty minutes, the cab stopped at a fine modern suburban house. Mrs Lestrange paid the cabbie, and rang the bell. The door was opened by an elderly woman in a black bombazine dress.

'Good evening, ma'am,' she said, standing back to let Mrs Lestrange enter. 'Did you have a nice dinner?'

'It was *very* nice, thank you, Mrs Benson. Is Mr Murchison still up? I might just have a word with him before I retire.'

'Yes, ma'am, he's still up, bless him. I think he's better than he was – more cheerful, you know.'

Mrs Benson only took quality people as guests in her house. Mrs Lestrange was obviously a lady of quality, but her friend Mr Murchison – well, he'd seen better days, that was for sure. He was supposed to be her friend, but – well, she wasn't one to gossip. She watched Mrs Lestrange as she knocked on Mr Murchison's door, and then made her way down the kitchen passage to the comfort of her little parlour.

'Any luck?' asked Mr Murchison.

What a ruin he was! His cheeks had fallen in, and his eyes were rheumy. His right hand shook with incipient palsy. He was only forty-three years old, but opium had had its destructive way with him.

Celia Lestrange took a cigarette from a silver box on the table, and lit it. It was a long, foreign affair, with a paper tube through which to suck the aromatic Balkan smoke.

'Any luck? Yes, quite a lot. A considerable number of people are attracted to the idea of funding what would be, in effect, a scientific expedition. I think my talks in London, and here in Oxford, should do the trick. I don't need to go to Cambridge after all.'

'And how was Dr Oakshott?' His voice was feeble, but it was that of an educated gentleman.

'He was much the same. Brilliant, but pusillanimous. I am working on him. I gave him the glad eye again this evening, and told him to apply once more to his rich uncle for the necessary funds. He will, you know!'

She crossed the room and kissed the frail man on the cheek. Then she retired to her own room.

Yes, Jeremy Oakshott was falling for her. What had he made of her marriage proposal? She could see from his eyes that he was attracted to her, and if she pretended to show contempt for his apparent weakness, that would stir him to some kind of positive action. As a scholar he was second to none, but he was a poor ornament of his sex.

That man had been there – that Jesuit priest who could read minds. What had he told Oakshott about her? Well, time would tell.

She opened the curtains, and looked out into the quiet, lamp-lit road. A tall, bearded man, a gentleman to judge by his dress, was reading a book by the light of a lamp-post. Oxford was an eccentric place, with eccentric inhabitants. She closed the curtains, blew out the bedside candle, and retired to bed.

Early on Saturday morning, Jeremy Oakshott stood in the misty cemetery at Botley, and watched as the body of Michael Sanders was lowered into a freshly dug grave. A friend of his, one of the clergy at St Lawrence, North Hinksey, had agreed to say the burial service, followed by the committal at the graveside. For old times' sake, he had bought a fresh burial plot; Michael would not lie in a common grave. Later in the year, he would have a modest stone erected.

Later the same evening, Oakshott descended to the furnace room in the crypt beneath the chapel at Jerusalem Hall, and consigned Vivien West's bloodstained Prayer Book to the flames. He was alone in the crypt, so no one heard his racking sobs as the golden sparks flew upwards.

'Jeremy,' said Jeremy's Uncle Ambrose, 'your Aunt Arabella

has made splendid progress since you brought her back from Frampton Asylum last month. She's now more than able to take her place as chatelaine of Hazelmere. I'll retain the nurse and the new maid for her. At least, for a time.'

It was the Monday after Jeremy had witnessed the obsequies of the friend of his youth, Michael Sanders.

The library of Hazelmere Castle had been designed to remind its owner of the gloomy and frightening chambers encountered in the gothic novels of Mrs Radcliffe. Book cases of black oak lined the walls, but the books crammed on to their shelves had never been read. Oakshott's architect friend told him that they had been bought from a dealer, who charged three shillings a yard. Two great chandeliers hung from a plaster ceiling writhing with fan tracery, modelled on that to be found in Gloucester Cathedral. The walls behind the panelling were of shoddy brick. The fan tracery was wrought in cracked and yellowing plaster.

'I want you to go upstairs and visit your aunt,' Ambrose Littlemore continued. 'Speak to her, and let her speak to you. I can assure you that she is much improved, now that she's her own mistress, and eating properly.'

Uncle Ambrose looked like a medieval ascetic, the type of man who would have liked to be walled up in an anchor-hold, but appearances could be deceptive. It would have been wrong to call him a recluse. He was certainly not a man who courted what people liked to call 'society', but he was fond of quiet gatherings with people of like mind, and when not prevented by arthritis he would ride out with the local hunt.

Hazelmere Castle, built in 1856, was a costly pile to maintain, a monument to Uncle's father, a very successful railway promoter, who had desperately wanted to be considered one of the gentry. One day, as Uncle was fond of reminding him, it would all be his, but such a liability was a dubious legacy. Uncle was a generous man within his own determined limits – limits which did not include funding archaeological expeditions.

'You should have received a letter from me on Saturday—'

'I did, Uncle. I expect neither of us wants to refer to it at the moment. You have made up your mind, and I respect your decision. Now, tell me about these new charities that you want to support.'

Jeremy had been standing by the fireplace, looking at the heads of grotesques and monks adorning its marble surround. The flames from the fire made some of the heads seem to nod and grin at him as his uncle was speaking.

'Come and sit here at the table,' said his uncle. 'Let me explain why I want to support these good folk.' He added, in a more gentle, almost shamefaced tone: 'I won't be giving them a fortune, my boy, just a couple of hundred each per year. I'm having their secretaries here for dinner, and a couple of public figures who might want to associate themselves with these charities, and I want you to be there, too. I'd written to them, suggesting Friday the twenty-first – this Friday coming – and they have all agreed.' With a sudden flash of humour, he added, 'Well, they're bound to agree, aren't they, when there's money in the offing!'

The smile faded, and Uncle's serious look returned. He seemed slightly ashamed of his cynical outburst.

'I want to do something to help women of our own class who find themselves reduced to poverty by illness or mental affliction. You'll realize, I think, that it was the plight of your aunt, and her long confinement to an institution, that had prompted me to take this action.'

'Admirable, Uncle!' cried Oakshott, and the old man looked at him with scarcely concealed surprise. His nephew seemed to be genuinely enthused by his plan.

Considering the contents of the letter that the boy had received on Saturday, it was little short of a miracle that Jeremy should have shown such sympathy for his idea.

'What are these charities, Uncle?'

'The first one is the Establishment for Gentlewomen in

Temporary Illness, which has a house at 90 Harley Street. It relieves the sick wives and daughters of professional men. And the other is the Ladies' Samaritan Society, at 23 Queen Square, Bloomsbury. They supply the wants of ladies who have fallen into epilepsy or paralysis. I think you'll agree, Jeremy, that they are worthy causes.'[1]

'They are, indeed. And will you continue your grant of £50 to the Prison Visitors' Association? That, too, is a worthy cause, and I have been an active member for over five years.'

'Indeed, indeed, my boy. Not only will I continue it, but I will raise the sum to £75. Now, go upstairs and visit your aunt.'

Oakshott had expected to find his Aunt Arabella mewed up in a gloomy, airless chamber, like those to be found in the pages of Jane Austen's *Northanger Abbey*. It came as a surprise to find that her suite of rooms had been newly decorated and furnished; Uncle Ambrose had evidently prepared for Arabella Cathcart's release from Frampton well in advance.

His aunt, too, had undergone some kind of transformation. Her long face still showed the lines of suffering that she had brought away with her from the asylum, but her complexion was now that of a healthy woman of sixty, and her eyes shone with a new interest in life. She was wearing a dress of mauve silk, complemented by a necklace of small rubies. There was nothing in her appearance or demeanour to suggest that she had just emerged from fifteen years in a mental institution.

'Come in, Jeremy,' said Aunt Arabella, 'and sit down with me at the fire. You've been avoiding me, haven't you? I'm afraid that I was confused and confounded when you came to fetch me away from Dr Critchley's madhouse.' She laughed. 'But I know very well who you are now, nephew, so there's no need for you to be afraid of me.'

---

1. The Establishment for Gentlewomen closed in 1948. The Ladies' Samaritan Society still exists.

'I'm delighted to see you so well, and in such good spirits, Aunt Arabella,' said Jeremy, relaxing in his chair. Surely that new wallpaper, with those stylized swans, posed among green rushes against a light cream sky, was the work of Walter Crane? Perhaps Uncle Ambrose was not as attached to the pseudo-gothic dark flocked papers to be found in the downstairs rooms as he pretended to be.

'I have been talking about you to your uncle,' said Aunt Arabella. 'He has told me all about your distinguished academic career, and lent me volume one of your work on the Crusades. I must confess that I found it too heavy going, but I can see its merit.'

Jeremy watched her as she took a small bottle from a table, and unscrewed its cap. She did so rather clumsily, leaning forward, and holding the bottle with a slightly trembling hand. Was Aunt Arabella showing incipient signs of the palsy? The bottle, he saw, was made of dark blue glass, covered in a filigree of gold, with a gold cap. She poured some of its contents on to a handkerchief, and dabbed her temples with it.

'Cologne,' she said. 'Dr Critchley wouldn't let any of us have perfumes or pomades of any sort. But now that I'm my own mistress, I have whatever I like.'

Aunt Arabella put the little bottle back on the table. Jeremy saw that it held a few novels, all published within the last few years. There was *Dracula*, and *The Picture of Dorian Gray*. And what was that third book? *The Time Machine*, by H.G. Wells.

Evidently his aunt was undergoing some kind of physical and mental resurrection.

'What do you think of your uncle?' she asked suddenly.

'Think of him?' repeated Jeremy, startled by this unexpected question. 'Well, I've always held Uncle Ambrose in high regard—'

'No, no, I don't mean that. I mean what do you think of his health? He's only sixty-five, you know, but you could take him for eighty. He's frailer than you'd think. I wonder how long he'll last?

He could drop dead at any moment. Or maybe he'll see us all out. You never know. But one thing is certain, nephew, if your uncle *does* die within a reasonable space of time' – she waved her hand with mock solemnity around the room – 'all this will be yours!'

Jeremy Oakshott said nothing for a while. He thought, what shall I do with it when it *is* mine? Pull it down? Sell it? One thing he would never do, he would never live in it.

Aunt Arabella had begun hemming some towels, in the way of ladies of her generation. Beside her on the table were a large pair of gleaming steel scissors.

Jeremy recalled the account that Dr Critchley had given of the event that had brought his aunt into the doctor's confinement and care. 'Miss Cathcart had become jealous of a neighbour's young daughter, a girl of twenty-two. She envied the girl's prettiness and liveliness, and also her intellectual ability. One day, while this girl was telling her about the latest book that she was reading, Miss Cathcart stabbed her in the back with a pair of scissors.'

Jeremy excused himself, and left the room.

On Tuesday morning, Jeremy Oakshott stood outside the forbidding gates of Oxford Gaol, talking to a cheerful man in his thirties, a man dressed in a threadbare pea-jacket, dungarees, and a battered peaked cap.

'Now, Patrick,' said Oakshott, 'we all know that you're not a real villain, but you stole wooden sleepers from the railway, and sold them to a not very scrupulous builder, and for that you got nine months. I've helped you all I can, and in that envelope you'll find enough money to catch a boat back to Dublin. I want you to go straight from this moment forward, and if you do what I ask I'll send you a money order in the post in a couple of weeks' time to help you on your way. Will you promise me to keep to the straight and narrow way?'

The Irishman's eyes filled with tears.

'God bless you, sir,' he said, 'you've been like a ministering angel to me. I won't let you down. And when I've done here, I'll go back home, and seek out an honest living.'

The man drew a sleeve roughly across his eyes, and stumbled away.

The warder had been watching them from a barred window beside the gates. Dr Oakshott had done well with Paddy Flynn. Paddy wasn't a real villain, and there was every chance that he'd live a straight and honest life once he got back to Ireland. He wondered what had happened to John Smith, another of the good doctor's cases, the violent thug who had twice got away with murder. One thing was certain: wherever he was, he'd be up to mischief.

8

A MURDEROUS NIGHT

AMBROSE LITTLEMORE'S VALET skilfully adjusted his master's white tie, and then helped him on with his tail coat. For a man in poor health, with a slight curvature of the spine, the master made an impressive figure once he was dressed for dinner. The formal evening clothes seemed to give him a kind of renewed confidence in himself. There were times during the day, though, when he appeared to be assailed by sudden onsets of self-doubt. It was a valet's duty to note these things, but never to comment on them.

He glanced around the cavernous bedroom, with its old faded tapestries, soot-stained vaulted ceiling, and vast marble fireplace, above which hung an oil painting depicting Judith slaying Holofernes. The many candles in the apartment only emphasized the overall gloom of the place. If the truth be known, Mr Littlemore would be much more comfortable in one of those neat, cosy villas that were going up everywhere.

'Is there anything else, sir?'

'No, thank you, Albert. I'll make my way downstairs presently.'

Albert Stead left the room, and walked along a dark passage that brought him out on to a panelled gallery, from which he could look down into the entrance hall of Hazelmere Castle. He quite liked the ancient suits of armour standing on their plinths around the walls, and the shields and swords displayed on the panelling.

He walked carefully around the great carved chair standing against the gallery wall. Mrs Tonkiss, the housekeeper, said it was a copy of the Coronation Chair in Westminster Abbey; maybe she was right.

There were to be six, all told, for dinner that night. The Master, Dr Jeremy Oakshott the Master's nephew from Oxford, a Colonel and Mrs Scott-James, Lord Arthur Farrell, and a Miss Jex-Blake. Miss Cathcart was slightly unwell, and had already had a light meal served in her room. The four guests were representatives of a couple of London societies. The Master contrived to look like a miser, but he was nothing if not generous.

He had reached the great curving staircase leading down to the hall, but it was not his place to use that means of getting to the ground floor. Instead, he opened a narrow door in the wall, and descended a musty spiral staircase that took him to the kitchen passage. Various savoury smells came from the direction of the kitchen. Dinner would be served at seven, and because of the six covers to be serviced, he would have to join Mr Jevons and the two girls to serve. There was just time to have a word with Bob Freeman before donning a fresh pair of white gloves.

He found Bob Freeman in the gun room, standing at the long barred window, and looking out across the front pasture. He could hear the roll of distant thunder, and knew that a storm was approaching. It had been close all day, but now there was a smell of rain in the air.

'I can give you ten minutes, Bob,' said Albert, 'and then I'll have to present myself at the pantry. What is it that's troubling you?'

Bob Freeman, a weather-beaten man of forty or so, dressed in a dark moleskin suit, turned from the window and produced a sheet of paper from one his pockets.

'Here, Albert,' he said, 'read this. I should have shown it to the Master, but I didn't want to frighten him. I can deal with this myself, but I want someone else to know about it in case I – in case something happens to me.'

Albert took the paper and went over to the window to read it. There was a single candle burning in the gun room, but a bright moon high in the sky had broken through the scudding clouds, and its light was sufficient for him to read. It was a message, written in capital letters with a pencil.

'A Fenian man is coming to the castle tonight to steal weapons from your gun room. He'll come across the south pasture at ten o'clock, so be ready for him. I know about your cousin. You'll want to strike a blow for him.' It was signed: 'Orange William'.

'Fenians! You should have told the Master, Bob. What did he mean by those words, "I know about your cousin"?'

'My cousin Eddie was working as a groom at the CID head-quarters in London ten years ago last May, when those fiends set off a bomb that blew the place apart. Eddie was maimed for life. He died in the workhouse last year. I don't know who Orange William is, Albert, but he struck the right note with me.'

'What are you going to do?'

Bob Freeman walked over to the gun-rack, and used a key from his own bunch to unlock it. He took down a rifle, and laid it care-fully on a table near the window.

'This is a lovely weapon, Albert,' he said, 'a Lee Enfield, and I'm going to oil it now, put the bolt in, and load it with a clip of bullets. When that Fenian man comes running across the lawn there' – he gestured towards the window – 'I'll be standing at the side door, and I'll let him have it in the legs. That'll bring the household running, and someone will send for the police.'

'Are you sure, Bob? It's not seven yet. Let me send down to the village for the constable. It'd be out of your hands, then.'

'I want revenge for poor Cousin Eddie, Albert. When he died, he left a wife and four children behind him in the workhouse. I'll stay here, as quiet as a mouse, and wait. Besides, I've a right to defend my Master's property.'

Albert Stead knew that there was nothing more to be done. Bob was the gamekeeper, and a fine shot into the bargain. Besides, it would serve the damned Fenian right if he lost the use of his legs for a while. Leaving the gun room, he made his way to the pantry.

Jeremy Oakshott sipped the dessert wine that had accompanied the gooseberry tart, and looked at his fellow diners. The dinner for six had been a success, and the four representatives of Uncle's charities were now fully at ease. Jevons, the butler, was well over seventy, but excelled at table service. Oakshott had seen the discreet hand-signals that the old man made to Albert the footman, and the two maids whenever it was time to remove a plate, or replenish a glass. Albert looked a little *distrait*, as though part of his mind was preoccupied with matters unconnected with serving dinner. Well, that was more than possible. People of his sort, like college scouts, had private lives, and private worries.

Uncle Ambrose was talking animatedly to Colonel Scott-James, an elderly retired soldier with white side-whiskers. The Colonel's wife was evidently confiding some domestic secret to Miss Jex-Blake, who sat beside her. Sophia Jex-Blake was dressed smartly but soberly in a dark silk evening gown, relieved at collar and cuffs with Brussels lace. Where one would expect to see a corsage, she wore a small gold watch attached to a ribbon. Her fair hair, parted in the middle, was uncovered. She had a round, pleasant face, and was blessed with a flawless complexion.

Lord Arthur Farrell, representing the Ladies' Samaritan Society, was an earnest young man in his thirties. He had spent most of the evening talking in low tones to his host.

Oakshott thought, where have I heard that name – Jex-Blake – before? It had been only recently that he had heard it, but in what context he could not recall. He saw a vigorous woman in her mid-fifties, a woman who carried with her an air of quiet command. Why was her name so familiar?

Yes! This was the woman who had helped to solve the mystery of Warden Fowler's death at St Michael's, working, so he had been told, in tandem with the prying, over-inquisitive Inspector Antrobus. She was a qualified doctor – both physician and surgeon; not a radical person, by all accounts; but she had persisted in pursuing her vocation, and was now rightly distinguished in her own profession.

Oakshott listened to the rain beating against the windows of the dining chamber. The curtains had not been closed, and he could see the bright moon hurtling across the sky as it sought to free itself from the embrace of the black rain clouds.

The dessert plates were removed, and a savoury of anchovies on toast was served.

'You're very quiet this evening, Jeremy,' said Uncle Ambrose. It sounded like a statement; it was, in fact, a question.

'Well, Uncle, I'm a little preoccupied with college matters at the moment, but I can assure you that I listened very carefully while Colonel Scott-James and Lord Arthur Farrell argued their respective cases. Like you, I can think of no worthier causes than theirs for you to support.'

'I'm glad to hear it,' Uncle Ambrose replied. 'I can tell you all now that I have already instructed my banker to make certain payments to both charities as soon as they receive my letter of consent – which will be sent to them in the next couple of days.'

There were murmurs of approbation from the guests, and soon afterwards the company moved into the drawing room, where coffee was to be served. It was yet another vast chamber, its floor covered by faded Turkey carpets. It was well lit by four great chandeliers suspended from the ceiling.

Oakshott looked at his watch. Twenty minutes to ten.

'Uncle,' he said, 'Colonel Scott-James was telling me before dinner that he had served in India as *aide-de-camp* to General Ogilvy in Madras. Why don't you show him the jewelled dagger that the Maharajah of Cawnpore gave to your father? The story behind that would be of great interest to all your guests, I think.'

'I should very much like to see it,' said the Colonel. 'I met the

Maharajah on a number of occasions. He was a very generous man, after his own fashion.'

'The dagger? Now, where have we stowed it?'

'Isn't it in that Indian cabinet in your dressing room, Uncle?' said Jeremy. 'I'll come with you to search for it, if you like.'

Uncle Ambrose rose from his chair and left the room, followed by his nephew.

'Tell me, Colonel,' said Sophia Jex-Blake, 'what kind of men *are* these native potentates? They're disgustingly rich, aren't they? Well, they must be, I suppose, if they can hand out jewelled daggers as presents.'

'Yes, ma'am, they're very rich, but very generous, when the mood takes them. The Maharajah of Cawnpore was very bountiful, you know, though a bit on the wild side. He tended to hit out at anyone or anything that caused him the slightest annoyance. I remember … Good God, what was that?'

All those present in the room knew that what they had heard was a shot – or perhaps two shots – coming from the grounds. Colonel Scott-James rushed to one of the windows, and peered out into the rainy night. He found himself looking across the pasture that came right up to the terrace on the south side of the castle.

'Damn this rain,' he cried. 'I can't see much, but there's an altercation of some sort going on out there. You ladies, stay where you are. Lord Arthur, come with me.'

They stood on the terrace, oblivious of the driving rain, and watched as two men carrying flaming torches aloft, ran across the moonlit pasture and bend over a man who lay face downwards on the grass. One of the men, grooms from the house, shouted a single word, which they could just make out above the noise of the rain: 'Dead!'

'Oh, gentlemen,' sobbed Bob Freeman, 'I never thought to kill him. I aimed for his legs. Come through here, into the gun room, and I'll tell you the whole story.'

Colonel Scott-James and Lord Arthur Farrell followed him into the room. Bob Freeman tried to light a candle, but his hand shook so much that Lord Arthur performed the task for him. The shadows receded, and Jeremy Oakshott spoke.

'Gentlemen,' he said, 'this man is my uncle's gamekeeper, Robert Freeman. Whatever he has done tonight, he has done with good intent.'

Out in the pasture, the two grooms had dragged the body into the shelter of the trees. One of them ran to them across the grass, and addressed himself to the Colonel.

'Sir,' he said, touching his cap, 'that man was felled by two bullets. One hit him in the left leg, and the other went straight through his heart, as far as we can tell. Shall I send someone into the village to fetch the constable?'

'An excellent idea, my man. Well done! Now, Robert Freeman, what is your account of the matter?'

Despite the seriousness of the business, Jeremy Oakshott smiled to himself. Trust an old military man to assume command as though it was his right to do so! Well, perhaps it was, all things considered.

'Early this morning, sir,' said Bob Freeman, 'I found a note pushed under that door, which is the side door of this gun room. It said – well, perhaps you should read it yourself.'

Freeman handed the Colonel the note that he had shown earlier to Albert Stead, the valet. The Fenians again! The Colonel recalled the frightful events of 1884. In February, a Fenian bomb had gone off in Victoria Station. On a single day, 30 May, the CID headquarters had been attacked, as had the Carlton Club, and the home of Sir Watkin Williams-Wynn, the Member of Parliament for Denbighshire. And this gamekeeper's cousin had been one of the Fenians' victims.

'Tell me what happened tonight,' said the Colonel, in gentler tones than he had so far assumed.

'Sir, as you can see, the side door to the gun room opens

directly on to the terrace. So while the master and his guests were in the dining room, I took up a position just inside that door, and waited. I was holding one of the hunting rifles, loaded and ready for use. There it is, sir, lying on that table.'

'Yes, a Lee Enfield, I see. A powerful weapon for a day's shoot. Not something you'd expect to see in a country gun room. What do you hunt round here?'

'There are plenty of deer in these woods, sir, and since the seventies there have been wild boar here. We used to have the old Baker muzzle-loading flintlocks here, sir, left over from the French wars. A wonderful weapon, sir. But the Master's father replaced them all with modern Lee Enfields.'

'Hmm.... Well, Freeman, that Fenian man chose a bad night for raiding, because there's a moon out. Odd, that....'

'Yes, sir. Well, sure enough, close on ten, I saw the man running across the pasture from the trees, his head bent down as though he was trying to make himself smaller than he was. I opened the door – it opens inward – raised my rifle, and took aim.'

Bob Freeman began to tremble, and it was an effort for him to stifle a sob.

'I hoped to shoot him in the leg, sir, and bring him down. I squeezed the trigger, and the room seemed to shake with the noise of the shot. The man staggered, but remained standing. And then another shot rang out, and he fell to the ground.'

'Another shot.... Could you have squeezed the trigger a second time? It happens, you know. Soldiers in the heat of battle often fire a second, or even a third shot, without realizing that they've done it.'

'I don't think so, sir. I'm not sure, though. Perhaps I did.'

The Colonel strode to the table, picked up the rifle, drew back the bolt, and peered into the breech. He pulled off the magazine, and examined it carefully.

'You did not fire a second shot, Freeman,' he said.

'I'm relieved to hear it, sir. I was mad with rage when I saw that fellow running across the grass to rob my Master. I didn't intend to kill him, but I'll tell you now, sir, I'm not sorry that I did. Will I – will I go to gaol?'

'You will not. You were protecting your Master's property, and considering the background of that man, you may also have been defending your own life. Besides, it would seem that the second fatal shot was fired by somebody else. You have committed no crime.'

'It's a dark mystery,' said Lord Arthur. 'Ah! Here's another member of the household staff. You served at table tonight, didn't you? Take this poor fellow away, and give him a glass of brandy. Meanwhile, gentlemen, we'd better rejoin the ladies, and tell them what's happened.'

They returned to the drawing room, and Colonel Scott-James regaled his wife and Sophia Jex-Blake with an account of all that had happened.

'A most unpleasant incident,' said Sophia Jex-Blake. 'But as neither Mrs Scott-James nor I had any part in the investigation, I propose that we be allowed to retire to bed. It's twenty to eleven. I expect a police constable will arrive soon, but there will be little for the poor man to do before the morning.'

'Quite right, ma'am,' said Colonel Scott James. He was feeling very pleased with himself, basking in the admiring glances of his wife. And why not? That Oakshott fellow was reputedly very clever, but he was a milk-and-water kind of a man, and young Lord Arthur couldn't be expected to take command.

'Quite right, ma'am,' he repeated, 'but correct form and order must be observed. The police must know immediately. That second shot – there's something very sinister about that— In God's name, what *now*?'

A piercing scream had stopped the Colonel in mid-sentence.

It seemed quite natural for them all to line up behind Colonel Scott-James as he made his way from the drawing room and out into the great entrance hall of the castle. The butler, and all the indoor servants, were standing in a huddle at the foot of the winding staircase, looking up towards the gallery. One of the two servant girls who had waited at the table was lying senseless on the landing. Ignoring them all, the Colonel strode up the stairs, followed by Lord Arthur and the ladies.

They found Ambrose Littlemore sitting motionless in the great throne of a chair that the housekeeper likened to the Coronation Chair. He seemed to be staring thoughtfully into space, but it was obvious to them all that he was quite dead.

'The strain has been too much for him,' said the Colonel gruffly. 'Over-excitement. His heart, I expect.' His wife was quietly weeping.

Dr Sophia Jex-Blake looked closely at Ambrose Littlemore's face. 'No,' she said, half to herself, 'not heart.'

To a little cry of protest from the Colonel's wife, she seized the dead man's shoulders and pulled him forward in the great chair.

'No,' she repeated, in a firm voice, 'not heart.' Seizing a candle burning in a sconce set in the wall, she held it down behind the figure, and bade them look at what she had found. 'I am sure that you can all see, quite clearly,' she said, 'that Mr Ambrose Littlemore has been stabbed to death. Stabbed in the back with a pair of scissors.'

The village of Hazelmere, remodelled at the same time that the castle had been built, consisted of a number of mock-gothic cottages, a medieval church, and a public house called The Farmer's Arms. On that particular Friday night, the bar was crowded with men and women who had tired of the rain, and quitted their cold dwellings for the comforts of the village inn. The landlord understood the needs of his fellow villagers, and on nights like this ignored the requirements of the hated Licensing Act. He closed when his last customer had left. Constable Roberts never set foot in a public house, having signed the pledge; but he was a discreet young man, who always gave notice if he was calling on official business.

At half past ten, the door was flung open, and a wild stranger made his entrance. He was panting, as though he had run through the village. He put two half-crowns on the bar counter, and asked for a bottle of gin.

The locals had stopped talking, and were regarding the stranger with surly suspicion. Ignoring the glass that the landlord placed on the bar, he drank the gin straight from the bottle. Suddenly, he began to address his silent audience. He spoke with a pronounced Irish accent.

'This night, my friends,' he cried, 'I have struck a blow for Queen and country. I have gunned down a Fenian man who came here to steal weapons from yonder great house. He lies dead, shot to the heart, and 'twas me that done the deed.'

His audience watched, fascinated, as he proceeded to take further great gulps from the gin bottle. Then he burst into song.

'Sure I'm an Ulster Orangeman, from Erin's isle I come,
To see my British brethren all of honour and of fame,
And to tell them of my forefathers who fought in days of yore,
That I might have the right to wear, the sash my father wore!'

The Irishman seized the gin bottle, and staggered towards the door. The landlord picked up the two half-crowns, and said, 'I'll get your ninepence change.'

'Keep it, keep it,' said the Irishman. 'Have a drink on me. It's a grand work that I've done this night!'

In a moment he had gone, and the drinkers in The Farmer's Arms broke out in a gabble of speculation. More beer was drawn from the casks, and the fire was banked up. It was scarcely half an hour later that Constable Roberts, accompanied by a groom from the castle, looked in at the door to tell them that a Fenian man had been shot dead while trying to steal guns from Mr Littlemore's gun room.

9

SOPHIA JEX-BLAKE

Sophia Jex-Blake stood at the window of Arabella Cathcart's bedroom, and looked out across the dew-covered pasture. It was just after six o'clock, and the sun had begun to tint the enveloping trees with morning gold. How quiet it was! She could see the carriage-road curving away towards the hidden entrance gates of the demesne.

The local constable had told her that detective police from Oxford would be arriving at the castle before seven. She wondered whether one at least of those detectives would be her newfound friend, patient, and collaborator, Inspector James Antrobus.

Son of a grocer, he had attended a grammar school until the age of 14, when he was obliged to leave, owing to his father's becoming trade-fallen. He had worked on a farm for a while, and then had joined the Oxford City Police when he was twenty. A widower, he had a daughter who was working as a pupil-teacher in Battersea.

Constable Roberts, to her way of thinking, was little more than a boy, unable, as yet, to realize his own potential. She and Colonel Scott-James had insisted that the body of Mr Ambrose Littlemore should be left sitting in the chair until the constable had arrived. The young man had examined the wound, and then carefully traced a trail of blood along the dim corridor and into the dead man's bedroom.

'I think he was stabbed there, ma'am,' he'd said, 'and then walked out of the room and along the passage until he began to feel faint, and sat down on that chair. I expect he died almost immediately after that.' She had agreed, and told him that people who were stabbed in the back often didn't realize what had happened to them, and would walk quite a distance until they collapsed.

While it was still dark, the body of Ambrose Littlemore was removed from the chair, and carried to the bedroom, where it was laid on the bed, and covered with a sheet.

Dr Jeremy Oakshott, the dead man's nephew, had volunteered the information that his Aunt Arabella had a pair of scissors similar to those that had been used to kill Mr Littlemore. A search of that lady's room showed that the scissors in question had disappeared.

It was strange how Sophia and Colonel Scott-James had, as it were, assumed command of the house and its inhabitants after the tragedy of Ambrose Littlemore's death. The Colonel had placated the servants, and had placed his own carriage and swift horses at Constable Roberts's disposal to make the ten-mile round journey to Oxford and back in order to report the two deaths to the duty officer at High Street Police Station, there being neither telegraph nor electric telephone in Hadleigh village.

For her part, Sophia had devoted herself to tending the stricken Miss Arabella Cathcart, who, on being told the news of her cousin's murder, had first had a fit of hysterics – in the medical, not the vulgar dismissive sense – in which she had wildly accused herself of Mr Littlemore's murder, and then had relapsed into what Sophia recognized at once as a catatonic spasm. Assisted by the resident nurse, who had shown great relief at her presence, she had administered a soporific – she always carried her 'doctor's bag' with her – that settled the unfortunate woman down, and then had sent the nurse to ask Mr Jeremy Oakshott to come and talk to her.

He was still there now, sitting in a chair beside Miss Cathcart's bed. He looked pale and shocked, and when he had accepted a glass of Hoffman's Drops that she had prepared for him, his hand had shaken almost uncontrollably. Unless he took great care, he would suffer a nervous convulsion.

She had asked him bluntly to tell her whether or not his relative had ever suffered from a mental disease, and he had told her the whole story. Miss Cathcart had been confined to an asylum for many years, and had only recently been released to her family. He told her about her killing of a young woman by stabbing her in the back with a pair of scissors.

She was relieved that he had made no futile attempt to protest Miss Cathcart's innocence. To do so would have sounded like a disguised accusation.

When the nurse had handed Miss Cathcart the little glass containing the soporific, she had had difficulty in grasping it; two of the fingers of her right hand seemed to be partly paralysed. She had unconsciously thrust her right shoulder forward, which had seemed to make her grasp more sure. Something stirred in Sophia's mind.

'Dr Oakshott,' she said, 'do you recall the name of the physician who tended your aunt during her confinement in the asylum?'

'What? Yes. Dr Samuel Critchley.'

Well, well, thought Sophia, that's very interesting. I *knew* it must have been he before ever I asked.

Suddenly, a carriage appeared on the drive, a light vehicle furiously driven by a police constable sitting high on the box. Her heart gave a sudden leap of pleasurable anticipation when she glimpsed its occupants as it turned towards the main entrance of the castle. Yes! It was bringing to their aid Detective Inspector Antrobus, and his irascible sergeant, Joseph Maxwell.

*

As the two detectives climbed down from the carriage, they were accosted by a gentleman whose anguished face suggested that he was burdened with a secret that had to be told immediately.

'Inspector Antrobus? My name's McArthur ... oh, hello, Mr Maxwell, it's nice to see you again. Inspector, there's something that I must tell you before you embark on any investigation of this dreadful crime. You see—'

'I'm sure you realize, Dr McArthur,' said Sergeant Maxwell in the stentorian tones that he adopted when wanting to spare his guvnor from unwelcome attentions, 'that Mr Antrobus must consult the police constable before questioning members of the family and household. But we'll certainly talk to you later.'

At that moment Constable Roberts appeared, and saluted. Both Antrobus and Maxwell raised their hats. Dr McArthur slipped unobtrusively back into the house.

'Sir,' said Roberts, 'I've made my headquarters in the gun room, which we can enter from this terrace. There are two murders, the first one of a man said to have been a Fenian, and the other of Mr Ambrose Littlemore, the owner of this castle. Here we are, sir. Let's go in, so that we can talk in private.'

'And so we meet again, Constable,' said Antrobus, 'and once more it's murder.'

Once settled in the gun room, the constable gave the detectives a full account of the shooting of the Fenian, and his suspicion that the man had been fatally shot by an unseen assailant immediately after the gamekeeper had hit the man in the leg. And then he told them about the letter that the gamekeeper had received, a warning of trouble to come from someone signing himself 'Orange William'.

'These murders, Constable,' said Antrobus, 'do you think they are connected?'

'At first, sir, I thought not. But then I wondered whether the first murder – the murder of the Fenian man – was in some way designed to create a diversion. When the shots were heard, everybody rushed out on to the terrace to see what had happened. This left some person unknown free to stab Mr Littlemore fatally in the back.'

They listened while Constable Roberts gave them a full account of what had happened. He had seen the body sitting dead in a great chair on the balcony overlooking the entrance hall. He had followed a trail of blood back to Mr Littlemore's room, and had concluded that he had been stabbed there.

'After I examined Mr Littlemore's remains, sir, I had his body taken to his room, and laid under a sheet on his bed. I was accompanied by a very remarkable lady, one of the guests, who covered and strapped up the wound in Mr Littlemore's back.'

'A remarkable lady. I wonder.... And the Fenian, out in the pasture?'

'I had him taken on a handcart into the castle court, and put on a table in the harness room next to the stables. The body was soaking wet, and has been covered with a horse-blanket.'

'Hmm.... I like your idea of a diversion, Constable. Two murders at more or less the same time, although apparently unconnected, does seem a mite contrived. Have you prepared lists of the household and the guests for me to look at?'

'Yes, sir. This one's a list of the household servants. You'll want to question Robert Freeman, the gamekeeper, who shot the Fenian man in the leg, and Albert Stead, Mr Littlemore's valet. He's very upset, sir, as he was much attached to his master. And this is the list of family and guests who were present. I've not allowed anyone to leave the premises until you have given the word.'

'Upon my word, PC Roberts,' said Antrobus, 'I'm very impressed with how you've conducted yourself over this business. I shall certainly let Superintendent Fielding know. We had little time to talk to you when we were here about the murder of Mr Sanders. Are you a native of Hadleigh?'

The constable had flushed with delighted pleasure at Antrobus's compliment.

'Yes, sir. I live with my wife Ellen and our new baby in Church Lane.'

'I'd like to acquaint myself with the geography of this house, Constable. The layout of the main rooms, the bedrooms, and what leads to where. Could you take us on a very quick tour?'

PC Roberts showed them the dining room and the drawing room across the hall, then took them up the main staircase to the bedrooms. In Ambrose Littlemore's great gothic chamber they saw the sheeted figure lying on the ponderous four-poster. There was a dressing room beyond, and then a small passage led to Miss Cathcart's room. Returning to the gallery, Roberts opened a door in the panelling and led them down a servants' staircase to the kitchen passage, which was filled with fitted cupboards and presses. From here, he led them back to the gun room.

'Very interesting, Constable,' said Antrobus. 'There are sinister possibilities in that half-hidden back staircase. Now, I suggest you go home for a while, and see how your Ellen and the baby are doing! If I need you again, I'll send someone down to the village to fetch you.'

When the constable had gone, Antrobus looked at the list of family and guests. Mr Ambrose Littlemore, now lying dead. Miss Arabella Cathcart. A Colonel and Mrs Scott-James. Beside their names Roberts had written: 'Colonel a great help.' Lord Arthur Farrell. Dr Jeremy Oakshott, nephew—

'Ah! Here he is again, Joe! Turn up any stone, and you'll find our Jeremy underneath it. He was here in the village on the very night that poor Michael Sanders was murdered. He's here now, on the night that his uncle is murdered, and a man shot dead in the grounds. And all those years ago, Sergeant, he was hovering in the wings when that poor girl was done to death. Jeremy Oakshott, scholar of the Crusades, and the wielder of a fine Italian hand! I don't like that man, and I'll tell you why. He's—'

Antrobus's words were driven away by a sudden violent bout of coughing. He tried to draw breath, but succeeded only in half choking himself. One of these days, thought Maxwell, he'll burst a blood vessel. After a good deal of wheezing, the stertorous breathing abated, and he sat back in his chair with a sigh of relief. At the same time, a thin stream of blood trickled from the side of his mouth.

'I sometimes think, sir,' said Sergeant Maxwell, who during the attack had stood at the window whistling 'The British Grenadiers', 'that you have too much of a down on Dr Oakshott. You take everything he does as a personal affront.'

'Maybe I do, and maybe I have just cause. Now, who else is on this list? Oh! Miss Sophia Jex-Blake! I wondered…. She's here, Joe!'

'Indeed, sir? Your lady friend. Well, she did well by us last time – it's just over a month since she solved that business at St Michael's College. But I think it's time, sir, that you flew the flag. The white flag, you know.'

Antrobus knew what this meant. He withdrew a white handkerchief from his pocket, and wiped away the congealing blood from his mouth and chin.

'Now, sir,' said Maxwell, 'what do you want us to do? Shall we divide the spoils?'

'Yes, we will. I want you to look into this business of the Fenian. Was it just coincidence that two murders took place on the same night? Or is Constable Roberts right in thinking that the first murder was a diversion? Find out all you can. I'll concentrate on the murder of Mr Littlemore. I'll see that doctor friend of yours first. What on earth can he want?'

The constable was panting with the exertion of running up the winding road from the gates.

'Sir!' he cried. 'The mystery of the Fenian's death is solved! Last night, soon after the man was shot dead in the pasture, a wild Irishman burst into the Farmer's Arms and ordered a bottle of gin. He said his name was Orange William, and he boasted that he had shot the Fenian dead. He sang a Loyalist song, called 'The Sash my Father Wore'. He paid for his drink, and made his escape.'

'Did he really?' said Antrobus. 'And after he sang the Sash, did he go on to sing "The Wearing of the Green'? Did he dance an Irish jig? What did he look like, this Orange William? Did he have a sprig of shamrock in his cap?'

'Sir—'

'It's all right, Constable. Take no notice. It's just that I'm in a questioning mood this morning, and your singing Loyalist seems rather too good to be true. When a man's committed murder, he usually slinks away. But your Irishman seems to have treated the company in The Farmer's Arms to a complete music hall turn. It doesn't ring true, and it makes me think that someone very clever is taking us all for a ride…. But you did well coming up here to tell me. Will you go, now, and question the late Mr Littlemore's valet, Albert Stead? Find out what he remembers about the events of this evening. And the girl who fainted on the landing. See what *she* has to say.'

'Sergeant,' he said when Roberts had left the room, 'go and examine the body of the Fenian in the harness room. When I've finished talking to Dr McArthur, I'll send him to you to extract the bullets. And after he's done that, examine the body from *our* point of view. You know the kind of thing I mean.'

Dr McArthur, who had been waiting impatiently for Antrobus to emerge from the gun room, accosted him immediately. 'Come into the writing room, Inspector,' he said, 'there's something I must tell you immediately – something about Miss Arabella Cathcart.'

'Were you a guest here last night, Doctor? Your name doesn't appear on my lists.'

David McArthur sighed. It was clear that this police officer could not be hustled into hearing what he was not yet ready to hear.

'No, Inspector, I was not a guest. I was summoned here at eleven o'clock last night. A footman came down to the village to fetch me. I am – was – Mr Ambrose Littlemore's physician. By the time I arrived here, all that was necessary had been done. You see, one of the guests was a distinguished woman doctor, whom I know quite well. She is a friend of ours. I met her when I was studying at the School of Medicine in Edinburgh in the late sixties. My wife met her there, too, when she was a nurse at the old Royal Infirmary.'

'You are talking about Miss Sophia Jex-Blake, aren't you? Well, she is also a friend of mine and, I may say, a colleague, too. So, Doctor, what do you want to tell me about Miss Arabella Cathcart?'

They had entered the writing room, a chamber designed to resemble a chantry chapel. This whole sham castle, thought Antrobus, is an affront to architecture.

'It is only just over a month, Inspector,' said McArthur, 'that Miss Cathcart was released, cured, from Frampton Lunatic Asylum. She had been incarcerated there, initially as a criminal lunatic, for fifteen years.'

'What had she done?'

'She stabbed a young woman in the back with a pair of scissors. The young woman died.'

'And Mr Littlemore, too, was stabbed in the back with a pair of scissors. *Her* scissors, so I am given to understand.'

'Yes.'

'And what is your stance in this matter, Dr McArthur? Are you accusing her, or defending her?'

'I believe that Miss Cathcart would have left Frampton Asylum cured, Inspector. Ignorance of modern medicine breeds fear and prejudice, but the curative processes employed by Dr Samuel Critchley have produced quite triumphant results. There are risks involved, of course, but they are worth taking. So I beg you not to jump to the obvious conclusion—'

'I never jump to obvious conclusions, Doctor; no detective ever does. But that name, Critchley.... Somebody told me about him. He inserts electrodes into the brain. Thank you for telling me all this, Dr McArthur. Let me assure you once again that I will not view Miss Cathcart with a jaundiced eye because of your revelation. I must leave you now, as there's much to be done.'

'Can I be of any use?'

'Yes, Doctor, indeed you can. I wasn't able to contact a police surgeon before I came here, so I'd be obliged if you'd examine the body of the so-called Fenian, and extract the bullets for me. We know that the man was shot twice, but not from the same rifle. Sergeant Maxwell is waiting for you.'

The body of the dead Fenian had been carried into the castle yard, and laid on a table in the harness room attached to the stables. Sergeant Maxwell stood beside the table, clutching his bowler hat to his chest. Villain he may have been, this Fenian man, but he had been shot first in the leg by Bob Freeman, and then through the heart by an unknown assailant. Only those who had suffered such a leg wound could know the appalling agony that followed it. The second fatal shot would have delivered the man from insufferable pain.

Insufferable! Maxwell's mind reverted to his time in Abyssinia, and the searingly hot March day at Gallarbat in '89, when his company – C Company of the Oxfordshire Light Infantry – had been routed by rebel fanatics, and the Emperor John IV had fled. Maxwell had suffered a leg wound much the same as the Fenian man's, and had thought that he would die of the pain. But he hadn't died. He had been invalided out of the army, where he had been a corporal drill instructor, and had joined the county constabulary as a uniformed constable. He had soon progressed to the detective branch, and had transferred to the City of Oxford Police in '92.

He awoke from his reverie when the door of the harness room opened to admit Dr McArthur, who was carrying his Gladstone bag. He looked tired and drawn, but greeted the sergeant cheerfully enough.

'So this is our murderous intruder, Sergeant,' he said. 'He looks an ugly, ill conditioned brute. Help me off with his clothes, will you? I'll examine the wounds, and then extract the bullets.'

With some difficulty, because of what McArthur called 'adhesions', they removed the dead man's outer clothing, and laid it aside. The body lay in a pool of congealed blood. In life, the Fenian had been a strong, muscular man. The massive bicep of his right arm was almost entirely covered by a tattoo, consisting of a coat of arms, the inscription 'Ashanti 1874' and the motto *Semper Fidelis.*

'Perhaps he came from Exeter,' said McArthur. 'I think that's their town motto.'

He opened his Gladstone bag and produced a case of surgical instruments. Sergeant Maxwell said nothing, but he thought, that's the badge of the Devonshire Regiment. They fought in the Ashanti war of '73 to '74, and this beauty must have been there. 'Always Faithful', that's what the Latin means. A rum kind of Fenian, this ex-soldier who records his military history on his arm for all to see. What was the doctor saying?

'Yes, it's gone straight through the heart, and unless I'm very much mistaken, it will have passed right through his body. You should find both the spent cartridge and the bullet itself somewhere around the spot where he was shot.'

With a sudden powerful movement the doctor turned the body over. Maxwell flinched as he saw the great gaping wound in the man's back.

'It's always like that, you know, Sergeant. A neat bullet hole in the front, and a massive injury at the back. That's what a .303 bullet does to the human body. Now let's look at the leg. Ah! You see? There's the bullet, lodged in the knee joint. It will have shattered both tibia and fibula on impact, rendering the limb useless.'

Using a probe and a pair of tweezers, Dr McArthur extracted the bullet, and dropped it into a tin bowl.

'The cause of death is quite obvious, Sergeant,' he said, 'but I had better perform a full post mortem examination. No, you don't have to be present! After that, I suggest that the remains be buried this evening in the churchyard here. As you will have certainly noticed, dissolution is beginning to set in. Here, inhale from this flask of spirits of hartshorn, to clear your olfactory passages. If Mr Antrobus is willing, I'll arrange all that is necessary with the sexton.'

Declining the smelling salts, Sergeant Maxwell gathered up the dead man's clothes and boots, and hurried from the room. A Fenian, hey? Fenian, my foot! He'd go and find PC Roberts, and see what he'd learnt from Albert the valet, and the swooning maid.

Maxwell found PC Roberts in the writing room. He was sitting at a desk in the window, reading through the entries in his notebook. Maxwell asked him how he was progressing.

'I interviewed Albert Stead, the valet, Sergeant,' he said. 'He was very upset. He seems to have been devoted to Mr Littlemore. He told me that his master had been in good spirits before dinner, and had showed no signs of agitation. Apart from that, there was little that he could tell me.'

'And the fainting maid?'

'She's one of three housemaids, Sergeant. Doris Collins. I know her quite well, as she lives with her parents in the village, and comes to work here in the evenings. She had been to check on the state of the candles in Miss Cathcart's bedroom while the company were still at dinner. Miss Cathcart was lying on the bed, apparently asleep. She had dined earlier, in her room. On the way back through the gallery Doris had seen Mr Littlemore sitting on that throne-like chair. She thought it odd that he should have been there, and asked him if he was all right. It was then that she realized that he was dead, and fainted clean away.'

'Well, Constable,' said Maxwell, 'there's not much to be learnt from those two, but I'll tell the guvnor what they said. I've brought the dead man's clothes with me to examine. Maybe you'd like to do the job yourself?'

PC Roberts examined the blood-stained jacket, carefully

searching the pockets. Then he turned his attention to the trousers.

'There's nothing in any of the pockets, Sergeant,' he said. 'No money, no papers, not even a handkerchief. That's odd, to my way of thinking. The shirt could have done with a wash. He wore boots, but no socks. The boots— Hello, Sergeant, look at that!' Stamped into the sole of each boot were the words: *HM Prison Birmingham*.

'Prison issue, given to an indigent prisoner on discharge. So our so-called Fenian's an old lag. Well, that's interesting. Now, where's that gamekeeper? Bob Freeman?'

'He's still in the gun room, Sergeant. Oh, I meant to ask you, talking of old lags, did you catch that foreign fellow you and Mr Antrobus were after?'

'What foreign fellow? What are you talking about?'

'Polonius, I think that was the name.'

'Oh, him. No, we never caught him. Slippery customers, foreigners.'

'Now, Robert Freeman,' said Sergeant Maxwell, 'you say that you aimed for the man's legs, in order to bring him down without killing him. How did you know that you'd be successful?'

'Well, Sergeant, I've been a gamekeeper for most of my life. I'm no stranger to guns. I knew the Fenian was coming, you see, so I loaded a rifle beforehand.'

'I see. So when you go out hunting – you've got deer and boar here, haven't you? – you shoot for their legs. All those spindly little legs. Most hunters aim for the flank. Why should you be different?'

In spite of his nervousness at being questioned, the gamekeeper could not help smiling.

'Years ago, Mr Maxwell, I was in the county militia. That's where I learnt to shoot like a soldier. And that's what I did last night.'

Maxwell picked up the rifle from the table, and felt its weight in his hands. Seven pounds, lighter and better balanced than the old muskets, and relatively easy to aim. He looked at the gamekeeper, who stood wretchedly near the open door of the gunroom. He's a decent man, he thought, a man who can't cope with the fact of having shot a man to incapacitate him, only to see that man killed by a second shot from another rifle, another .303 Lee Enfield.

'You've done nothing wrong, Mr Freeman,' said Maxwell. 'Why don't you try to get some sleep? If this matter comes to trial, you'll be needed as a witness, but that's not the same as standing in the dock.'

From somewhere in the house someone began to sound a gong. Even though the Master had been murdered, his family and guests required their breakfast.

When the gamekeeper had gone, Maxwell turned his attention to the gun racks. There were five Lee Enfield rifles still secure in their slots; an empty sixth slot showed where Robert Freeman's rifle had been fixed. The sergeant proceeded to make a close and careful inspection of the five rifles. In keeping with responsible practice, they were all minus their bolts. Squinting down the barrels of the first four, Maxwell saw that they were quite clean. The fifth rifle, though, had clearly been fired recently, and not cleaned with a 'pull-through'.

Maxwell placed the rifle back carefully in its rack. Somewhere in this room there would be a locked drawer, in which the bolts were kept. He could use one of his own pick-locks to open it and examine the bolts, but there was no need. Whoever had fired the fatal shot, the shot that had killed the Fenian, had almost certainly been someone who lived in Hazelmere castle.

10

THE ESPIED SPY

'Sir,' said Sergeant Maxwell, 'while all these gentlefolk are having their breakfast, let you and me go for a stroll in the pasture. Walls have ears.'

It was the dawn of a beautiful September day, and the strong sun had driven away the morning dew. They walked through the rough grass until by unspoken consent they stopped at the place where the Fenian man had fallen dead. Maxwell dropped to his knees and carefully examined the area. If the bullet had passed right through him, then it would be here, somewhere in the topsoil. Yes! There it was. And over there, gleaming in the morning sun, was the brass shell case.

'Well done, Sergeant,' said Antrobus. 'You haven't opened your mouth since we left the house. Did Dr McArthur extract the bullet from the Fenian's leg?'

'He did, sir. And he wasn't a Fenian. He had a big patriotic tattoo on his arm, showing that he'd served in the British Army in the Ashanti War. And his boots, sir, were prison issue: Birmingham Gaol. Whatever reason he had for coming here, it wasn't to steal rifles.'

'No, and Orange William never held much credence with me. It's all been staged. It's Oakshott! He's laughing at us, that prim, fastidious little man; he's taunting me – *me* – by deliberately sailing close to the wind—'

'There's more, sir,' said Maxwell. 'I examined all the rifles in the gun room, and found that another one had been fired, and the person who fired it hadn't had time to clean it. Bob Newman fired the first shot from the rifle that he'd pre-loaded. Somebody else – somebody in the house – fired the second shot that killed the so-called Fenian. It was an inside job, sir. All this business of Fenians and Loyalists is a smoke-screen.'

'You're right, Sergeant. And so was PC Roberts. It was a diversion to bring the family running out of the house while that man stabbed his uncle to death. He's trying to blame it on the aunt!'

Sergeant Maxwell fixed his attention on a point somewhere in the woodland adjoining the pasture. He removed his black bowler hat, and clutched it to his chest. Antrobus prepared to be chastised.

'With all due respect, sir,' said Maxwell, 'you're drawing wild conclusions which could get us both into trouble. I grant you the diversion, because that's what it clearly was. But how do you know it was caused by Dr Jeremy Oakshott? You've not interviewed him yet, sir. Just because you don't like him doesn't mean he's guilty.'

Inspector Antrobus sat down on the grass, and lit one of his Richmond 'Gem' cigarettes. He inhaled deeply, coughing out the smoke in short bursts. He looked up at his sergeant, who was still gazing into the wood.

'"She sat, like patience on a monument, smiling at grief." Do you know who said that, Sergeant?'

'No, sir.'

'It was Shakespeare. Well, not Shakespeare himself, but one of his characters. But there's no need for *you* to stand there like a monument. I take your chiding in good part, because you're right. I need to talk to Oakshott, and to that colonel. And when I've done that, I'll take great pleasure in renewing my acquaintance with Miss Sophia Jex-Blake.'

*

'We meet again, Inspector,' said Jeremy Oakshott, 'and once again under the most melancholy of circumstances.'

Oakshott seemed to have aged since Antrobus had last seen him. His face was pale and drawn, and his eyes red-rimmed. His hands trembled, as though he had received a profound shock.

'As though'? The man's uncle had been murdered only hours ago. And if that wasn't bad enough, he would surely know that he was the prime suspect. It was common knowledge that he would inherit his uncle's fortune, which was enormous. No wonder that he seemed on the edge of a nervous breakdown.

'Melancholy indeed, Dr Oakshott,' said Antrobus. 'Pray let me offer my condolences. I hope you will not be offended if I ask you to account for your own movements last evening?' Was it guilt at his own blind condemnation of the man that made him speak so civilly?

'We were all at dinner, Inspector. At twenty to ten, I asked my uncle to fetch a jewelled dagger that he had been given as a present, in order to show it to Colonel Scott-James, who had an interest in such matters—'

'How did you know that it was twenty to ten, sir?'

'What? Oh, I happened to look at my watch. I am a little short-sighted, and could not see the time on the mantel-clock. Uncle was not sure where the dagger was to be found, so I offered to go with him.'

'Did you indeed? And what happened then?'

'We went upstairs—'

'Which stairs did you use? You once told me that you are a professional scholar, used to sifting detail. Please try to be more precise in telling me your story.'

Jeremy Oakshott flushed with anger. Really, this man was insufferable.

'I resent your tone, Antrobus,' he said hotly. 'You are scolding me as though I was a recalcitrant little boy. You have never liked

119

me, and I know that you have been prying into my past. I have complained about you to the Rector of my college, and I understood that he had spoken to your superintendent.'

'I am sorry if I have offended you, sir,' said Antrobus. 'I can assure you that personal animus does not enter into the matter. I am merely following the procedures that any detective must employ in order to get at the truth. Please continue your account. By which stairs did you mount to the first floor?'

'By the main stairs. That was the nearest way to reach Uncle's room. When we got there, we went through the bedroom and into the dressing room, where there is a large Indian cabinet. We looked through the drawers, but could not find the jewelled dagger. "Go down and make my excuses, Jeremy," he said. And then ...'

'Yes, sir? And then what?'

'He said that he'd go and look in on Aunt Arabella, to see if she wanted anything. She had not been very well that day.'

'And did he?'

'I don't know. I left him, and made my way along the gallery. It was then that I heard what sounded like a shot. No, not "sounded like": it *was* a shot. I hurried downstairs as fast as I could. This time, I used the servants' staircase, which is accessed from a door at the end of the gallery. Hearing voices in the gun room, I ran down the kitchen passage and out on to the terrace, where I joined the others. And it was in that period of time after I left Uncle and the maid Collins screamed, that – that someone stabbed Uncle in the back.'

Antrobus remained silent for a while. Oakshott was a bold, inventive man. If he had planned to murder his uncle, he would quite brazenly state that it was he who had asked Mr Littlemore to fetch the dagger, and equally brazenly announce that he had offered to go with him. All done in the open, and then told to *him*. And even now, he was casting suspicion on his Aunt Arabella by saying that his uncle had proposed visiting her moments before he was murdered with her scissors. Had any of that account been true?

There were other possibilities. Oakshott could have accompanied his uncle to his room and immediately stabbed him to death. He could then have dragged the body out into the gallery, propped it up on the great throne-like chair, and then made his way downstairs by the servants' staircase. Oakshott could have concealed a loaded rifle beforehand in one of the many cupboards lining the walls of the kitchen passage. There was a door leading out of the silver-room directly on to the terrace, and from a hidden vantage point there, he could have waited for the first shot to be discharged before firing his fatal shot. He would just have time to replace the rifle in its rack, but not to clean it.

That hypothesis suggested other possibilities. The ex-felon posing as a Fenian could have been in his pay, lured by some subtle argument to come running across the pasture at the right time for him to fall into a trap. The letter from Orange William could have been Oakshott's composition. And Orange William himself, boasting of his assassination, could be another of Oakshott's dupes. What if—

'Thank you, Mr Oakshott,' he said. 'I'm sorry that you took offence at my methods of questioning.'

Oakshott did not seem to hear him.

'I buried my friend Michael Sanders in Botley Churchyard the other day,' he said. 'And now I must arrange the obsequies of my poor uncle. How I wish that I could just be going about my quiet pursuit of learning at Jerusalem Hall! I'll go now, if you don't mind, Inspector, and see how my poor Aunt Arabella is bearing up to the loss of Uncle.'

He gave Antrobus a perfunctory bow, and left the room.

'I tried to keep everybody calm, Inspector,' said Colonel Scott-James. 'We heard the shots, and Lord Arthur Farrell and I ran down to see what was afoot. We found the gamekeeper in a blue funk, but managed to get the story out of him.'

'Was Dr Jeremy Oakshott there, Colonel?'

'Yes, he was there. He spoke up for the gamekeeper. Said he was a *pukka sahib*, you know. Bit of a milksop, but decent at the core. Oakshott, I mean. It's a mystery, though. The Fenian was shot twice, once by Freeman, and then by somebody else. Must have been hiding in the shadows. A third party. But you'll find out all that, Inspector. As for Ambrose Littlemore, well, who could possibly have stabbed him?'

'Could it have been Dr Oakshott?' asked Antrobus. He treated the Colonel to a smile, hinting that his question was not meant to be taken seriously.

'What? No, because he was there with us, on the terrace. I can't think *who* could have done it. Mind you, Oakshott's the heir, you know – he'll come into hundreds of thousands of pounds by his uncle's death. But there, as I've told you, he couldn't have done it. He was there with us, on the terrace.'

'My dear Detective Inspector, I am delighted to see you again!'

Antrobus had found Miss Jex-Blake sitting at a table in the cavernous library of Hazelmere Castle. She looked out of place surrounded by the black oak shelves full of unread books, beneath the gimcrack plaster ceiling with its fan-vaulting copied from that in Gloucester Cathedral. She had been sipping a cup of coffee, but on seeing Antrobus she hastily put it down on its saucer, and half rose from her chair in unconscious defiance of the usual convention.

'My pleasure likewise, ma'am,' said Antrobus, bowing gravely. It was a gesture of affectionate regard. Miss Jex-Blake was wearing a morning dress of some dove grey material, with plain white linen collar and cuffs. She looked just as he had last seen her, with her fair hair parted in the middle, her pleasant face animated by a welcoming smile.

'Come here, sir,' said Sophia, 'and sit on that chair. I have been waiting patiently here since breakfast, hoping that you would seek me out. How are you? How are you managing?'

'I'm very well, thank you, ma'am. Keeping active, as they say.'

'Do they? Well, you're a little more hunched in the shoulders than when last I saw you. You would benefit from a long period of bed-rest, but I know that you would find it insufferable.

'Now, are you going to tell me what you've found out so far about the murder of my host, Mr Ambrose Littlemore? And about the other man, the one who was shot dead in the grounds? The girl who brought me this coffee told me as much as she knew, or thought she knew.'

Antrobus did not reply, and his face grew stern beneath the close black beard. For a moment, Sophia wondered whether she had presumed too much in speaking so familiarly with this Crown Officer of the Law. After all, she had only known him for a couple of months.

'Oh, Miss Jex-Blake,' he said at last, 'I am very ill at ease with this case. Before ever these murders occurred – yes, both deaths were murders – I have had the uncanny feeling that one man, one wicked, cunning man, has been leading me by the nose, planting clues for me to find, turning up at the scene of another murder so that I would suspect him, and then ensuring that he had a water-tight alibi to frustrate my attempts to catch him out in his villainies.'

'Does this wicked man have a name?'

'He's secretly laughing at me, leading me from place to place, as though saying, "Look here, look there!" knowing that I will find nothing. I'm the hunter hunted, the espied spy. He anticipates my every move—'

'And does this wicked man have a name?' Sophia repeated. 'Tell me about him. Tell me the whole story. There may be ways in which I can help you. I have done so before.'

James Antrobus told her all about Jeremy Oakshott, the tragic death of Vivien West, and the fate of her killer, Margaret Meadows, who had ended her days in a Cheshire asylum. He told her about the brutal murder of Michael Sanders, and how Oakshott had contrived to be in the village on the very night of the murder, and how Sergeant Maxwell had discovered that he had been in the sight of others for the whole day and night.

'So you have made up your mind that that pleasant, gentlemanly scholar, Dr Jeremy Oakshott, is a brutal cut-throat? Incidentally, how did you find out about this Margaret Meadows? The girl who murdered Vivien West?'

'I visited the incumbent of the little town where those three had lived in their youth – Vivien, Oakshott, and Michael Sanders. He introduced me to a retired wardress of the asylum in question, who told me the truth about that poor girl's death.'

Antrobus gave Sophia a full account of his visit to Henning St Mary, his conversations with the young Rector, Hezekiah Daneforth and the indomitable Miss Probert.

'Hmm.... Most interesting. And what about the man in the grounds?'

'I have information about him, ma'am, but I'll keep it to myself for the moment. The story of the so-called Fenian will only cloud the issue.'

He stopped speaking, and after a few moments' silence, he muttered, 'For these and all my other sins that I cannot now remember—'

Sophia held up a hand to stop his mock confession.

'I think I can see a solution,' she said. 'I am going to prescribe you some steel drops, to be taken in coconut water. You are seriously run down, Mr Antrobus, which is why you are becoming obsessive about Dr Oakshott. You want to run about, probing and questioning, but you can't exert yourself physically as you used to do. Meanwhile, let us be done with this obsession, and look at some interesting facts.'

Antrobus suddenly felt more like his own self. Ever since his visit to Henning St Mary he had felt tired and wasted. Now, the brisk, no-nonsense words of his doctor friend were already beginning to have their effect. Yes, he would take the steel drops, and anything else that she cared to pour down his throat.

'I want you to concentrate for a moment, Mr Antrobus, on the death of Mr Ambrose Littlemore. I spoke to the local constable, a young man called Roberts, who had established to his own satisfaction that Mr Littlemore had been stabbed in his own room, and had then walked into the gallery, where he had collapsed into the great chair. It was a very sound interpretation of the facts. People who have been stabbed in the back, as I told him, often do not realize what has happened to them, and will often walk some distance before they collapse. What do you think of Roberts's reasoning?'

'I think it's worth considering. But an alternative reading of the evidence – the bloodstains in the passage, and so on – could be that the killer dragged the body of Mr Littlemore out of his room and into the gallery, placing the body on the chair.'

'Why?'

'To give the impression that the murder had taken place in the gallery. He had openly announced that he was going to accompany his uncle upstairs in order to search for the jewelled dagger, so he wanted to distance the crime from his uncle's room.'

'You are still obsessed with poor Dr Oakshott. You want him to be guilty because you don't like him. I have myself manhandled the corpse, and can assure you that it would be no easy task to drag it along the gallery. For one thing, Mr Littlemore was possessed of large skeletal mass. He looked frail and thin, but he was very heavy for his age and physical makeup; he weighed, at a guess, twelve stone. And secondly, the wound in the back would have begun to bleed profusely, and the assailant would have noticed this. When I first examined the body, it was sitting in a pool of scarcely congealed blood. Yes, I think that PC Roberts's view of the matter is the right one.'

Miss Jex-Blake opened her reticule and brought out a little leather-backed notebook. She donned a pair of gold-framed spectacles, and read one or two pages of what were evidently her own notes on the case.

'Have you examined Mr Littlemore's body yet?' she asked.

'Not yet. Dr McArthur is conducting a post mortem on the remains of the Fenian here, in the stable wing. He's doing that for form's sake, having first extracted a bullet from the man's leg. Later this morning I shall have Mr Littlemore's body conveyed in a closed van to Oxford mortuary.'

'Hmm…. Well, I expect you know your own business best. And when do you plan to release the guests? Myself, the Scott-Jameses, and Lord Arthur Farrell?'

'You are all free to go. All I will need are your addresses, in case I have to contact you. Have you been a guest in the house, ma'am?'

'No. I'm staying with Dr and Mrs McArthur, here in the village. They are old friends. I came up here last night to dine, and to help persuade my unfortunate host to contribute to a worthy charity that I support. After the shooting and the stabbing, I remained here to look after Miss Cathcart. More of that later.

'Now, I have examined the dead body of Mr Littlemore, and have noted down my conclusions. I used my fingers and a probe from my instrument case to make my examination. The weapon – a large pair of tailor's scissors – was still *in situ* when I first saw the body in the gallery. Someone, presumably PC Roberts, removed them when the body was laid on the bed. They had been placed on a towel, and put on a small table near at hand.'

Antrobus thought, I did *not* know my own business best. I should have done all this myself. I should have taken McArthur with me to examine Mr Littlemore's body first. The Fenian was a mere diversion. But my obsession with Oakshott threw me off course. What was she saying now?

'The blow, delivered to the right side of the body, had been a very powerful one, Inspector, penetrating the thoraco-lumbar fascia, glancing off the pelvic bone, and then passing through the intercostal space between two of the floating ribs, rupturing the heart. Part of that statement is based on physical exploration, and the rest is a description of likelihood, based on personal knowledge of the body's structure.'

'A very powerful blow, then?'

'Yes, indeed. The assailant was almost certainly standing behind Mr Littlemore when he struck the blow. And now let me tell you about Miss Cathcart. After her cousin's death she was in a state of collapse, which could have had very serious consequences without medical attention, which I was able to give. I had observed Miss Cathcart's difficulty in holding things like drinking glasses; she needed to hunch her right shoulder forward in order to make her grasp more effective. I recognized this condition as being one of the results of electro-convulsive brain therapy, a risk of nerve and muscle damage that a bold practitioner of such a therapy is prepared to take. I knew at once that this lady must have been a patient of the distinguished mental specialist, Dr Samuel Critchley—'

'Critchley! He was the doctor who ministered to that wretched woman Margaret Meadows, the woman who murdered Vivien West. As a result of his tender ministrations, she died within hours of his sending galvanic shocks through her brain.'

'You express the matter too dramatically, Mr Antrobus. Dr Critchley is a most distinguished man, with a European reputation. But the point I am making is this: if anyone were to suggest that Miss Cathcart repeated her earlier delinquency by stabbing her cousin to death, then they will be wrong. As a result of the shocks given to her brain, she is incapable of delivering any kind of blow. For her, stabbing anybody is a physical impossibility. She can scarcely lift either arm above waist height.'

So much for Oakshott's attempt to implicate his aunt, thought Antrobus. He had declared that his uncle had wanted to visit Miss Cathcart in her room, where, presumably she had stabbed him, or failing that, accompanied him back to his own room, and stabbed him there. But Miss Jex-Blake had shown that this could not possibly have happened. He took her point about being obsessive: he had almost yielded to persecution mania. But he would not let Oakshott out of his sight.

'Now, Inspector Antrobus,' said Sophia, returning her notebook to her reticule, 'are you prepared to give me free range in making enquiries? Will you support me if I come to you with fresh evidence? This afternoon, I am going back to Oxford to stay the week with Elizabeth Wordsworth at Lady Margaret Hall. We can meet there, if we need to confer.'

'I give you *carte blanche*, ma'am. What do you propose to do?'

'Well, first, I will visit Dr Samuel Critchley. There are certain things I'd like to discuss with him. And then, I will go down to Henning, and ask some questions there. There were some things in your account of your visit there that rang alarm bells—'

'Indeed, ma'am? And what alarm bells were they?'

'Not another word, Inspector. I will write you a prescription for steel drops, which any chemist will make up for you. Farewell, until we meet again!'

11

THE DAPPLED PARTRIDGE

JEREMY OAKSHOTT STOOD with the other mourners among the monuments in Hadleigh churchyard, and watched as the coffin of his Uncle Ambrose was lowered into the grave. The vicar, the Reverend Matthew Parkinson, had just told them that they were mere sojourners here on earth, destined to achieve fulfilment somewhere else.

Man that is born of woman hath but a short time to live, and is full of misery. He cometh up, and is cut down like a flower; he fleeth as it were a shadow, and never continueth in one stay.

An inquest on Uncle had been opened and adjourned on Monday evening, following a post mortem examination at the police mortuary earlier in the day. Both necessity and decency decreed that he should be buried today, Wednesday. It was surprising how many people had turned up for the funeral. Poor Aunt Arabella was in full mourning, hardly recognizable beneath her long black veils. Mary McArthur stood beside her, and behind them her husband David, who throughout the service had thrown her a number of anxious glances. But Aunt Arabella had borne up surprisingly well, once the initial shock of Uncle Ambrose's death had passed.

It was time to cast some earth upon the coffin. It was the custom, but it seemed crude and barbaric to him, a gratuitous attack upon someone who had already endured the ultimate assault.

The service of committal continued. It had literary merit, but was dreary beyond measure. He and his aunt were Uncle Ambrose's only living relatives. Apart from the McArthurs, the other black-clad figures thronging the churchyard were business acquaintances of his uncle, directors of the railway and engineering companies in which Ambrose Littlemore and his father before him had invested a considerable competence, and reaped a vast fortune. There were other people watching the burial, the family servants, and farming folk from the village, standing among the trees at the far side of the graveyard.

The committal came to an end, and the company began to leave the churchyard. For a moment, Oakshott thought that he saw the tall man with tinted glasses in the throng. Who was that fellow? He seemed to be everywhere. The two gravediggers emerged from behind some tall headstones, and Oakshott gave them a half-sovereign each. The vicar approached the McArthurs, and he heard them arranging a rubber of whist for Thursday evening. Thus life went on.

It was mid-afternoon before the wine and cake had been consumed, and the company had dispersed, the phalanx of carriages rolling away down the long drive of Hazelmere Castle. Among family and servants there was a feeling of relief that things could now return to something approaching normality. Jeremy Oakshott went to visit his aunt in her suite of rooms on the first floor. She had retained her mourning dress, but had removed the long crepe veils. Her hair was being tidied by her French maid, Adèle, who curtsied and left the room as he entered.

'Adèle is a good girl,' said Aunt Arabella. 'She came from a London agency, and I have had her for a month now. She's delighted that I speak to her in French.'

'Aunt,' said Oakshott, 'you've weathered the storm very well, and I hope that you will not be subject to further shocks. The reading of Uncle's Will takes place in Oxford on Friday. What do you intend to do after that? Do you want to remain here? Or will you look for another house somewhere in the county?'

'I have no particular attachment to Hazelmere Castle, Jeremy: it's not as though I grew up here, or indeed lived here for any length of time. But I should like to stay here for a few months, and then perhaps venture abroad for a while. I have been re-establishing contacts with some friends I made at finishing-school in Switzerland, and one of them has suggested that I stay with her at Nice during the winter. After that, perhaps I'll look for a small house.'

Oakshott watched her as she crossed to her dressing table and took up the bottle of dark blue glass which contained her cologne. She poured a few drops on to a handkerchief, and applied it to her temples.

'Jeremy,' she said, 'would you please do me a great favour? As your uncle's death was unnatural, the police may wish to sift through his papers. I want you to look through them, and remove anything that you feel should be seen by the family only. I believe there is a factor here who has charge of all Ambrose's business correspondence.'

'Yes, Mr Sturgeon runs Uncle's business office, and he's already been in touch with Merryweather and Partners, Uncle's solicitors. We shall both meet them on Friday, when the Will is read.'

'I know nothing of Ambrose's private affairs,' Aunt Arabella continued. 'After all, I have spent the last fifteen years in an asylum. Go through his desk, Jeremy, and secure anything that you think should be kept from prying eyes. Here are his keys. I think I shall lie down now, until dinner time. Send Adèle to me as you go out.'

Tomorrow, if all went well, he would be back in Oxford, back at Jerusalem Hall, where he could immerse himself in things academic, and – yes, contemplate the enrichment of his rather drab life by drawing closer to Celia Lestrange! In the autumn of '95, if rumour was to be believed, a vacancy would occur at All Souls. If he returned in triumph from the mooted expedition to Syria, that Fellowship could be his.

He had constantly underestimated his own position in academia. He already had a European reputation as an expert on the Crusades. How that reputation would be enhanced when he had interpreted the historical significance of those ancient fragments that Celia was holding secretly for him to read!

Yesterday, a genial little man called Todd, partner in a building concern in Birmingham, had come to see him by appointment. He had walked all around the great house in the morning mist, his legs thrust into Wellington boots, his head covered by a tweed cap. He had puffed away at a clay pipe, and had said nothing until his inspection was complete. Then he had stood in the pasture, looking back at the towering pile of Hazelmere Castle.

'What needs to be done here, Guvnor,' said Mr Todd, removing his clay pipe from his mouth, 'is for you to hold a grand sale. What you don't want to take with you, let a whole crowd of folk buy from you at giveaway prices. You could have a big marquee on the pasture. Then dynamite the whole place. We can do that for you. It's better and cheaper than demolition brick by brick.'

'And what would that cost, Mr Todd?'

'I can't give you an exact figure, yet, Guvnor, but it would be in the region of £300. If you wanted us to take it all away, and leave the site pristine, as we say, then it will cost you £500.'

'I'll leave the matter alone for a while, Mr Todd,' said Oakshott. 'I'll let you know one way or the other in a few weeks' time.'

His uncle been fond of reminding him that one day the place would be his. Well, by the look of things, it was going to cost him £500 simply to raze the monstrous edifice to the ground!

It was quiet in Uncle Ambrose's great gothic bedchamber. The bedding had been removed from the four-poster, and its feathered plumes seemed to have drooped in mourning for its late occupier. Jeremy stood for a moment, looking at the hideous paintings and the writhing sculptures around the empty fireplace. He could feel no lingering presence of his uncle in the room. Ambrose Littlemore had left Hazelmere for good.

Jeremy used the keys to open the top drawer of the Indian cabinet standing in the dressing room. There, in its shagreen case secured with golden clasps, he found the jewelled dagger that had belonged to an Indian potentate. The second drawer down contained bundles of correspondence, much of it yellowed with age. There were letters from long-dead relatives, with stories of marriages, births and deaths. There were receipts for member-ship of one or two London clubs – had Uncle ever frequented those places? Nearly an hour passed, and Jeremy had not found anything worth keeping from prying eyes. He and Aunt Arabella were Uncle's only kin. Most of these old letters were of interest to neither of them, and, when the time came, they could be con-signed to the flames.

But what was this? A letter, still in its opened envelope, from Alfred, Lord Tennyson! What possible connection could a reclu-sive retired businessman have with Britain's Poet Laureate? It was only two years since Tennyson had died. This letter was dated 7 October 1890, and was written on House of Lords notepaper.

My dear Littlemore,

There was nothing at all presumptuous about your writing to me. I remember you well. We met at Wordsworth's funeral in '50, and I was impressed by your refreshing, if unorthodox, views on his poetic output, particularly the offerings of his later years. We met again at that dinner given by Disraeli at the Athenaeum in '68. I forget who it was for. Some luminary of the moment, I suppose.

Let me answer your question. Yes, I composed those lines at the suggestion of a friend who had known the family of the dead girl, and who had told me her tragic story. This friend came to see me in the Isle of Wight. It was an amusing challenge to put the poor girl into a sonnet, with hidden meanings, and so forth. Only those who knew her will recognize her in my lines!

Are you a hunting man? If so, you'll see at once that I have described a 'rough shoot', where one takes pot shots at anything that moves once the dogs have 'walked it out', as the saying goes. Anything that falls out of the sky or runs from cover. It's not like a specific shoot, for grouse, or deer – or boar, when you can find it. Rough shoots are usually for men only, but as you can see here, it's THE GIRL who's at the shoot. You will appreciate that she, like the partridge, is also 'fleckt with blood', and that her 'Immortality' (vide the last line) is that of death. It's not an orthodox Christian thought, but then, I have never been orthodox in anything. I suppose I'm a pantheist of a sort. I called the poem 'The Dappled Partridge', but I don't think it appears under that name in the various anthologies.

Oh, why make a mystery of it? I'll tell you my friend's name. It was Michael Sanders, a young fellow of great promise who, I believe, fell on evil times in later life. He had been a friend of the Eltons, from whom he had heard of Hallam's death at Vienna.

Please don't noise this letter abroad. It's private to you.
Ever yours sincerely,
Alfred Tennyson

Jeremy Oakshott put the letter down, and entered the world of his past. He saw Vivien West, delicate, ethereal, preparing for the actual rough shoot that Tennyson had described in his sonnet. It had always seemed a paradox to him that so gentle a creature should have loved the hunt, and that on more than one occasion she had ventured out alone, accompanied only by the dogs and the beaters.

Michael Sanders had known Tennyson! Who could have

imagined such a thing? And he had prevailed upon England's greatest poet to enshrine Vivien's story in verse. Oakshott suddenly felt sick, and the air in the quiet dressing room seemed to choke him. It was as though an invisible hand were clutching at his throat.

He made his way to the library where, among the yards of books bought to fill the shelves, he found an edition of Tennyson's poems. The poem about Vivien was called simply *Sonnet*.

She took the dappled partridge fleckt with blood,
And in her hand the drooping pheasant bare,
And by his feet she held the woolly hare,
And like a master-painting where she stood,
Lookt some new goddess of an English wood.
Nor could I find an imperfection there,
Nor blame the wanton act that showed so fair—
To me whatever freak she plays was good.
Hers is the fairest life that breathes with breath,
And their still plumes and azure eyelids closed
Made quiet Death so beautiful to see
That Death lent Grace to Life and Life to Death
And in one image Life and Death reposed,
To make my love an Immortality.

So Sanders had known all along. Tennyson's poem was filled with Michael Sanders's love and grief, rendered immortal by the superb poetic artistry of the Laureate. Yes, Sanders had known, and so, of course, had Uncle, to whom the letter had been addressed. This letter must not be seen by Antrobus. He would carry it off, and hide it among Aunt Arabella's correspondence. It would be too dangerous to take it back with him to Jerusalem Hall.

Oh, Vivien! Vivien!

Alone in the great library, no one heard his convulsive sobs.

Back in Oxford the next morning, Jeremy Oakshott decided to call at Blackwell's bookshop in Broad Street, to see whether a consignment of books that he had ordered had arrived. He skirted the Radcliffe Camera and took a short cut through the buildings of the Bodleian Library. As he crossed the central courtyard, he saw the Honourable Mrs Lestrange in conversation with a seriously crippled man, leaning heavily on a stick. He was well dressed, but there was something not quite English about his appearance. He was accompanied by a youth, who seemed to be a servant of some kind.

Oakshott watched them, unobserved, as they spoke earnestly to each other. Mrs Lestrange was carrying a heavy leather valise. The crippled man pointed to the youth, and she handed the valise to him. With some difficulty he extracted a wallet from an inside pocket, and took from it an envelope, which he handed to Mrs Lestrange. Then he limped away, supported by his young servant. What a mysterious woman she was! Oakshott waited until she had gone through the gate opposite the Indian Institute, and then continued on his way down the steep steps into Broad Street, and Blackwell's bookshop.

Mr Marcus Merryweather looked doubtfully at his visitor. It was all very well assisting the police with their enquiries, but one's clients' interests were paramount. Mr Merryweather's offices were above a high class grocer's establishment in Cornmarket. They had been there for over fifty years, and so had Mr Merryweather. At one time lithe and dark-haired, he was now stout and bald.

'You see, Inspector Antrobus,' he said, 'it's not good form to discuss a client's affairs without his knowledge and consent. I have already secured both Miss Cathcart and Dr Oakshott as my clients, following the sad demise of Mr Ambrose Littlemore.'

Really, Inspector Antrobus was looking very poorly. His close black beard only served to emphasize the extreme pallor of his face. His cheeks were showing the hectic spots on the cheekbones that betokened advance consumption.

'What exactly was it that you wanted to know, Inspector? I can reveal nothing about Mr Littlemore's Will until tomorrow. The legatees must be the first to be informed of its terms.'

'I should like to be present at the reading of the Will, Mr Merryweather. I have sound reasons for making that request. I promise you that I will say nothing, or interfere in any way with your own proceedings. As I am currently investigating the murder of Mr Ambrose Littlemore, I think I am entitled to hear the provisions of his Will.'

'Well, although it's somewhat irregular, I'll allow you to be present. After all, I know you to be an officer of the highest repute. You will not question the legatees?'

'Certainly not. In fact – I see you have another room leading off this one. Perhaps I could sit in there, with the door partly open?'

'Ah! I see what you're up to! You want to catch the look on people's faces when I read the terms of the Will. I must confess, Inspector, that it's something that I like to watch myself. Yes, by all means sit in the back office. Anything else? I have a client calling at eleven.'

'Can you give me some details about the Hazelmere Castle estate? Is it a valuable property? There is no need for you to be specific.'

'It's not really an estate at all in the legal sense, Mr Antrobus. The castle stands in 150 acres of forest land, but they are on a 150 years' lease from the De Boulter family. The so-called castle, you know, is practically worthless – poorly built for show in the wake of the Railway Mania, for a man who had more money than sense. No, what matters to the principal legatee is the vast fortune left by Mr Littlemore. It is, in fact, far more than the family probably realize. But then, you'll hear all that on Friday.'

'The principal legatee being Mr Jeremy Oakshott?'

Mr Merryweather shook his head good-humouredly.

'You'll hear all about it on Friday, Mr Antrobus. Until then, my lips are sealed!'

Friday 28 September was a day that James Antrobus would never forget. He had presented himself at Mr Merryweather's office just before ten, when a morning mist was beginning to rise, leaving the Cornmarket bathed in a weak but welcoming sunlight. He settled himself in the back office, with the door partly ajar, and awaited the arrival of the legatees.

The clock at Carfax had just finished its elaborate chiming of the hour when footsteps on the stair heralded the arrival of Jeremy Oakshott, accompanied by his aunt, Miss Arabella Cathcart. Both were clad in full mourning. Oakshott carried his silk hat in his left hand. Dressed in this necessarily formal habit, he looked more impressive than usual. His face betrayed nothing of what must surely have been an inner excitement. Miss Cathcart murmured a greeting, and accepted the chair that Merryweather drew out for her at the polished table. Oakshott sat down opposite her, and Antrobus watched him as he slowly removed his black gloves, and dropped them into his silk hat.

'Well, well,' said Mr Merryweather, rubbing his hands together in what looked like satisfaction, 'the auspicious day has arrived when you must hear the testamentary dispositions of the late unfortunate Mr Ambrose Littlemore.'

He opened a cardboard folder which his clerk had earlier placed on the table, and pretended to glance over its contents. It was a bit of an anti-climax to have no more than two chief legatees. Lack of numbers somehow lessened the dramatic capabilities of the event. Was Antrobus watching? He could just see him if he squinted a little and peered through the crack in the inner office door. He cleared his throat.

'Miss Cathcart, Mr Oakshott, I am about to read to you the terms of a new Will executed by the late Ambrose Littlemore, of Hazelmere Castle, in the County of Oxford, Esquire, Gentleman, executed and witnessed on Friday, 14 September, 1894. This supersedes his previous Will, made on 8th December 1893. There are minor bequests to servants, totalling £300. Then follow these two major bequests, as follows. I will read aloud Mr Littlemore's own words.

'"To my nephew, Jeremy Oakshott, of Jerusalem Hall, Oxford, I leave my house entitled Hazelmere Castle, together with its contents, as itemized in the attached Schedule. To my dear kins-woman, Arabella Cathcart, currently residing with me, and formerly of Frampton House, in the County of Oxford, I bequeath the sum entire of my monetary estate, all cash deposits and invest-ment paper of all kinds, for her sole use; and do stipulate that her bequest be administered by a Trust, to be set up by my family's men of business, Merryweather and Partners, in conjunction with Deloitte and Company, Chartered Accountants, of Basinghall Street, London."'

In the back office, Inspector Antrobus listened in disbelief. It was supposedly common knowledge that Jeremy Oakshott was to inherit his uncle's vast fortune. Now, it transpired, this great deposit of wealth would go to the spinster aunt, the woman who, many years earlier, had murdered a young woman by stabbing her to death with a pair of scissors.

He looked at Jeremy Oakshott, sitting opposite his aunt at the table, and felt the shock of a sudden and terrible uncertainty. Oakshott's face betrayed nothing but kind and cordial interest. He stretched his arm across the table, and took his aunt's hand in his.

'There now, dear Aunt Arabella, you are safe and secure for life. I know that nothing can really atone for your years of suffer-ing, but to be mistress of a vast fortune should go some way to make up for the years that have been lost to you.'

Antrobus felt that the sure foundations of his world had begun to shift. He had been wrong all the time about Oakshott. There was no rancour in the man's voice, no sign of disappointment or spite. Had he made the renowned scholar a victim of his own irra-tional obsession? The aunt was saying something.

'Jeremy, your uncle must have taken leave of his senses! I must

139

insist that you and I share this bequest. I have few needs, and have much to atone for, but you—'

'No, Aunt Arabella,' he said, in a kindly but firm tone, 'the bequest is yours entirely. That's what Uncle wished. In any case, I have means of my own. Now, you can purchase your own villa at Nice, if you so wish, and establish yourself in French society. A new life, Aunt! You can leave the dark shadows of the past fifteen years behind you.'

He means it, thought Antrobus. He's shown not the slightest trace of anger or indignation. How could I have been so incredibly wrong?

'I have already begun to set up the Trust for you, Miss Cathcart,' said Merryweather, 'and it will be operative within the next fortnight. Deloitte will transfer all monetary deposits to Coutts and Company. All paper investments will be placed in the hands of one of their accredited brokers.'

'Can you give us both an idea of the extent of our bequests?' Jeremy asked.

'Yes, indeed, Dr Oakshott. The house, and its contents, should yield you about £1,500. I scribbled a few figures last week, which is why I can give you that provisional sum. I expect you will want to demolish the house. The land, of course, is entailed to the De Boulter Estate.'

Merryweather seemed very pleased to have furnished Jeremy with these figures.

'As for your bequest, Miss Cathcart, I can say that the amount has proved to be far larger than was supposed. Mr Littlemore had made some spectacularly successful investments during the last three years. The sum involved amounts to £1,254,000.'

The legatees rose from the table, and in doing so, Jeremy Oakshott caught sight of Inspector Antrobus in the back office. His face flushed with anger, and he strode across the room to confront him.

'Antrobus! You came to spy on me, did you? And Merryweather

connived in your sneaking attempt to discompose me. We'll talk about that later, Merryweather. There are other solicitors in Oxford.'

'Sir—'

'You thought that I murdered my uncle in order to inherit his fortune. God knows what else you thought I had done. Well, let me show you *this.*'

Jeremy Oakshott took a letter from the inner pocket of his frock coat and all but thrust it into the inspector's hand.

'Read it! And after you have done so, maybe you will set out to find my uncle's killer.'

It was a letter from Ambrose Littlemore to his nephew Jeremy Oakshott, dated 14 September, a week before he was murdered.

My dear nephew,

I want you to know that I have very recently written a new Will, duly witnessed, in which, as before, I leave you Hazelmere Castle and its contents. The bulk of my estate, which will now be something over £1,000,000, I have left in Trust to your Aunt Arabella. I know that you will acknowledge the justice of this bequest. She suffered much, because her mind was deranged. She is not the only member of our family to have been tainted with madness, but she has atoned for her crimes, condemned to incarceration, and rendered a cripple through the electric therapy that she endured.

Think well of me, Jeremy. I will always hold you in regard, and follow your academic career with the greatest interest.
Your affectionate uncle,
Ambrose Littlemore.

'I knew the terms of Uncle's Will a week before he died. I received that letter the day after poor Michael Sanders was murdered. I had only slender expectations from my uncle, as his letter shows. Did you think I murdered him to inherit a sham castle that is worth only a few hundred pounds in real terms? I am prepared to forget your intolerable persecution if you will now set out to find who murdered Uncle, and who murdered my friend Michael Sanders. You have wasted valuable time.'

'Sir,' Antrobus stammered, 'I am devastated. I can only apologize—'

But Jeremy Oakshott had stormed out of the room.

'Mr Merryweather,' said Arabella Cathcart, 'I should pay no attention to what my nephew said just now, if I were you. About changing solicitors, you know. He knows perfectly well that he can do nothing of the sort. We've been tied up with Merryweather since Farmer George's time.

'Now. I won't pretend that this legacy has not come as a complete surprise, because it has. I have lived out of the world so long that I am not prepared for its shocks and surprises. Nevertheless, I strongly disapprove of what Ambrose has done. I can't think whatever possessed him to leave Jeremy with nothing. Dear boy! You saw how pleased he was at my good fortune. It was Jeremy who fetched me away from Frampton House. He has been sorely tried of late.'

'Yes, indeed he has. You saw how he rushed out of the room after he'd confronted Antrobus with his folly. He clattered downstairs and out into the Cornmarket as though all the devils in hell were at his heels! There is his hat, and there are his gloves. He's quite forgotten about you, Miss Cathcart. If you like, I'll walk you down to the Clarendon, and you can stay there until the silly fellow comes back.'

'Mr Merryweather,' said Arabella Cathcart, 'I want you to draw up a Will for me. Setting aside all the mumbo-jumbo you lawyers use, I wish to leave everything unconditionally to Jeremy when I die. Can you do that?'

'I will do it this very day, Miss Cathcart, and if you come in on Monday, which is the first of October, you can sign it, and my two clerks will witness it. I think you are doing the right thing. October! In a few days, the undergraduates will be flooding back, and the old city will change its character once more. We will hear the ringing of bicycle bells in all the streets, and there will be riotous uproar once again at night, when inebriated youth finds itself pursued by the Proctors, with their human bulldogs in attendance. Ah, well! One is only young once. Here's Mr Oakshott now.'

Jeremy, looking rather shamefaced, appeared at the door. He was holding a very large bunch of flowers.

'A peace offering, Aunt Arabella,' he said, 'for dashing off as I did. I couldn't stand being in the same room as that fellow any more. I went across to the market and bought you these flowers. As I came back, I saw Antrobus skulking away towards Carfax.'

'Well, they're very nice flowers, but you will have to carry them with you all the way to the station. Better still, you can give them to poor Mr Merryweather. You are going to see me off, I suppose?'

'Yes, indeed. There'll be a carriage waiting for you at the Halt. By the way, Merryweather, don't pay any attention to what I said about – er – another solicitor. I was carried away by that lugubrious man's presence. Please accept these flowers as a token of my regard. Come, Aunt, let me call a cab to take us to the station.'

12

DELUSIONAL SPASM

SOPHIA JEX-BLAKE AND Sergeant Maxwell walked together in the fragrant gardens of Lady Margaret Hall. The close-cropped lawns were still redolent of summer, but the trees were starting to show the golden tints of autumn.

'As the matter stands, mum,' said Sergeant Maxwell, 'Mr Antrobus is thoroughly put out by recent events. Nonplussed, if there's such a word. He was so sure that Dr Jeremy Oakshott was guilty of his uncle's murder that he wouldn't listen to me, or to the Superintendent. Now he's swung the other way. Dr Oakshott is as pure as the driven snow. And there the guvnor sits, immersed in routine paperwork. He's thinking of handing over the case to Inspector Corbett at Cowley Police Office.'

Sophia looked at the man who had come to seek her out at Lady Margaret Hall. He wore a long, black overcoat, meticulously buttoned up, and was clutching his bowler hat to his chest. It was a stance that seemed to be habitual with him. When not speaking, he was unconsciously gnawing his walrus moustache. He was no stranger to her, but now she was seeing him in a fresh light. She could see the concern for Antrobus in his eyes.

'And what's your view of the matter, Mr Maxwell? Do you also believe that Dr Oakshott is as pure as the driven snow?'

'I'm undecided either way, mum. When Mr Michael Sanders was murdered, Dr Oakshott was "on the spot", as we say, but Dr and Mrs McArthur had him in their sights for every moment. When Mr Littlemore was stabbed to death, Dr Oakshott was standing on the terrace with Colonel Scott-James and Lord Arthur Farrell. Mr Antrobus was forced to admit that Oakshott could not have murdered Michael Sanders, but he believed that he could have murdered his uncle. Would you like me to tell you his reasoning?'

'If you would be so good.'

'Mr Antrobus suggested to me that Oakshott went upstairs with his uncle, ostensibly to fetch that diamond dagger, and straight away stabbed his uncle to death with a pair of scissors concealed about his person. He then dragged the body into the gallery—'

'Yes, I have heard this theory. My own suggestion is that Mr Littlemore walked from the room of his own volition, not realizing that he had been stabbed.'

'I'm sure you're right, mum. Mr Antrobus believed that Oakshott stabbed his uncle and then rushed down the servants' staircase, picked up a rifle which he had previously hidden in one of the cupboards in the kitchen passage, ran through the empty silver room, and slipped out on to the terrace. He could have concealed himself behind one of the buttresses there, and when the first shot was fired at the Fenian man, he would have fired his own rifle with intent to kill. He had no time to clean the weapon, but put it back in its rack and swiftly joined the Colonel and Lord Arthur on the terrace. It would have been an almost suicidal risk, mum, but it could have been done. I can state as a fact that a second rifle was fired, and returned to its rack uncleaned, and that it must have been fired by someone in the house.'

'It's very interesting, Sergeant. It also implies that Oakshott must have known the so-called Fenian if he was so quick to silence him. Two murders within the space of fifteen minutes. And Mr Antrobus has now abandoned his hypothesis?'

'When Dr Oakshott proved beyond all shadow of doubt that he had no motive for killing his uncle, my guvnor collapsed. You need the three things, mum, motive, means and opportunity. Dr Oakshott had the means and the opportunity, but no valid motive. He would have been risking his neck for £1500.'

'Hm.... Can *you* fire a rifle, Mr Maxwell?'

'Yes, mum. I was in the Army at one time.'

'What about Mr Oakshott? Was *he* in the Army?'

'About fifteen years ago, mum, he was in the county militia. Quite a few university gentlemen were in the militia in the late seventies and early eighties.'

'Did Mr Antrobus know that?'

'He didn't, mum, not until I'd told him. You see,' said Maxwell, 'a detective sergeant is left to pursue his own enquiries, as we say, and keep his findings to himself until he thinks his guvnor should know about them. I didn't tell the guvnor about Oakshott being in the militia at first, because I didn't want to fuel his growing prejudice against him. But I told him in the end.'

'I see. Now about that jewelled dagger—'

'I have a friend who keeps a jeweller's shop in the Cowley Road, mum. I got him to come out to Hazelmere Castle and look at it. He said that all the stones set into the dagger were made of coloured glass. I thought as much. Even maharajahs and suchlike aren't going to give away fortunes to all and sundry. It's different, of course, when they send gifts to Her Majesty. I haven't had time to tell the guvnor that, mum, but I will at the first opportunity.'

'So, no hidden fortune there. Now, Sergeant, you've told me that Mr Antrobus has hidden himself away. What do you want *me* to do?'

'I want you to rouse him out of his torpor, if that's the right word. He'll listen to you, mum. I believe you were going to make some investigations yourself. The last time you did that, you turned that particular case upside down.'[1]

1. *An Oxford Tragedy*

They had reached the tennis court near the boundary of the Parks. Maxwell stood quite still, waiting to see what Sophia Jex-Blake would say.

'Where is he?' she demanded.

'He's in his office in the High Street, mum, drawing up duty rosters for traffic patrols. He's been real bad this morning, mum, coughing, you know, and spitting up blood.' A spasm of pain crossed his usually impassive face. 'I sometimes think that I'm going to lose him one of these fine days. Superintendent Fielding says he's dying before our eyes.'

'Superintendent Fielding is not a qualified doctor, Mr Maxwell, and should watch what he's saying. Very well. In an hour's time I will call upon Mr Antrobus and shake him out of his depression.'

'Shake, mum? I hope you'll use no violence.'

Sophia laughed.

'No physical violence, Mr Maxwell, I promise you. But I *will* do violence to his lethargy. I was going to go my own way, but now I'm going to take him with me, whether he wants to come or not. Give me one hour, and you will see.'

'Come with you? I can't, Miss Jex-Blake. I have put myself under heavy censure over this business. I am surprised that Dr Oakshott has not taken further measures against me.'

Antrobus was sitting behind a table in his High Street office. It was strewn with folders and graphs, and loose sheets of paper, covered in pencilled notes.

'Upon my word, Inspector,' said Sophia, 'I believe you are enjoying your misery! Come, I have the cure for all your ills.'

'The steel drops?'

'Those, yes. But I have something equally effective.'

She opened her reticule, and produced two train tickets.

'I was going to go my own way, but now, as I've just told you, I think I must take you with me. You can't be left alone. I am going to visit Dr Samuel Critchley, the distinguished mental specialist. I have questions that I wish to ask him, and where a direct approach fails, I will resort to wheedling. Come with me. I have purchased two train tickets. You will not want to leave me out of pocket.'

James Antrobus laughed. There was no gainsaying this determined woman, who was both physician and friend.

'This is outright blackmail, madam,' he said. 'I am appalled at your underhand tactics to make a fellow conform to your wishes. Very well. I shall accompany you. Sergeant Maxwell will give these wretched schedules to one of the constables. Come, ma'am, I am entirely at your disposal.'

'I expect Sergeant Maxwell will make investigations of his own,' Sophia ventured.

'Oh, yes, I'm sure that he will. And when he judges the time is right, he'll tell me the result of those investigations. That's how he and I work. We don't tread on each other's toes. He doesn't much like formulating theories, but he's a meticulous investigator. But enough of him. Let us turn our attention to Dr Samuel Critchley.'

Frampton Asylum was not as Antrobus had imagined it. No bleak, prison-like heap of granite; it was in fact a simple, elegant, late Georgian mansion, its white stucco gleaming in the morning sun. The extensive grounds were somewhat overgrown, which gave the place an air of privacy and seclusion.

And there was nothing sinister about Dr Critchley, a comfortable red-faced man with a shock of white hair. He received his visitors in what was evidently his study.

'Your fame has preceded you, Dr Jex-Blake,' said Critchley. 'I am delighted to meet you. I read your paper on Unhealed Lesions in *The Medical Mirror* with great interest.'

'You are very kind, Doctor,' said Sophia. 'Your paper on Self-Generating Convulsions of the Cortex in *The Lancet* last May was truly ground-breaking.'

That's taken care of the civilities, thought Antrobus. Now these two physicians can get down to business. He had been introduced to Critchley as Mr Antrobus; the name had clearly meant nothing to him, which was probably just as well.

'So how can I be of help, Dr Jex-Blake?' Critchley asked.

'I am sure that you are aware, Doctor, of the recent murder of Mr Ambrose Littlemore at Hazelmere Castle. He was stabbed in the back with a pair of tailor's scissors. His cousin, Miss Arabella Cathcart, was confined here at Frampton in 1879, and released this August gone. Can you assure me that she is completely cured? I have long been an admirer of your electro-convulsive treatments.'

'I take it, ma'am, that you are a friend of the family? I realize that you are aware of the crime that brought her here: the stabbing of a young woman with a pair of scissors. But I can assure you, Miss Jex-Blake, that Miss Cathcart is completely cured. When she came here, she had fallen into a fixed delusional spasm. She—'

The doctor glanced questioningly at Antrobus.

'You can speak safely before my colleague,' said Sophia. 'He has my full confidence.'

'I said that Miss Cathcart came here in the ineluctable grip of a delusional spasm. Her symptoms were almost identical to those characterized by Grein and Steinberg in their classical experiments at the House of Mercy in Nuremberg. She had stabbed a young woman to death, but could not understand that this was both a moral and a forensic crime. It was murder, of course, but she was found unfit to plead by reason of insanity, and came here. She was a danger to others, and was confined to a cell here for six months. She received both psychiatric counselling and drug therapy, which calmed her considerably, though the delusional spasm still remained.'

Sophia glanced briefly at Antrobus. Her lips formed the words: *Ask a question.*

'Dr Critchley,' said Antrobus, 'what was the nature of that delusional spasm? How soon was it before she became free from it?'

'It was a very interesting delusion,' said Critchley. 'I had met only one case of it before, but that was when I was working in a different hospital. Come through into the operating theatre. I can consult the relevant papers there.'

They followed Dr Critchley down a long corridor which took them to a modern extension at the rear of the building. It consisted of a large rectangular room, lit entirely by a skylight, and containing two operating tables, covered in dark rubber, and fitted with leather restraints. Between the tables stood a console, displaying a number of dials and heavy brass switches.

Antrobus shuddered. He was no stranger to operating theatres, but this one succeeded in frightening him. He could imagine Miss Cathcart secured by those leather straps while her brain was exposed, and invaded by electric probes.

'We have our own generators here,' said Dr Critchley, proudly, 'so we have no need of batteries of jars. Now, in this filing cabinet I have the details of Miss Cathcart's case, together with a full account of the treatments she received over the course of fifteen years. Sit down at that table. I'll join you in a minute.'

He rummaged through one of the drawers in a filing cabinet and removed a bulky cardboard file.

'Here we are,' he said, joining them at the table. 'Let me see.... In July 1880, a man was sent here from Warwick, under one of the usual restraining orders issued by the Home Office. The man is long dead, so I shall tell you his name. Robert Grant was an undertaker, who worked with an assistant, a young man called Thomas Cave. Grant became convinced that Cave was what he called at his trial "a limb of Satan", bent on driving Grant's soul from his body and into one of the corpses being prepared for burial.'

'A classic symptom of dementia præcox, according to Heinrich Schule,' said Sophia. 'Do you think that was the case with Robert Grant?'

'Possibly. There is much to ponder in Schule's work. In Grant's case I was content to diagnose epileptic insanity.'

'What did Grant do to Thomas Cave?'

'He stabbed him in the back with a pair of garden shears,

prepared him for burial, and took him in the hearse to the local cemetery, where he buried him in a grave that had been freshly dug for someone else. His deed was discovered when a funeral cortège arrived at the cemetery the next day. It was a grotesque affair altogether.'

'And how did this case affect Miss Arabella Cathcart?' Antrobus asked. If he didn't ask a question, these two doctors would talk about their dreadful mysteries until the sun went down.

'As often in these cases, Mr Antrobus, Robert Grant could see nothing wrong in what he had done, and was proud to tell others of his exploit. Miss Cathcart lent a willing ear, and in the September of that year she began to recount the details of the crime as though she herself had committed it. The death of Thomas Cave became an *idée fixe*. She transferred Grant's whole psychosis to her own mind and personality, so that it was *she* who had brought about the destruction of Thomas Cave, the "limb of Satan", *she* who had been practising as an undertaker. Like Robert Grant, she was proud of what she thought she had done.'

Dr Critchley extracted a sheet of shorthand notes from Arabella Cathcart's file.

'Here, let me read you part of a conversation that I had with Miss Cathcart on 7 February 1882. "Cathcart: 'I waited until Thomas Cave and I were alone in the embalming room, and stabbed him to death with a pair of scissors. I could hear the demon leaving him with a scream of rage. Although a woman, I found the physical strength to lift him into a coffin...." And so it goes on. She had fallen into a very severe delusional spasm. She continued to believe in this delusion for three years, but after the twentieth application of the electrodes to the cortex it completely disappeared. From that time forward – June 1884 – she had no recollection of the business, and when I told her about it, and showed her my notes, she was dumbfounded.'

'If she thought she was Robert Grant,' said Antrobus, 'what

happened when she continued to meet the real Robert Grant?'

'No, no, Mr Antrobus,' said Dr Critchley, 'you don't understand. She had appropriated Grant's crime, in all its detail, to herself. She was, all along, aware of her identity as Arabella Cathcart. Whenever she encountered Grant, she spoke to him of other things.'

'You enter the dark chambers of the mind, Doctor,' said Antrobus, 'places which I, as a layman, would not dare to enter.'

'All alienists do that, Mr Antrobus, because we hope to bring some light to those dark places of the mind. Miss Cathcart's was a difficult case in many ways, and it was only this year that I was able to say that she was fully cured. That is a *fact*, Dr Jex-Blake. Miss Cathcart was cured at the expense of severe damage to her nervous system, involving some wasting of the upper limbs; but cured she is! She is now completely sane.'

Sophia Jex-Blake glanced at Antrobus. His eyes were shining, and some healthy colour had rushed into his cheeks. What was it in Critchley's gloomy narrative that had caused this change in her friend?

'You said that you are a layman, Mr Antrobus. I assumed that you were Miss Jex-Blake's medical assistant.'

'No, sir. I am a detective inspector in the Oxford City Police—'

'Ah! And you suspected Miss Cathcart of murdering her cousin, because of her previous history. Well, I am quite certain that she did no such thing. Arabella Cathcart is as sane as you or I.'

Critchley's words seemed to signal that the interview was over. But James Antrobus had one more question to ask.

'Dr Critchley,' he said, 'am I right in thinking that you came across a similar case of delusional spasm earlier in your career? I refer to a young woman called Margaret Meadows—'

'Yes, indeed, Mr Antrobus. I alluded to that case earlier. Fancy you knowing about that! It was when I was at Prenton Bridge Criminal Lunatic Asylum in Cheshire. Let me see, it would have been in 1880. Meadows's case was similar to that of Miss Cathcart, but very much more obscure. She described a murder that she had committed, but it was proved to our satisfaction that she could not have done the deed that she described. We never determined whether she was describing an actual murder that she had witnessed, or whether the whole thing was an independently generated illusion, of the type Etmuller has described. She was still under treatment when I left Prenton Bridge later that year. The most challenging cases were waiting for me here at Frampton, including that of Miss Arabella Cathcart, so I never heard what happened to Margaret Meadows.'

'I was told that she died soon after you had performed your electrical treatment on her brain.'

'Indeed? Well, I'm surprised to hear that. I thought that she would have recovered sufficiently well to lead a tolerable life under constraint. But then, the path to success is strewn with earlier failures. It's nearly fifteen years ago now, Mr Antrobus. Who told you about Meadows's death?'

'It was a retired wardress from Prenton Bridge, a Miss Probert. I'm sure that you will remember her.'

'Joanna Probert? Yes, indeed. An excellent, dedicated woman. I rather fancied that she had died; I'm pleased to find out that I was wrong!'

Once they were settled into a first-class carriage on the train to Oxford, James Antrobus began to talk about delusional spasm.

'That was a wild surmise on my part, Dr Jex-Blake. About Margaret Meadows having suffered from a persistent delusion. What I heard from Miss Probert when I visited Henning St Mary was that Margaret Meadows had confessed to her that she had murdered Vivien West. Miss Probert stated this as a fact. She spoke with great authority, and showed a remarkable memory for detail. I found her to be a very forceful woman.'

'Your praise for this lady is clearly masking an inner doubt.'

'It is, ma'am. That was why I asked Dr Critchley whether the case of Margaret Meadows had been a case of delusional spasm, like that of Miss Cathcart, and he answered in the affirmative. He said that Meadows had *not* committed the murder to which she apparently confessed on her deathbed. So who is telling the truth? DrCritchley, or Miss Probert?'

'Excellent, Inspector! It is evident to me that you are no longer down in the dumps. Here is another thought for you to ponder. Miss Probert was a wardress at an asylum in Cheshire. Is it more than coincidence that she apparently lives in Henning St Mary, the *fons et origo* of the leading characters in this drama?'

'By Jove, Miss Jex-Blake, I'd not thought of that! Yes, why was she there, in Henning? Miss Probert has some explaining to do….'

'She has. Sooner rather than later, we must pay a surprise visit to Henning St Mary, and beard the good wardress in her den. But it would be wise for us to visit that asylum in Cheshire first. I think that the truth of this whole mystery will lie there for us to discover.'

A greater contrast between Frampton House and Prenton Bridge Criminal Lunatic Asylum could not be imagined. Prenton comprised six forbidding four-storey ward blocks surrounded by flagged yards and high brick security walls. It had been built away from the main roads in the middle of a dense wood.

Sophia Jex-Blake and James Antrobus had given themselves a day's respite before setting out once again by train to Chester, where they had changed to a smoky little engine pulling one third-class carriage, that took them along a single-track line to the village of Prenton Bridge. They were received by Dr John Lucas, the Superintendent, a white-haired man in his late sixties, in his heavily-barred office in the first of the four blocks.

'We currently have 217 inmates,' he told them, 'all of them dangerous criminal lunatics. I have sixty warders, ten of whom are female. We impose a number of therapies, including electric shock treatment, upon those inmates who could benefit from such treatment. Otherwise, it's largely a case of guard and restrain.'

It had been agreed between the two of them that Inspector Antrobus should take the initiative on this occasion. Prenton Bridge was a government hospital, more formal and official than Frampton House.

'Dr Lucas,' Antrobus began, 'I am going to ask you to cast your mind back fourteen years, to 1880. In that year you received a patient here, a woman called Margaret Meadows. She had been found guilty of mutilation and murder—'

'Yes, indeed, Inspector, Margaret Meadows. I remember her well. She was brought here on the strength of a warrant from one of the Masters in Lunacy, and was placed in the hands of a gentleman who was my junior colleague at the time, Dr Samuel Critchley, who moved that year into private practice in Oxfordshire. Critchley, as I think you know, now has a European reputation as a practitioner of convulsive therapy.'

'Did Margaret Meadows prove to be a difficult subject?' asked Dr Jex-Blake. 'Mr Antrobus and I both know Dr Critchley; he recalled that Meadows was subject to delusional spasm.'

'She was. She had to be supervised constantly, because in addition to her delusional complex, she was physically violent. Dr Critchley undertook to treat her by subjecting her exposed brain to electric invasion. We had no generator in those days, and Critchley employed banks of Leyden jars to produce the necessary shocks.'

'Do you think he was prone to take risks, Dr Lucas? I'm speaking as one physician to another.'

'He did take risks, yes, but in my view they were necessary risks. He was – is – a brilliant man, Dr Jex-Blake, with many successes to his name. He and I were dealing with criminal lunatics of the most debased sort.'

Dr Lucas got up from the chair in which he had been sitting, and began to pace round his office. Something, some memory perhaps, had disturbed his equanimity.

'It was a tragic affair altogether, the case of Margaret Meadows. I will admit to you now that it should never have happened.'

Antrobus recalled the words of Miss Probert in her account of Margaret Meadows's treatment at Prenton Bridge. The therapy had been very successful; unfortunately, the patient had died within six hours. There had been a kind of smug satisfaction in her words. At least Dr Lucas saw the affair as tragic, something that should never have happened.

'Meadows was in the custodial charge of my senior Wardress, Joanna Probert, an extremely competent woman, who exercised a vigilant watch over Meadows at all times. But there: one cannot always anticipate the outcome of these situations.'

Dr Lucas sighed, and shook his head sadly. 'Such tragedies occur only rarely, I am glad to say, but when they do happen, they leave their mark for many years afterwards.'

'I believe she is buried here, in Prenton?' said Antrobus. He recalled Miss Probert's mild indignation at the idea of a criminal lunatic being buried in the churchyard of Henning St Mary.

'Yes. Let me take you out into the grounds. You may as well see her melancholy resting place.'

They followed Dr Lucas across a bleak yard to a brick wall containing a door which had been strengthened with steel plates. An attendant warder unlocked the door, and they passed out into an overgrown clearing among the trees. They could both see low headstones half concealed by tall grass.

'Here we are,' said Lucas, parting the grass in a section of the field set slightly apart from the other graves. Together they read the inscription on the stone.

In Memory of Joanna Probert, Wardress,
Died 11th August 1880,
Aged 35 years.
"O LORD, thou hast seen my wrong; Judge thou my cause."

'I don't understand,' said Antrobus. 'Miss Probert is lying in that grave? I have seen that Biblical text quite recently on another headstone. It was at the grave of a young woman who had been murdered.' He contrived to keep his voice steady. There was a tremor in his voice as he recalled being shown the grave of Vivien West at Henning St Mary. 'Are you saying that Miss Probert was *murdered*?'

James Antrobus's question rang out like an accusation. Dr Lucas seemed taken aback.

'Yes, poor Joanna was indeed murdered. But I assumed you knew that.... Have we been talking at cross-purposes? It was her wish to be buried here,' he continued, 'because she had lived at Prenton Bridge for so many years. She had no family, you know. But it's getting chilly out here in this desolate place. Let us go back into the house. Poor Miss Probert! I have never forgotten her.'

13

OUR LADY OF REFUGE

'TELL US WHAT happened to Miss Probert,' said Antrobus. 'You say she was murdered. Was her murderer ever caught and punished?'

He saw the doctor blush with evident embarrassment, which was what he hoped would be his reaction. Something reprehensible had been covered up in this secluded haven for lunatics, and this was the moment to demand the truth.

'I thought you knew,' said Lucas. They had regained his study, and the doctor had motioned to them to sit down. He looked more than merely preoccupied. 'It happened on 11 August, 1880. It was a hot, sultry day, and we had sedated most of the inmates, who were resting in their cells or bedrooms. Joanna – Miss Probert – was in the dispensary, checking over the chemists' receipts. I was in here. Later – after it happened – one of the male attendants told me that he had seen Margaret Meadows walking into the dispensary, and heard her greeting Miss Probert.'

'Why was she not in a cell? The woman was clearly a danger to others.'

'Meadows was making excellent progress, Miss Jex-Blake, and we had allowed her a certain measure of freedom. After half an hour, I went out into the passage and along to the dispensary. Miss

Probert was lying on the floor. Her—' Lucas stopped speaking, and held his head in his hands. Antrobus finished his sentence for him.

'Her throat had been cut from ear to ear.'

Dr Lucas, pale as a sheet, rose from his chair.

'How did you know that?' he whispered. Antrobus ignored the question.

'What happened to Margaret Meadows?'

'She had fled the scene of her crime, and nothing was seen of her from that moment onwards. She had escaped from the house. The knife that she had used – a common kitchen knife – was found where she had thrown it on the carriage-drive. How she got out of the house I never discovered.'

Antrobus looked at Dr Lucas with growing distaste. Once rid of his murderous patient, he had done nothing. Did these people think that they had no civic duties? He felt a sullen throbbing in his left lung, and his throat filled with blood. Damn this consumption! Would he ever be free of it? He swallowed, but the throbbing continued. He saw that Dr Jex-Blake was observing him with what he would have described as 'clinical interest'. She had tended him in bad times before, and never made a fuss.

'Did you report Miss Probert's death to the police?' he managed to say.

'I … What? Meadows was a certified lunatic. I agonized over having her sought out and charged with murder. She was never seen again. The deed had been done, and nothing could bring Joanna Probert back to life.'

'Listen, Dr Lucas,' said Antrobus, arching his back to relieve the throbbing. 'What you did was, at the least, criminal negligence, and at the most, the condoning of a homicide. You allowed a dangerous madwoman to roam free. Did you even consider what further vile deeds she may have gone on to commit?'

'She disappeared entirely,' faltered Dr Lucas. 'She was never seen again.'

'Then let me tell you about a woman whom I met on Wednesday 12 September. She lives in a little Herefordshire town called Henning St Mary. This lady told me that her name was Probert, and that she had once been head wardress here, at Prenton Bridge—'

'But that's impossible!'

'Not if you take into account delusional spasm, or mania, or whatever you alienists choose to call it. This woman told me that she was Miss Probert, and that she had had particular charge of a lunatic woman called Margaret Meadows. Meadows had been subjected to electrical treatment, and had shown much improvement. However, she soon entered into a physical decline, and the ward physician told her, Probert, that Meadows would die within six hours.'

'But this is nonsense! There was no physical decline!'

'Clearly not, sir. But let me finish. *My* Miss Probert said that Meadows sent for her, and confessed to the murder of a girl called Vivien West eight years earlier. She had been consumed with jealousy, because a man called Michael Sanders had rejected her overtures. She hated Vivien West, who loved Michael Sanders, and had cut the girl's throat from ear to ear. Now, sir, to whom do you think I was speaking that Wednesday, in Henning St Mary?'

'Your Miss Probert – what did she look like?'

'She was a very impressive woman, strongly built, and with grey hair. She was well dressed, and well spoken. She walked with the aid of a stout stick, and leaned forward heavily on her right side. I wondered whether she might have suffered a stroke—'

'No, no,' cried Dr Lucas, wringing his hands, 'the stick, and the right-side lunge are the results of electro-convulsive therapy. Allowing for differences brought on by ageing, you have described Margaret Meadows.'

Antrobus rose to his feet. He would leave the contrite doctor to his own devices for a while. It was necessary for him now to bring Dr Jeremy Oakshott back into focus.

'Dr Lucas,' he began, but was stopped by an agonizing stab of pain in his left lung. At the same time, he felt the upward rush of a pulmonary haemorrhage. He had just time to see Sophia Jex-Blake rise from her chair before he lost consciousness.

At first, all he could hear was a mere jumble of echoes, but very soon the sounds resolved themselves into words. He tried to open his eyes, but found that he had not the strength to do so. He could hear his own flat, stertorous breathing, but felt no pain. That could only mean that he had received an intravenous injection of morphia.

'His left lung is virtually useless,' someone was saying, 'but it can still maintain an acceptable breathing function. I strongly urge you to let me perform an artificial pneumothorax.' Who was that speaking? Perform a *what*? He had collapsed just as he had more or less bullied the truth from the disturbing Dr Lucas. What had been the upshot of that? Hush! Dr Jex-Blake was saying something.

'His left lung is badly compromised by tubercular lesions, Dr McKay. Do you think it can sustain an induced collapse? Of course, I defer to your specialist knowledge of consumption.'

'He needs lung rest while allowing the body to rest, Miss Jex-Blake. A pneumothorax will achieve this, while bringing the patient a great measure of relief from pain and stress. Will you let me proceed? We cannot afford to wait for him to wake up from the induced stupor to give his consent.'

'Will you administer ether?'

'No. We cannot compromise the airways any further. He will feel very little pain, as you know. Once I have penetrated the pleural cavity he will be fine.'

Antrobus was no stranger to hospitals. The smell of coal gas, and the series of little 'pops' told him that the strong gas-lights over the operating table had been lit. In a moment, he would sense the bright glow behind his closed eyelids as the lamps were pulled down on their flexible tubes. The voices became blurred once more, and in a moment he felt a sharp pain in the chest. The sound of hissing air followed, and he felt the gentle pressure of a hand on his chest. A moment later, he had relapsed into a calming sleep.

Antrobus opened his eyes, and saw Sophia Jex-Blake sitting on a chair beside his bed, reading a newspaper. Evidently, he had been removed from the theatre, and was now lying comfortably in a small white-washed room lit by a single window, and with a framed print of Da Vinci's 'The Last Supper' hanging on the wall in front of him. What had they done to him? Would he be able to speak?

'Where am I?' he ventured.

Dr Jex-Blake put her paper aside, and regarded him through her little round reading-glasses. She looked very smart in a dove grey morning dress, with matching bonnet.

'You are in the Chester Royal Infirmary,' she said, 'and in order to spare you the effort of speaking, I will tell you what we have done to you. There is a pulmonary specialist here, a Dr McKay. He didn't believe that I was a doctor at first, but after I had proved to him that I was not some eccentric, middle-aged lady with mania, he agreed to look at you. Your haemorrhage was a very serious one, and took far longer to abate than we had hoped. When it was under control, he suggested that we perform an artificial pneumothorax to relieve pressure on your left lung. Your lung is surrounded by a kind of sac called the pleural cavity. If one introduces gas or air into the cavity, the lung collapses in on itself, allowing it to rest. You will stay here in the Infirmary for three days—'

'But the case! I have Oakshott in my sights again—'

'Be quiet, Mr Antrobus. You mustn't talk yet. Just listen to me. You will stay here for three days, at the end of which time Dr McKay will refill your lung with air, by means of a special syringe. You will receive further refills in the ensuing months – they can be performed by any hospital – and thus your damaged left lung will undergo healing.'

Antrobus attempted to sit up, but found he had been strapped to the bed.

'For goodness' sake, Mr Antrobus, will you be still? If you don't behave, I'll leave you to the tender mercy of the nurses. We will forget your sufferings for the moment, and talk about the business in hand. Certain facts are now becoming clear. We know that Miss Probert is long dead, and buried at Prenton Bridge Criminal Lunatic Asylum. The woman whom you met, the woman calling herself Miss Probert, is almost certainly the delusional and deranged Margaret Meadows. Do we know what crimes Meadows actually committed?'

'She—'

'Will you be quiet? I'll have you sedated, James, if you go on like this. My question was a rhetorical one: I intended to answer it myself. Margaret Meadows committed acts of mutilation and murder. Miss Arabella Cathcart committed an act of murder. Both women were placed under the care of Dr Samuel Critchley. Two murderesses, Inspector, both placed in the hands of the same doctor.'

Antrobus squirmed under the leather restraints. He was bursting to speak, but knew better than to disregard his doctor-friend's instructions.

'Yes,' said Sophia, 'I can almost hear your mind working. Now here's another rhetorical question: what new condition developed in both women? The answer is, they both developed delusional spasm. Miss Cathcart believed she had murdered a young man called Thomas Cave. How did she come to think that? She listened to the story that Robert Grant, the deranged undertaker, told her, and appropriated his crime to herself. Happily, the delusion faded with the years, and she was cured.

'Margaret Meadows believed that she had murdered Vivien West. Dr Lucas was adamant that she had done no such thing. Her delusion, alas, remained with her, but then came an added complication: she underwent role-exchange, and in her own mind became the wardress whom she had murdered. To her, the wardress was still alive, and not a burden on her conscience. Furthermore, in her role as wardress, she had distanced herself from the belief that she had murdered Vivien West. It may be that she is not beyond some kind of redemption. But she has never been cured.

'Now, James, Robert Grant told Arabella Cathcart that he had murdered Thomas Cave. Who told Margaret Meadows that he had murdered Vivien West?'

'Oakshott!'

'Yes, perhaps you were right all the time. Oakshott possibly knew that Margaret Meadows would appropriate his confession to herself. Or maybe he knew her well, and in some kind of agony of remorse, confessed to her that he had murdered Vivien West. That, however, is mere surmise at the moment. Incidentally, I will forgive you for that vocal outburst. Do you feel fairly comfortable? Is there any pain?'

'Very comfortable. No pain at all.'

'Good. Now I'm going to tell you about the cerebellum. It's an area at the back of the brain that controls such things as balance, language, and the regulation of emotions such as fear. It also affects some aspects of memory. The good Dr Critchley has always taken risks, and I suspect that, in subjecting the cerebellum of both women to electrical impulses, he went too deep into the cortex, and triggered their propensity to suffer from the severest forms of delusional spasm.'

Dr Jex-Blake stopped speaking, and folded up the newspaper that she had earlier discarded. She looked at the man strapped to the bed. Was she to lose him? Surely not. But inspector or no inspector, he would have to do as he was told. Three days, and he would be standing on his feet again. Meanwhile …

'Inspector, while you are here, I intend to go down to Henning St Mary, and investigate the woman who calls herself Joanna

Probert. Why is she living there? Henning is the place intimately connected with Jeremy Oakshott, Michael Sanders, and the murdered girl, Vivien West. I will do all I can to probe the mystery of those three.'

'Do you want Sergeant Maxwell to go with you?'

'No. He has enquiries of his own to make, no doubt. I'll go alone, and rely on my woman's wit to find out what I want to know.'

'Will you undo these straps?'

'No. You must lie quite still for at least another hour. Contain your soul in patience, Mr Antrobus, while Maxwell goes about his business, and I attempt to unlock the secrets of Henning St Mary.'

'I'm so very pleased to meet you, Miss Jex-Blake,' said Mrs Daneforth. 'I know a lot about you, because I was a nurse before my marriage, and so much admired your struggles for women's talents to be recognized.'

Well, thought Sophia, that's a good start. She had been drawn to the Rector's wife as soon as she had set foot in the rectory. Miriam Daneforth was an attractive, fresh-faced woman, with a friendly manner towards strangers. Sophia had wondered how to introduce herself – how does one introduce a snooper? But Mrs Daneforth had asked no questions, and had ushered her into the pleasant sitting room of the rectory.

'The Rector is out visiting at the moment. Monday morning is always busy for him. There are times when—'

She was interrupted by the arrival of Mary-Jane and Beth, followed by their protesting nurse maid.

'Oh, ma'am,' cried Annie, 'I'm ever so sorry. They wanted to see the lady, and I couldn't stop them coming in.'

Sophia Jex-Blake opened her arms.

'Come here, girls,' she said. 'Let me see you. What lovely little things you are!'

The children showed no shyness, and clung to Sophia's skirts.

Beth solemnly placed a rag doll on her lap.

'How old are they, Mrs Daneforth? Five and three? You must both be delighted with such healthy, lively little daughters.' She cupped little Mary-Jane's face in her hands, and looked closely at her cheeks and neck. 'Has this little one suffered from a high fever? I can see the traces of a non-blanching rash on her neck.'

'Oh, yes, ma'am. She was only two and a half, and I was terrified that I might lose her. The doctor gave me some Carswell's Powders to give to her in warm milk, which I did. But I think I got her better by a lot of cuddles, and bathing her wrists and forehead with cologne. It was summer, so I had her out in the garden a lot. I think fresh air can help cure fevers.'

The young mother blushed.

'There, I must not tell a doctor what works and what doesn't.'

'On the contrary,' said Sophia, 'I'm inclined to agree with you. A mother has a right to trust her own instincts where her children are concerned.'

She gently disengaged the little girls, who were taken out of the room by Annie.

'I have a lovely, quiet house in Edinburgh,' said Sophia, 'and I sometimes take patients there to recuperate. It's a beautiful place, called Bruntsfield Lodge. Well, I was visiting some people once who had a little visitor, a boy of ten, who had fallen ill with a high fever. It was not a household that was used to boys, and the little fellow was left largely to his own devices. I took him away with me to Bruntsfield Lodge, and we looked after him there until he completely recovered. I took him for rides, you know, and generally mothered him. And when it was time for him to go home, guess what he did? He flung his arms around my neck, and kissed me!'[1]

Sophia Jex-Blake laughed. It was pleasant to recall that little boy after so many years.

'But I must tell you why I have called here to see you. Not

1 M.G. Todd: *The Life of Sophia Jex-Blake* (1918) p. 484

so long ago, a friend and patient of mine, Detective Inspector Antrobus, called here to see the Rector—'

'Yes, indeed! My husband told me all about it. How is Mr Antrobus?'

'He's not very well, I'm afraid. He's confined to hospital in Chester at the moment. But he apparently had a most interesting conversation with a lady called Miss Probert. She seems to have had a very successful career in the care of lunatics, a subject that interests me greatly. I was hoping that you could tell me where she lives. I am staying at the Anchor in High Street until tomorrow afternoon. Could you furnish me with Miss Probert's address?'

Sophia saw a cloud of wariness cross the young mother's face. What on earth was the mystery surrounding Miss Probert? Everybody seemed intent on shielding her from outside attention. But then, they almost certainly did not realize that she was Margaret Meadows, a woman who had once lived in this town at the time of Vivien West's murder, and, presumably, lived there still.

'It is so very difficult, Miss Jex-Blake,' said Mrs Daneforth. 'Miss Probert was allowed to come here as a special favour to my husband, who had been urged by the Archdeacon of Warwick to offer Mr Antrobus every assistance. Oh dear! She's—'

Young Mrs Daneforth seemed suddenly to make up her mind.

'You have been a most welcome visitor to me, Miss Jex-Blake,' she said, 'and after all, you are not the police. I will write down the place where you can find Miss Probert, but it's doubtful whether she will agree to speak to you. She lives about a mile from here at a hamlet called Carter's Spinney. If you ask at the Anchor, one of the grooms will take you out there in their dog-cart.'

Miriam Daneforth sat at a desk and wrote rapidly on a sheet of note paper.

'There you are, Miss Jex-Blake,' she said. 'I do hope that we can meet again. Let me see you out. I can hear the girls gambolling in the hall. They've escaped from Annie again.'

'It has been a pleasure to see you and your dear children, Mrs Daneforth,' said Sophia. 'Please give your husband my compliments when he returns.'

It was only when she had regained the road fronting the rectory that she opened the sheet of paper, and read the address written on it.

Sanctuary of Our Lady of Refuge
St Mary's House, Carter's Spinney, Herefordshire.

The Sanctuary of Our Lady of Refuge proved to be a large sandstone house standing in secluded grounds on the skirts of a straggling hamlet. The man driving the dog-cart drew up at the gates.

'There it is, mum,' he said. 'I'm not allowed to drive through the gates, but it's only a short walk to the house. A man called Mullins guards those nuns with his life. Very protective of them, he is.'

'Would you say that it's a nursing home?'

'Well, it's by way of being a home for lady loonies, mum. They're very brave, those nuns. Although they're Catholics, they take all sorts in there.'

'I shan't be more than an hour in there, I expect,' said Sophia. 'I saw an ale-house in that little hamlet as we passed through. Here's a three-penny bit. Go and refresh yourself until I return.'

'We call this a house of refuge,' said the Mother Superior, 'because the women we look after are incurable, and no other institution will offer them sanctuary. They are deeply afflicted mentally, and many are also physically ill. The woman known as Miss Probert is one of them.'

The Mother Superior wore the black habit and deep starched wimple of the Canonesses of St Augustine, an ancient nursing order. She was a woman in her fifties, with a no-nonsense air about her that appealed to Sophia Jex-Blake.

168

'We are all trained nurses – I received my training at University College Hospital – and I can assure you that all the sisters here know about your valiant work for the recognition of women as fit subjects for medical training. Now, Doctor, what do you want of me?'

'I want you to tell me about Miss Probert's mental state. I could prompt you, Reverend Mother, but that would be self-defeating.'

'Miss Probert – when she *is* Miss Probert – is an upright and law-abiding member of society. Miss Probert is taken into town – into Henning, you know – by Mullins, our general factotum, where she visits the circulating library, takes tea in one of the cafés, and joins one or other of the coteries of gossiping women for the day.'

The Mother Superior stopped for a moment, and glanced round the soberly furnished room that was her office. It was part study, part dispensary. Apart from a crucifix on one wall, there was nothing to suggest that the Sanctuary was a religious house.

'And then there are times when Probert is somebody else. A weak, fearful woman, racked by a guilty conscience, recalling dreadful crimes that she may or may not have committed. On those occasions, she is quite unfit to leave the house – indeed, she would be terrified to do so. I have listened to what most people would call her "ravings", and feel very strongly that at one time she had assumed an identity belonging to someone else.'

'When she is in that *persona*, Mother, does she call herself Margaret Meadows?'

'Ah, I see you know a lot about this poor woman. Yes, she becomes Margaret Meadows. And yet … We have a resident physician here, of course, and he thinks that Margaret Meadows contains the shadow of a third entity – these are his words, you understand. When she describes how she cut the throat of a young girl in Henning many years ago, Dr Freud believes that she has absorbed the deeds of another person into her own *psyche*.'

'Your doctor sounds more like an alienist than a physician.'

'Well, he is, I suppose. He is visiting from Austria, and staying with us for a few months. He is very interested in our patients. But of course, he is a trained physician, and is well able to administer treatment to our patients when necessary.'

'What treatments do you give to your patients when they become frantic?'

'We use kindness, reassurance, human things of that nature. We sit for hours with a disturbed patient, talking, reading Scripture, or poetry, or even singing. One of my colleagues, Sister Margaret, has a beautiful soprano voice, and she will sing gentle, soothing airs, accompanying herself on the harpsichord. No lithium, Doctor, no galvanic invasion. Just practical love. We are these women's last hope.

'And now I'll tell you something else about Miss Probert. She is suffering from a terminal disease – a physical disease, and both Dr Freud, and the London specialist whom I called in to examine her, tell me that she has only a few weeks to live. You visited the Rector of Henning, Mr Daneforth, I expect? Well, he too knows that Miss Probert's days are numbered. She has quite rightly been the subject of police interest. But I devoutly hope that she will now be left to see out her days here in peace. Whatever crimes she may have committed, it will be for Providence to mete out judgement.'

Sophia Jex-Blake rose from her chair, and shook hands with the Mother Superior.

'I thank you for receiving me today, Mother,' she said. 'I agree with you that this demented woman must not be further disturbed. Whatever her secrets, they can remain here with her. I am both friend and physician to Inspector Antrobus, and I know that, at my instigation, he will now dismiss Margaret Meadows from his investigation.'

At the far end of Henning High Street, and reached down a narrow lane bordered with drooping willows, lay the ancient and picturesque buildings of Corbet's Almshouses.

'You'll find some very knowledgeable old ladies there,' the landlord of the Anchor had told her, 'particularly old Mrs Pepper, who's over ninety, so they say. She was in service for many years with a family called Rowe, who were friends of the Wests. She knows all the local myths and legends.'

Armed with a bag of groceries, Sophia Jex-Blake called upon Mrs Pepper in her neat little dwelling in Corbet's Almshouses. She was shown into the sitting room, one of three small rooms in her house, the other being a bedroom and a kitchen, with a coal range. Mrs Pepper was indeed very old, and walked with a stick, but her eyes were bright with interest in all that was going on.

'Oh, yes, ma'am,' she said, 'I remember them all. After all, it's only just over twenty years ago that Vivien West had her throat cut. At my age, you forget what you did last week, but twenty years ago is as clear as day.'

'Vivien was a beautiful girl, wasn't she?'

'Oh, yes, she was. Very delicate to look at, refined, you know. But she *was* a flirt! She'd play one lad off against another, and laugh at them both. She was very self-assured, was Vivien. She'd go out with the shoot, and come back smeared with blood from the birds she'd shot. She was very popular with that set – the shooting gentlemen. She rode well, too.'

The old lady sighed, musing on the follies of the past.

'They both loved her, you know,' she continued, 'Mr Michael and Mr Jeremy. Mr Michael Sanders loved her dearly in a quiet, devoted sort of way, and she loved him partly for that, I think. He was staunch and true, was Mr Michael. Mr Jeremy Oakshott, now, he was one of those men who can be consumed by passion, and that's how he loved poor Vivien.'

'And which of them did *she* love?'

'She loved Mr Michael, as I said, she really did. She chose him in the end, but on the Friday before the wedding, she was murdered. It was terrible. Mr Michael never recovered from losing her. He took to drink, and went down in the world. He left these parts, and travelled around the country as a salesman. Restless, you see. And then, in the end, he was murdered, too. Well, of course, we all know who did *that*.'

'What do you mean, Mrs Pepper?'

'Well, it must have been Mr Jeremy, because it was Jeremy who murdered Vivien West. He was consumed with jealousy, and he blurted out his hatred to a poor mad girl who he was friends with, Margaret Meadows, her name was. And after he'd crept up on poor Vivien in the garden and cut her throat, he went and confessed to daft Margaret. For weeks afterwards she'd go round the town muttering to herself about the murder, and some people thought that *she* must have done it. So did she, in the end. But she didn't do it, it was Jeremy.'

'How can you be so sure, Mrs Pepper?'

'He was always a bit of a milksop,' the old lady continued, ignoring Sophia's question. 'He couldn't cope with a girl like Vivien. Somebody heard him propose to her, all passion and madness. She just laughed at him. She couldn't help it. So in his mad jealousy he killed her. No one said anything, of course, though a few of us knew well enough. Humble folk kept what they knew to themselves in those days. And now he's a professor, or some such, at Oxford, or maybe it's Cambridge. Poor Michael must have found out, and so Jeremy killed him, too.'

'But this is all surmise, isn't it, Mrs Pepper?'

'Surmise? Oh, no, ma'am. You see, when he killed Vivien West, *somebody saw him do it*. But it's best to leave these old, unhappy things alone. Asking your pardon, ma'am, but did you know any of the gentlefolk in Upper Henning?'

'No, Mrs Pepper. I've only heard about them from people who knew them in past years. Upper Henning? Is that another village?'

'Oh, no, ma'am, it's just the part of our village where the gentry live. It's just about time for my daily walk. Would you care to come with me? I'll be able then to show you where they all lived – the Oakshotts, the Wests, and the Sanders.'

Sophia gladly assented, and waited for the old lady to put on her bonnet and shawl. Although walking with a stick, she was evidently quite sound of wind and limb. They walked along a number of narrow lanes until they emerged at a wide flight of steps which took them up to a narrow green, flanked with sub-stantial villas standing in their own grounds.

Mrs Pepper stopped, and pointed to a granite house to their left. It stood in a walled garden, and was entered through a pair of iron gates.

'That house, ma'am,' said Mrs Pepper, 'is Wellington Lodge, the residence of Mr and Mrs Percy Edwards and their children. He's a corn factor, and chairman of the parish council. Well, in the olden days, it was lived in by Mr Bertram Sanders, who was something to do with Hereford Cathedral. He lived there with his wife Joan and his son Michael. Michael was an only child. You can see all their houses from here, ma'am, all the folk who figured in that old tragedy.'

'Is that a school I can see, further up the green on the left?'

'It is, ma'am. That road is called School Lane, and that's Henning Grammar School. The nice sandstone house attached to it is where the headmaster lives. Mr Chivers, he's called. But in the old days, that's where the Oakshotts lived. Mr Oakshott was the headmaster then, a very clever man, so they said. I can't remem-ber his wife's name. His son Jeremy took after him when it came to cleverness, though I never heard tell of him committing any murders, like his son did.'

Mrs Pepper took Sophia's arm and together they walked up School Lane. Opposite the school, on the other side of the green, a fine eighteenth-century town villa stood in its own extensive grounds. Its stuccoed walls gleamed white in the sun, and Sophia fancied that she could hear the sound of children playing in the walled garden. Mrs Pepper placed a finger to her lips, as though enjoining silence.

'That's Priory House, where the Wests lived. They lived here in Henning, but they owned extensive lands in Worcestershire. Mr Theodore West was a gentleman by birth, one of the Wests of Seaton Style. He was a kind man by nature, and a true country-man. He was Master of the Foxhounds, and a magistrate. I can see him now in my mind's eye, though he's dead these many years. His wife was a beauty – I don't know where she came from. Some folk said that her family were in trade. And Vivien was their daughter. Poor, lovely girl! No one who had seen her would ever forget her.'

They crossed the green, and walked quietly up to a gate in the rear wall of the house. Mrs Pepper invited Sophia to look through it to the garden beyond.

She saw a grass arbour, shaded by tall bushes on the far side. Flowering shrubs occupied the space on either side of the wall. By looking beyond the line of tall bushes she could see Priory House basking in the sun. If there had been children playing in the garden, they were not there now.

'That's where it happened,' Mrs Pepper whispered. 'In that patch of grass between the gate and the line of bushes. It was a favourite spot of Vivien's, especially in the summer, when it was cool and shady. She was sitting there in a basket chair, reading the marriage service in the Prayer Book. Jeremy Oakshott crept through that gate like the felon he was, and cut her throat from behind.'

Sophia felt that she had fallen under the spell of the old woman, who remembered the past so vividly. But she forbore to make any reply to her bold assertions about Jeremy and the murder of Vivien. Mrs Pepper had said earlier that there had been a witness, but she seemed to have forgotten about it.

'So there, ma'am,' said Mrs Pepper. 'That's Upper Henning. But the folk you're interested in have long gone. There's nothing left here but memories. Mr Chivers has been at the school for nigh on fifteen years. Mr Percy Edwards and his wife have lived at Wellington Lodge for nearer twenty. And Priory House is the home of Sir Edward Phillips, the merchant banker.'

'What happened to the Sanders family, and the Wests?'

'Mr and Mrs Sanders both died of pneumonia one severe winter, and when Mr Sanders's Will was read, he'd left Wellington House to his widowed sister, and just a couple of hundred pounds to Michael. I think Michael had disappointed him, you see. He'd sent him to one of those public schools, but nothing came of it. And then, after Vivien was murdered, a lot of people wondered. The widowed sister sold the house to Mr Percy Edwards.'

'And the Wests?'

'They couldn't bear to live there after Vivien died. They upped sticks and left, and bought a country estate in Oxfordshire. Mr West died of grief within the year. Mrs West's still alive, and lives on the estate that they bought.'

The old woman turned to look at Sophia with a kindly and respectful interest.

'Those buildings, ma'am, that school, and the great houses, hold nothing of the folk who once lived in them. The Wests, and the Sanders, are nothing but shadows.'

They made their way back to the wide flight of steps that would take them away from Upper Henning. Presently they came to a row of workmen's cottages.

'Do you see that first cottage in the row, ma'am?' said Mrs Pepper. 'Well, a little boy of ten called George Potter lived there in 1872. Like all boys of that age he liked to go exploring – snooping, some called it. And on the day that Vivien was murdered, young George was hidden in the shrubs behind the garden wall of Priory House. He was playing Indians, or hermits, or something. And while he was there, Vivien came down with her book and sat in the basket chair. George knew that he'd get a wigging if he was discovered, so he stayed put.

'And while he was hidden there, he saw Jeremy Oakshott sneak through the gate in the wall, and tiptoe across the grass, with a knife in his hand. Vivien, who was reading the marriage service in her prayer book, half turned round, so George said, with a smile on her lips. It was then that Jeremy leaned forward and cut her throat from ear to ear. George said that his face was the face of a demon. He turned and fled the scene. No doubt he went straight home and washed the knife under the sink-pump. You saw yourself, ma'am, how near the headmaster's house was to Vivien's home.'

The door of the cottage opened, and a young, sun-bronzed man in his thirties came out. He raised his cap to the two ladies and walked rapidly away in the direction of Priory House.

'And this boy – I expect he was ill for a time, wasn't he? I don't suppose he could even bear to tell anyone what he had seen.'

'That's so, ma'am. He was very ill for some weeks, with a fever of the brain. And he told nobody for years. He only confided in his mother after Jeremy Oakshott had left Henning for London. Most of us here know the truth of the matter, but we have always chosen to say nothing. It's fear, you see, ma'am, fear of what Jeremy Oakshott might do if anyone here chose to open their mouth. Least said, soonest mended.'

'And this George Potter – I suppose he's another shadow, like the Wests and the Sanders.'

'Oh, no, ma'am. That was George Potter who came out of the cottage just before. He's lived there all his life. He's the gardener to Sir Edward Phillips at Priory House.'

14

JEREMY OAKSHOTT'S DAY

O<small>N THE MORNING</small> of 8 October, the day of Sophia Jex-Blake's visit to Henning St Mary, Jeremy Oakshott rose early, breakfasted in hall, and then went in search of his friend Jonathan Grigg. The satisfying thing about Grigg was that he wasn't ambitious. He was quite content to vegetate in Jerusalem Hall, working away at his research into what he called 'reference toxins'. It would have been a social gaffe to ask him what that meant, as to do so would force him to give a little lecture in reply, which in its turn would have been a gaffe. One did not air one's knowledge in front of a colleague working in a different discipline.

The quadrangle was full of newly returned undergraduates, calling to each other in the loud and confident tones of young men who had been born into a privileged élite. Still, most of them were good, steady fellows, who would do well when they went out into the world. Several of them greeted him cheerily, and he returned their greetings in kind.

Jonathan Grigg occupied a set of cramped rooms in a little eighteenth century afterthought to Jerusalem Hall known as Green's Yard. It was an unlovely, triangular court, containing a door that took one out into Bacon's Lane. Green's Yard also housed the kitchen middens. Grigg's quarters consisted of a sitting room, a bedroom, and two interconnecting rooms that had been set up as a chemical laboratory. All these rooms were pervaded with that acrid smell of chemicals typical of such places.

Grigg, clad in an old dressing gown, looked up from the bench where he was peering into a microscope, and waved Jonathan to a chair.

'You're an early bird, Oakshott,' he said. 'What brings you here this morning? How's your aunt? Is she coping in that vast barracks of a place she lives in?'

'She's coping very well,' Jeremy replied. 'Besides, she has plans to move abroad. She's already been in contact with a French architect who proposes to build her a villa in Nice. I think it's a splendid idea.'

'It's certainly an advantage to be extremely rich.'

Jeremy looked at his friend, who had turned his attention once more to his microscope. When pursuing his professional interests, he always wore a long white laboratory coat. With his genial red face and ample greying moustache, he looked very like Mr Jelkes, the man who kept the pharmacy in Queen Street.

Jeremy Oakshott wandered into the second room of the laboratory, and regarded the array of bottles and flasks lining the walls. Salts of Mercury, Mercuric Chloride, Strontium Hydroxide. Spirits of Salt. Hydrocyanic Acid. Dimethyl Mercury. There seemed to be several bottles of each chemical, and in a rack at the end of each shelf was a collection of ampoules containing lesser quantities of the same substances.

Jonathan Grigg came into the room holding a sheaf of papers. He leaned against the door-post, regarding his friend quizzically.

'I suppose you know the properties of all these mysterious substances,' said Jeremy. 'What they are, and what they do.'

'Well, yes,' said Grigg. 'I do. What have you got there? For goodness' sake, Oakshott, put it back on the shelf! That's Dimethyl Mercury, one of the most dangerous chemicals that you can find. Just a sniff of its vapour is enough to kill you. When you're working with that particular chemical, you have to wear a mask over your face, a sort of hood.'

'And has it got any practical use?'

'Well, it's possible that it could be bonded to a target molecule to form a powerful bactericide – but I don't know. Professor Oddling's blown cold on the matter, and I'm inclined to agree with him. But why did you come to see me?'

'I wanted to know what you feel about that subscription list, the list of donors to Mrs Lestrange's coming expedition to Syria. You had your doubts—'

'Yes, I did. I'd treat whoever got that list up with extreme caution. The trouble with you, Oakshott, is that you've got your head in the clouds. You live a large part of your life in the Middle Ages! Two of those subscribers are dead – I checked up on that, and found it was a fact. Sir Jacob Chantry died in 1890. Sir Philip Margrave, the merchant banker, died in '91. Just be careful, old fellow. Don't let your admiration for Mrs Lestrange lead you into Queer Street.'

Jeremy Oakshott walked up the uncarpeted flight of stairs that would take him to the premises of Hodge's Bank, which were situated above a fruiterer's shop at 31a Queen Street. It was a warm day, and the scent of apples and peaches accompanied him as far as the little glazed outer office of the bank, at the top of the stairs. An elderly clerk looked up from a ledger. Yes, the gentleman was expected. Would he care to wait a few minutes until Old Mr Hodge was free?

Hodge's Bank was as sound as the Bank of England. It had occupied various premises in the Queen Street area of Oxford for over 200 years. It didn't believe in ostentation, and was content to occupy a few rooms above a shop; it had for many years placed its gold by arrangement in the vaults of Parsons, Thompson, Parsons & Co in the High Street.

Next March, the Honourable Mrs Herbert Lestrange – Celia!

– would lead a new expedition to Krak des Chevaliers, and he would accompany her as specialist historian. She had unearthed a horde of ancient manuscripts waiting for him to interpret their meaning. When he had incorporated his findings into the text of Volume II of his work on the Crusades, its publication would become a sensation.

Six thousand pounds.... A fortune, but he must acquire it. Would old Hodge agree to a loan of that magnitude?

Old Mr Hodge had been so called to distinguish him from his son. The son had predeceased him, but the epithet remained as a fossilized part of his name. He was much advanced in years, and seemed to be physically sustained by the starch and stitching of his attire. Frail and attenuated, his old eyes sparkled with a sort of youthful awareness of the present, its needs and its demands.

Oakshott sat down on a leather-covered bench in the cramped office, and waited for the old banker to speak. (He and Celia would marry somewhere fashionable in London, and follow the ceremony with a reception for leading academics and patrons. Would she agree to that? Almost certainly....)

'You say here, in your letter, Dr Oakshott, that you want me to advance you a loan of £6000. I'm sure you'll agree with me that £6000 is a lot of money.' He added *sotto voce*: 'A very great deal of money, if the truth be told.'

'I agree with you, Mr Hodge,' said Oakshott, 'and I do not take the matter of my request lightly. But by part-funding Mrs Lestrange's coming expedition to Syria, I will be expanding my own scholarly reputation, and will secure myself considerable rewards.'

Old Mr Hodge permitted himself a little wintry smile. He picked up a document on his desk, peered at it, and threw it down again.

'Your enthusiasm does you credit, Dr Oakshott, and I have no rooted objection to advancing you the money. But I shall require security for so large a loan—'

'Of course; I fully realize that. I can offer as security my recently acquired property, Hazelmere Castle—'

This time, Old Mr Hodge laughed. It was a singularly unnerving sound.

'Hazelmere Castle, Dr Oakshott, is worth no more than £1500, as you well know. The property market is depressed, and has been for most of this decade. Hazelmere Castle. *Castle?* Dear me! What was it Tennyson said about such edifices?

"Awe-stricken breaths at a work divine,
Seeing his gewgaw castle shine,
New as his title, built last year."

'That describes Hazelmere to a tee. All plaster and pretence. Do you have anything that you can offer me?'

'I have considerable expectations—'

'Ah! Now we are talking. I was waiting for you to say that. Your aunt has recently inherited a vast fortune. And a friend – never mind who – has told me that she has named you as sole heir in her will. If you will formally offer me an open claim on your inheritance, I will advance you the £6000 immediately, at a rate of interest of four per cent per annum, without restriction. You can repay the interest of £240 yearly, and the capital sum whenever it is convenient for you to do so, either whole or in part.'

Jeremy Oakshott tried his best to stifle the gasp of relief that sprang to his lips. The old banker had frightened him by quoting Tennyson, which recalled that sonnet, *The Dappled Partridge*, with its grim secret meaning. Now he felt totally reassured. Aunt Arabella would not live for ever.

Old Mr Hodge slid a sheet of paper across the desk.

'My clerk has already drawn up the necessary document, assigning me an interest in your inheritance. I knew you'd agree to that. But let us say no more about the gewgaw castle.'

His heart beating with excitement, Jeremy appended his signature to the brief type-written document.

'I could give you a counter-cheque, payable to your good self,' said Hodge, 'but I would not advise it. Instead, let me urge you to accept a banker's draft. You can give that to whomever you please, without the bank having to approve your choice. As a matter of fact, I have such a draft here; it only needs my signature.'

The old banker signed the draft with a quill pen, blotted it, and handed it to Oakshott, who took it with a trembling hand. He rose, and shook hands with Hodge.

'A final word before you go, Dr Oakshott. You are engaging on something airy, a future project, which as yet has no substance. You could buy a whole row of terrace houses with that money, and rent them out for profit. But this expedition – it's a gamble, not an investment. Be sure of what you do.'

Oakshott went straight from Hodge's Bank to the Clarendon Hotel in Cornmarket, where Mrs Lestrange was waiting for him. She looked very smart in a dark green wool suit, with a matching short cloak. Although no connoisseur of women's clothes, he knew enough to see that her suit had come from one of the London fashion houses.

'Well, Jeremy? Did your banker see sense?'

'He did, Mrs Lestrange – Celia.'

He drew the banker's draft from his pocket, and handed it to her. She glanced briefly at it, and put it into her reticule, at the same time removing a picture postcard, which she handed to Oakshott. It showed a fine, porticoed and pedimented church, crowned with an elegant clock turret.

'This is St George's, Hanover Square, in Mayfair,' said Mrs Lestrange. 'It is the church where I would wish to be married. I assume that you are a member of the Church of England?'

'Yes, yes. Celia, my mind is reeling! When do you propose that we—'

'I see no reason why we should not marry this month. You can come up to London and obtain a Special Licence from Doctors' Commons. Now, I am leaving Oxford this very day. Come up to town this Friday, the twelfth, and call upon me at my house at 4 Mountjoy Street, Mayfair. I want you to meet some other members of the expedition team, including the epigrapher, and the Arabic translator. And then you can take a cab to Doctors' Commons.'

She stopped speaking, and laid her hand on his arm.

'Jeremy,' she whispered, 'am I rushing you into an action that you might come to regret? Do you want to wait longer, to learn more about me? It's not my wish to seem forward or unwomanly. Since my husband died, I have become accustomed to fending for myself.'

'Dear Celia, you need have no qualms on the matter. I feel that a whole new world is opening up for both of us. I feel—'

'Enough. I am so elated that I will soon burst into tears if we pursue the matter further! I must leave you now, or I will miss my train. Till Friday, then, dear Jeremy. Be sure to remember the address: 4 Mountjoy Street, Mayfair.'

Mrs Lestrange rose, and walked rapidly out of the lounge.

Mrs Benson stood at the landing window of her boarding house in Dragonfly Lane, Park Town. The garden, and the pavement outside, were crowded with chests and cases. It was vexing to lose two lodgers at once, but there were people clamouring to stay with her, and next week both suites of rooms would be occupied once more.

Mrs Lestrange had been a most welcome guest, a lady of quality, and a famous name, apparently, in academic circles. She was sorry to see her go.

Mr Murchison, her friend, had been a quiet, tidy man, but much reduced, as the saying went. They were friends, those two, but there were friends and friends. Still, it was not for her to say anything. They'd both paid fully to the end of the month, which was very handsome, really. The pantechnicon would arrive soon, to take all their things away. A cab had been hired for three o'clock, to take them to the station. They were going away together, which made you think – but she was not one to gossip.

Jeremy Oakshott walked out of Cornmarket, along Magdalen Street, and so into the wide, tree-lined boulevard of St Giles. The leaves were beginning to show a touch of autumn, but it was a pleasant day, with white clouds scudding across a clear blue sky.

A new life was beckoning! Soon, he would be free of the provincial restraints of Jerusalem Hall. Once married to Celia Lestrange, he would move out of his cramped bachelor quarters in the ancient college, and buy a fine, detached house in North Oxford. Later, perhaps in December, he would purchase a town house in London, after due discussion with Celia. They would start their joint adventure there.

He passed Pusey House, built ten years earlier as a memorial to Dr Pusey, one of the architects of the Tractarian movement. A High Church friend of his from Magdalen had taken him there to hear a talk on marriage as a sacrament. Well, very soon now, he would be involved in that sacrament himself.

Oh, Vivien, Vivien!

Bits of recent conversations now came to blight the pleasure of his walk. What had the old banker said? 'This expedition – it's a gamble, not an investment. Be sure of what you do.' He was right: he was building castles in the air. And Jonathan Grigg had told him that very morning that two of the signatories to Celia's subscription list were dead, and could not have put their names forward. What did it mean?

As he passed the gothic archway leading into the Jesuit church of St Aloysius, Jeremy saw the black-clad figure of Father Cuthbert Linacre SJ standing in front of the clergy house. He was in earnest conversation with the tall, bearded man who wore tinted glasses.

Well, the man was probably a Catholic. A foreign Catholic of some sort.

Linacre had claimed that three volumes of Captain Lestrange's letters had been written by Celia. Forgeries! Linacre had known Captain Herbert Lestrange well, or so he claimed. What was he to think? Nothing ventured, nothing gained.

He had walked far enough. It was time to get back to Jerusalem Hall. He crossed Woodstock Road, and began the pleasant walk back into Broad Street. It was as he passed St John's College that he suddenly remembered something else that Father Linacre had said. 'There's no money there, you know. That's why she's for ever holding those fund-raising events.'

He turned in to the Broad, and felt a few spots of rain falling on his face from an errant cloud. Nature, evidently, was showing her sympathy for his sudden and chilling misgivings. The scholarly part of his nature reminded him then that English scholars called that sort of thing the 'pathetic fallacy.'

'It's very kind of you to ask, Mr Gates,' said Sergeant Maxwell. 'Yes, Inspector Antrobus is much better, and walking in the hospital garden. He's still in the Radcliffe, but will be back in the office by Thursday. I thought we were going to lose him this time, though.'

Sergeant Maxwell and Mr Gates were sitting in the back bar of the Worcester Arms, a little free house tucked away in a court behind Beaumont Street. In a city dominated by Morrell's Brewery, it was a treat to enjoy two golden pints of Allsopp's India Pale Ale.

'I don't usually come this far down,' Maxwell continued, 'but I wanted to consult you on a private matter. Private to the likes of you and me, if you get my meaning.'

Mr Gates knew exactly what he meant. Joe Maxwell was a policeman. He, Frank Gates, was a warder in HM Prison Oxford. They were both sporadic attendees at Cowley Road Methodist Church.

'I want to ask you about boots, Mr Gates. Prisoner's boots.

When you get a new batch of villains, do you kit them out with boots?'

'We do, Mr Maxwell. They get a pair of pants and a jacket with broad arrows, and a little cap to match. Likewise, a pair of stout boots. We've an interesting programme of activities for them to follow, including work in the shale yard, and on the treadmill. If they're indigent on discharge, we give them a pair of boots free. Boots are very important for our lags.'

'And where do they come from? The boots, I mean, not the lags.'

'They come from Birmingham Gaol. They supply smaller prisons like ours with boots and clothes. Is there any special reason for asking, or don't you want to tell me?'

'I'll tell you with pleasure, Frank. Last month we were summoned to look at a man who had been shot dead – murdered, you know. When we took off his boots, we found that they had "HM Prison Birmingham" stamped on them.'

Maxwell rummaged in one of the pockets of his overcoat and produced a sheet of paper, which he handed to his friend. It contained a drawing, in various coloured crayons, of a large tattoo, depicting a coat of arms, the words 'Ashanti 1874' and the motto *Semper Fidelis*.

'That was tattooed on our dead man's arm,' said Maxwell. 'I wondered whether it means anything to you. The man was supposed to be a Fenian, but we don't believe that.'

'By George, it does mean something!' cried Mr Gates. 'That, and the boots. I think your dead man was a villain called John Smith. He was released on 5 September gone. I don't know about him being a Fenian, but I can tell you that he was a dangerous, evil man. Robbery with violence was his speciality, with the accent on violence. We know that he'd committed two murders, but he got away with both by threatening witnesses. He's no loss, I can tell you.'

'John Smith … Was that his real name?'

'Yes, it was. I can lend you our file on him, if it would be any good. John Smith ... Wait till I tell the others. These gentlemen are wasting their time, in my opinion.'

Mr Gates drained his glass, and looked expectantly at Maxwell.

'Yes, I think we could both do with another pint. I'll get them in a minute. Gentlemen, you say. You've lost me there, Frank. What gentlemen?'

'Oh, I mean the prison visitors. They're good-hearted folk, Joe, but they don't live in the real world. There was one of them visited Smith every week. He brought him a Bible, and some tracts, and a few eatables that we let them have. He'd sit in that man's cell for an hour. When you opened the spy-hole you'd see the two of them there, sitting side by side on the bunk, talking.'

'And how did John Smith react to all this visiting? Did he read his Bible?'

'He did. Very meekly and quietly, but with a mocking smile playing about his mouth. He read the tracts, too. God knows what he was up to. And when the day for his release dawned, Dr Oakshott was there, to talk to him and give him some money.'

'Dr Oakshott? Dr Jeremy Oakshott, of Jerusalem Hall?'

'Why, yes, Joe. Don't sound so startled! Dr Oakshott is a marvellous kind gentleman, who's been a prison visitor for years. He was wasting his time with John Smith, but he did have his successes. We had a young Irish chap, Patrick Flynn, who was inside for stealing railway sleepers. Dr Oakshott was here, too, when Flynn was released. He gave him some money, and I heard Flynn say: "God bless you, sir, you've been like a ministering angel to me. And when I've done here, I'll go back home, and make an honest living." He will, too, I've no doubt. He was one of Dr Oakshott's successes.'

Sergeant Maxwell rose, and went to the bar, where he ordered two more pale ales. Frank Gates was proving to be a very welcome mine of information. He paid for the ales, and brought them back to the table, being careful not to spill any of their precious contents.

'This John Smith – are you *sure* that was his real name? All kinds of villains call themselves John Smith. Was he a loner? Or did he have a mate? That kind of killer usually has a cringing, cadging lieutenant to run errands for him, or provide him with an alibi.'

'He *did* have a mate, a man called Joel Tasker, who came from Northampton. He was what I'd call a craven swaggerer. Quiet-spoken, but a villain by conviction. You know the type I mean. As a matter of fact, Tasker visited Smith just days before he was released. They were busy whispering to each other in the visiting room. Tasker did a three-month stretch with us a couple of years ago, for receiving. But he was all smiles and swagger when he came here as a civilian visitor. "Nice to see you again, Mr Gates," he said. I felt like kicking him out into the road!'

'You've helped me a lot this morning, Mr Gates,' said Maxwell. 'When this business of John Smith is brought to a conclusion, we'll meet here again, and I'll give you all the details.'

Sergeant Maxwell bade his friend farewell, and walked thoughtfully up Beaumont Street. He had been right. Smith, a villain in Oakshott's pay, lured into a deadly trap, and done to death. What had Smith done for Oakshott, that his mouth had to be closed for ever by a bullet through the heart? As he passed the Randolph Hotel the answer to his own question came clearly into the forefront of his mind. Smith had been hired to murder Michael Sanders, while Oakshott flaunted his alibi in front of his friends the McArthurs. And Patrick Flynn … He, too, had surely been in Oakshott's pay. Could he have been the lively Orangeman who had entertained the denizens of the Farmer's Arms in Hazelmere village?

As Jeremy Oakshott walked through the gatehouse of Jerusalem Hall, Tonson the porter came out of the lodge. He looked worried and apprehensive.

'Dr Oakshott,' he said, 'a man has come to visit you. He

wouldn't give his name, but he said he had some urgent news to impart to you.'

'A man? What kind of man, Tonson? I was not expecting anyone today.'

'Well, sir, he claimed to know you, but, asking your pardon, sir, he was not a gentleman, in fact he was quite a rough, ragged fellow, with a sort of knapsack on his back. I thought of summoning the beadles, but he was quiet-spoken enough, and seemed anxious to see you. I told him to sit on the bench in the quadrangle until you returned.'

'How long has he been here?'

'Just over an hour, sir.'

As Oakshott entered the quadrangle, he saw the man in question get up from the bench. Could it be some indigent friend of Sanders? He wore a suit that had seen better days, and a battered billycock hat. His face, now wreathed in smiles, had the ravaged complexion of a chronic drunkard. Perhaps he was some old crony of Michael Sanders. Well, if half a sovereign would get rid of him, he could have that.

'Dr Oakshott?' said the man, raising his hat. 'I'm pleased to meet you, sir. We had a mutual friend, you know, now dead. Perhaps you could spare me a moment of your valuable time?'

Yes, this was some cadger, and Michael Sanders, no doubt, was the 'mutual friend'.

'You'd better come in, my man,' he said. 'I can let you have a few minutes of my time.'

The man followed him into his study, and without being invited, sat down in an armchair. He took the knapsack off his back, and slammed it down on Oakshott's desk, sending some papers flying. Jeremy suddenly felt threatened and alarmed.

The man opened his knapsack and produced a pair of field glasses.

'Do you know what they are, Dr Oakshott?' he asked. The man had sprawled back in his chair, with his legs stretched out in front of him. His voice was not unpleasant, but he looked at Oakshott with a kind of loathsome familiarity.

'They are field glasses,' said Jeremy. 'Do you wish me to buy them? I will give you a sovereign for them, and then you can be on your way, my good fellow. I have important work to do.'

'Have you, sir? Have you really? And in the midst of all your important work, sir, can you recall the night of Friday 21 September just gone?'

Jeremy Oakshott sat down in his chair at the desk. Oh God! Who was this frightful, quiet-spoken man whose every word held menace?

'It was on that date, Dr Oakshott, that I watched through those field glasses while my friend John Smith— Ah! I can tell from that little cry that you know who our mutual friend is! It was through those glasses that I saw John Smith run across the pasture at Hazelmere Castle, as you'd told him to do, and it was through those glasses that I saw *you*, half-hidden behind a buttress, with a rifle in your hands. Some lackey in the castle, standing at an open window, fired a shot, and got Smith in the leg. And then *you* fired, Dr Oakshott and hit him in the heart. I *saw* you. I saw it all. So what do you propose to do about it?'

Jeremy Oakshott glanced despairingly around the room. What could he seize to brain this vile intruder, to batter the life out of him? There was nothing, and in any case, the man was strongly made, and no doubt ruthless.

'John Smith told me how you visited him in prison, and gave him tracts and Bibles. He also told me how you recruited him to kill a friend of yours, and promised to give him £1000 once he'd done the deed. You arranged all that while you were visiting him in his cell in Oxford Prison. But John Smith never worked alone. He always had a second-in-command, to check that all was as it should be. Sometimes it would be me, sometimes somebody else. But he was never alone.'

The man produced a clay pipe from his ragged coat, filled it from a pouch, and asked Oakshott for a match. Jeremy pointed to a matchbox on the desk, and the man lit his pipe and puffed away for a while. Then he laughed.

'John Smith wasn't the best kind of company for a gentleman,' he said. 'He was a violent, vicious man, with two murders under his belt. But he was also stupid – killers of his kind often are. He told me how he was to make away with this friend of yours, this Michael Sanders, on 7 September. He was to lie low for a few weeks, and then come to visit you at Hazelmere Castle on the night of the twenty-first. You told him that you were going to create a diversion in the house, something to do with private family business, and while everyone was running around in a panic, Smith was to run across the lawn and hide in a little thatched garden shed. You, Dr Oakshott, would come out there, unseen by anyone in the castle, and pay him £1000 in gold.

'Now, that kind of arrangement would have sent alarm bells ringing in my mind, but John Smith was stupid, as I said. He was shrewd enough to get me to go with him, but a wise man would have asked for a meeting by daylight, and in some public place. So he ran across that pasture and into your trap, Dr Oakshott, and was killed by your own hand. So as I said before, what do you propose to do about it?'

'What do you want?'

'I want £1000 in gold, or Bank of England notes. Once I've got that, you'll never see me again, and your secret will remain safe with me. A thousand pounds, the sum that you pretended you were going to give John Smith. Get it together, and I'll come for it on Thursday.'

'I don't know your name.'

'There's no need for you to know.'

'A thousand pounds is a fortune. How do I know that you won't be back for more?'

'You don't. And that's the price you have to pay for murder, Dr Oakshott. But I give you my word, for what it's worth. God knows,

I might have died of drink before that fortune's spent. A thousand pounds in gold or notes, and you'll never see me again. Don't bother to get up: you look as though you're going to faint. I'll see myself out.'

15

GUY LOMBARDO EXPLAINS

JEREMY OAKSHOTT WALKED along a depressing lane of slate-roofed houses in St Ebbe's and stopped at a decidedly superior residence, with crisp lace curtains on the windows, and a polished brass plate beside the door, bearing the legend: *Captain C. P. McKerrow*. Should he demean himself by calling on this man? He had no choice.

He rang the bell, and in a moment a bright little servant-girl showed him into an ornate and overheated sitting room. There was a quantity of flashy gilt furniture, heavy drapes of some oriental material, and a florid marble grate, in which a heaped-up fire was burning. The little maid asked for his calling-card – he had not expected that – and bade him wait for a few moments.

Presently, Captain McKerrow, a stout, well-fed man with a round perspiring face, came into the room. He wore an elaborate smoking-jacket and a tasselled silk cap, neither of which looked amiss on him. Despite his name, his swarthy complexion was more suggestive of the Levant than of Scotland.

'Well, this is an honour,' said McKerrow, glancing at Oakshott's card. 'A scholar, and an ornament of our great university. Perhaps you have come to see me to, er...?'

He paused delicately, his cold wary eyes fixed on his visitor.

His refined voice held a slight foreign intonation.

'I'll be quite blunt with you, Captain McKerrow,' said Jeremy. 'I am in urgent need of £1000. I need it before Friday of this week. I've heard of you, sir, and of your reputation. There are some people in this university who would call you a loan-shark—'

'And don't you think that's cruel, Dr Oakshott? Cruel, and uncalled for. I have devoted my life to helping people in distress. Desperate people come to me and plead with me to advance them a sum of money to save them from ruin and disgrace. I have never rejected any such appeal. I give them a loan, and tell them that there will be no limit to the time that they will need to repay it. They can take fifty years if they like. *You* can take fifty years, if you feel so inclined.'

McKerrow clasped a pair of beringed hands together, and looked judicially at his visitor.

'I have known lives that could have been shattered for want of a few pounds at the right time. I never refuse them. Many unkind things are said about people like me, but virtue is its own reward.'

I shall choke if I have to stay in this hot room much longer with this loathsome hypocrite, thought Jeremy.

'Will you lend me £1000 or not?' he demanded.

'I will, Dr Oakshott, I will. Goodness me, how blunt you are! Would you care for a glass of sirop de cassis?'

'No, thank you. Of course, you will want some kind of security—'

The beringed hand waved away any talk of security.

'Your fame has preceded you, Dr Oakshott. When I received your little note yesterday, I asked a friend of mine about you, and he told me of your impending good fortune – a great legacy, due to you on the demise of your good aunt. Now, here is what I will do. I will lend you £1000 now, and you can repay me when it is convenient. My rate of interest for this kind of instant transaction is forty-five per cent, compounded yearly.'

Jeremy Oakshott tried not to show the cold shock that overcame him as he heard this statement of terms. Well, he needed that money, and this was the only way to get it. He dared not approach old Hodge in Queen Street so soon after borrowing a fortune from him. And if he asked his aunt to lend him the money, she would want to know why he wanted it. He could hardly tell her that it was to pay off a blackmailer. McKerrow would be allowed to have his own way. Never mind; he would not be poor for much longer.

'That is very satisfactory, Captain McKerrow,' he said. 'And when do I receive the money?'

'Now, sir, as soon as you've signed this little note that I've prepared for your signature. That's right. Come through here, to my strong-room. Do you want gold or Bank of England notes?'

'Gold, I think. Will you be able to call me a cab?'

'I will, sir. My maid will do it. Now, here is the strong-room.'

They entered what was in effect an enormous steel safe. A burly man, who had been standing there, remained in the strong-room, but turned his back on them both.

'That man is there to see fair play,' said McKerrow, 'but it's none of his business to see my clients. Everything between you and me is utterly confidential.'

He unlocked a drawer, and removed a leather bag, tied at the neck with red string.

'One thousand pounds, sir,' he said. 'Come back into the parlour, and my maid will summon a cab. Meanwhile, if you are at any time in need of help, you have only to call upon me.'

On Wednesday, Jeremy gave the first of his series of lectures on the First Crusade to an eager gathering of second year undergraduates who were studying medieval history. These lectures were always popular, and were held by arrangement in the magnificent hall of Merton College. As always, it smelt of beetroot. Evidently it was a favourite vegetable of the college cook, who served it, so the legend went, with every meal.

'It began, gentlemen, as a pious pilgrimage from the Christian west, a pilgrimage that soon transmuted into a military expedition by Catholic Europe to regain the Holy Land, lost centuries earlier to the Muslims. But you know all that, don't you? You learnt that at your mother's knee, or rather, in the stuffy classrooms of your schools.' (A little tremor of laughter. He was always good with undergraduates.)

'But I want to take you away from Pope Urban and his crusade, further into the past, to the Levant, as it existed in the year of Our Lord 632 ...'

He talked for an hour. Some of his audience sat spellbound, engrossed in what he was revealing to them. Others wrote rapidly in their notebooks. When he had finished, he dismissed them, and was delighted when one young man, whose square cap sported the gold tassel of a nobleman commoner, thanked him personally for his fascinating lecture.

When he left Merton, and made his way into the High Street, he felt that the likes of McKerrow, and the nameless fellow who had wanted £1000, were mere shadows in comparison with his fellow dons, and the throngs of eager young men to be found in lectures and tutorials, on the river in the college eights, and on the cricket and rugger fields. All those people were part of his secure world, the world of academe.

It was only this year that his peaceful, fulfilled life had been disturbed by ghosts from the past and new terrors from the present. Michael Sanders, a shell of the handsome young man of the seventies, had fallen so low that he had come to blackmail him. That word, of course, had never been used by either of them, and he had pretended to be more than willing to help an old friend in need.

An old friend! He had hated Sanders for winning Vivien's hand all those years ago, and when the man had presented himself at Jerusalem Hall, a pathetic wreck, he had been surprised to find that his ancient hatred burned as strongly as ever. He had watched Sanders as he sipped his tea, and talked quietly of the old days.

He had alluded to Vivien's death, adding the chilling words: 'They brought in a verdict of "murder by a person or persons unknown", but a lot of people wondered.'

Those words had told him that Sanders knew the truth. Perhaps he had always known. But time and weakness of character had dealt badly with Michael Sanders. To him, no doubt, Vivien was no more than a sad and sentimental memory. It was the present need to survive that had occupied him in his later years. So he, Oakshott, had sat there watching him, his hatred of the man rekindled. They had last met ten years earlier, when he had made it clear to Sanders that any attempt to rekindle a so-called friendship was unwelcome and unwanted.

Curse him, the cringing wreck! In youth, so smilingly confident, he had taken Vivien from him. If he had not done so, she would be alive today, and married to *him*.

He had talked to John Smith in his cell at Oxford Prison, and had offered him £1000 to make away with Sanders. He himself made certain that he could be fully accounted for by David and Mary McArthur by arranging for the removal of Sanders while he was staying with them for a few days of whist, which included a visit from the local vicar, a noted devotee of the game. And so, in the early hours of Friday, 7 September, John Smith had killed Sanders, and had got away unseen.

He felt no guilt at all, but he had been horrified when that fellow Antrobus had told him that Sanders's killer had chosen throat-cutting as his method of disposal. It was sheer coincidence, but it had brought back frightful memories long buried in the darker recesses of his mind.

He had never intended John Smith to continue his murderous career. Dead men, as the saying went, tell no tales. He had told the man to run across the pasture towards the little thatched garden shed, where he would be paid £1000, and the dull fellow had accepted this as a reasonable thing to do. Fool! He had stood hidden in the shadow of a buttress, and when Smith came stumbling into his sights, he had shot him dead. Good riddance. The prison warders knew that he had got away with two murders. Well, he'd paid the price now.

The other prisoner due for release, Paddy Flynn, had been quite a different matter. He was essentially redeemable, a foolish fellow who had yielded to temptation, and had been sent to prison. He had apparently acted the part of 'Orange William' to perfection, and had then returned immediately to Ireland. It had been a pleasure to forward him quite a nice sum of money to tide him over until he procured some decent employment.

He would continue his charitable work as a prison visitor. With luck, he would never have to abuse the privilege of free access to the prisoners again. It was worthwhile work, and many a wretched fellow had been put back on to the paths of righteousness as a result of his exertions.

Next morning, Smith's accomplice, the man who would not give his name, arrived at Oakshott's rooms in Jerusalem Hall. He seemed slightly surprised that he had £1000 ready and waiting for him. He received the heavy bag of sovereigns with an almost deferential air, and as he left the room, he said, 'I meant it you know, Guvnor. You'll never see me again, as I'm going abroad. You've nothing more to fear from me.' Oakshott felt an overwhelming feeling of relief. Something about the man's demeanour had convinced him that he was speaking the truth.

Friday dawned bright and clear. Oakshott rose early to give himself time to dress more carefully than was his custom. He chose to wear a black suit with a full-frocked morning coat, a black waistcoat with matching white liner, and his best silk hat. From a flower stall in Queen Street he bought a carnation for his buttonhole.

Did he wish to impress Celia? Well, why not? And then, he wanted to cut a figure with the learned men who would be assembled to meet him at her house in Mountjoy Street. When the

London train drew in to Oxford station, he settled himself in an empty first class carriage, closed his eyes, and gave himself over to daydreaming. He submitted himself to the mesmerizing rhythm set up by the train's clattering over the track, and within a few minutes, he had fallen asleep.

Vivien! She was smiling at him, but it was a smile of amused condescension. She wore a green tweed skirt and jacket, and her face and hands were smeared with blood. How could such a fragile, beautiful creature enjoy the cruel violence of the chase? The blood came from the brace of partridge that she was holding. She had just walked out of the wood, accompanied by a young lad, one of the beaters, who was carrying her gun, open at the breech. The boy touched his cap, but he too greeted him with a kind of pitying smile.

He opened his eyes, and saw the stream of black smoke from the engine passing the carriage window. On either side, the clay fields of Oxfordshire stretched out to the horizon. Once again, his eyes closed....

'Oh, Jeremy, you're such a milksop! Why shouldn't a country girl follow country pursuits? There's more to life than books, you know!'

Michael Sanders came along the lane to greet her. He looked handsome, full of vigour, with a zest for life. Oakshott watched the look of glad greeting that she gave him, and hated him all the more. They turned away from him, and walked together side by side, deep in whispered conversation. She still held the partridges, oblivious of the blood that dripped from them on to her skirt.

She took the dappled partridge, fleckt with blood ...

It was on that occasion, long in the past, that a new, more insane hatred, a hatred of the girl whom he would never cease to love, had welled up in his heart.

At Paddington Station, Oakshott hailed a cab to take him on what was to prove a long and tiresome journey to Mayfair. They arrived at the corner of Mountjoy Street at just after eleven o'clock. Number four was a fine, four-storeyed town house, its front door reached by a flight of three stone steps. The door gleamed black in the morning sun. The brasses were highly polished. Evidently the Honourable Mrs Lestrange kept a good staff of servants.

Oakshott rang the bell, and the door was opened by an old butler dressed in rusty black.

'Yes, sir,' said the butler, 'how can I be of service?'

'I have an appointment to see the Honourable Mrs Lestrange this morning. My name is Oakshott. Dr Jeremy Oakshott.'

'Indeed, sir? Well, I'm sorry, but you must have the wrong house.'

'This *is* number four, Mountjoy Street?'

'It is, sir. This is the residence of Mr and Mrs Abraham Rosheimer. Mrs Lestrange, you say? No, sir, there's no one of that name living in Mountjoy Street.'

An impatient voice from somewhere in the house called out, 'What is it, Vokes? Who's calling?' The old butler wished Oakshott good day, and firmly closed the door.

Oakshott stood in a kind of trance on the pavement. Had he misheard Celia when she gave him this address as her residence? He glanced down the road, and saw the bearded man with the tinted spectacles standing a few doors away, looking at him.

Enough! This man had appeared on the periphery of things once too often. He walked rapidly towards the man, who stood his ground, and to Oakshott's surprise, raised his hat in greeting.

'Sir,' said Oakshott, 'I think this is the fifth occasion on which I have seen you observing me. I demand to know who you are, and why you are following me in this offensive manner.'

'Dr Jeremy Oakshott, I think?'

The swarthy 'foreigner' spoke with an educated London accent.

'Yes. And who are you?'

'My name is Guy Lombardo, and I am a licensed private detective.'

'Indeed, sir. And you are following me?'

'Oh no, Dr Oakshott. Not *you*. If you'll share a cab with me, I will take you to Ford's Hotel, in Manchester Street. It's a nice, old-established place, not far from Baker Street. When we get there, I'll tell you what I am doing, and where *you* fit in the scheme of things.'

Jeremy Oakshott and Guy Lombardo sat in two overstuffed chairs in the parlour of Ford's Hotel. Lombardo had ordered coffee, and neither man spoke until the waiter had arranged everything on the table, and retired.

'Now look here, Lombardo,' said Jeremy, 'this is all very well, sipping coffee and making ourselves comfortable. But what is this all about? What—'

'Contain your soul in patience, Dr Oakshott, while I tell you the whole story. Some two months ago, I was approached by a Mr Neville Chantry, the elder son of the late Sir Jacob Chantry, the industrialist and supporter of worthy causes. He had found that his late father's name had been placed on a subscription list designed to raise money for an archaeological expedition to Syria. Mr Chantry knew that his father's name had been used without his consent or knowledge.'

Lombardo sipped his coffee. Jeremy said nothing. He dreaded to hear what the detective was going to reveal.

'I was naturally given access to Sir Neville's papers, and there I found a letter from the Honourable Mrs Herbert Lestrange, asking him to subscribe to her coming expedition to Syria in the spring of 1895. Sir Neville's secretary had attached a note to this letter, saying that his employer had declined to be associated with the project, but had sent her a cheque for £5 as a gesture of goodwill ... Your coffee's going cold. Why don't you drink it?

'I won't tell you how I followed that cheque from the bank to the clearing-house, and then to the receipt ledgers of Mrs Lestrange's bank. It's a complex process, and its details have to remain secret. But the outcome of the matter was this: Sir Neville

Chantry's cheque for £5 had become a cheque for £500 when it was credited to Mrs Lestrange's account. Fraud and forgery, you see. Do you want to hear more?'

'Yes.' Oh God! He could see where all this was leading.

'I and my agents probed further into that list. Another defunct philanthropist, Sir Philip Margrave, had also sent Mrs Lestrange a cheque, this time for £50 – it was a *bona fide* donation – and that cheque had also grown to £500 before it reached Mrs Lestrange's bank.'

Mr Lombardo leaned forward in his chair, and tapped Oakshott on the knee.

'I saw you give something to Mrs Lestrange in the lounge of the Clarendon Hotel, in Oxford – I was shadowing *her*, you understand, not you. I couldn't see what it was. But there is a Catholic priest in Oxford who knew Captain Herbert Lestrange well. I introduced myself to him, gave him the gist of my investigation, and asked if he could help me in any way. He told me that Mrs Lestrange was drawing you into her net. That piece of paper that you gave her in the Clarendon – I hope it was not money?'

Oakshott groaned, and placed his head in his hands. What a vain fool to think that such a woman as Celia Lestrange could have had any interest in him! He had been duped.

'It was a banker's draft for £6000.'

'Then you have lost that money, Dr Oakshott. Mrs Lestrange's power to deceive lay in her great erudition. She was indeed a scholar of antiquity, fluent in Arabic, Greek and Latin. But she had long tired of academe, and had set her sights on more exciting things, or so my agents tell me. Father Linacre knows that the books ostensibly written by her husband were, in fact, written by her. Forgery again.'

Jeremy Oakshott had mastered himself. He drank his cold coffee, and looked at the mysterious man with the tinted glasses. With his waxed beard and moustache, he looked like a prosperous merchant banker.

'There's more, isn't there, Mr Lombardo?'

'Yes, there's more. I have discovered that a man living at the same lodgings in Oxford, a Mr Murchison, is in fact Captain Herbert Lestrange. He did not perish in Egypt. My agents have ascertained that he fell victim to acute alcoholism, and for a time lost his faculties. He was concealed out there in Egypt by the family of a faithful native servant, while his wife gave out that he was dead. He has more or less recovered now, but he is a physical ruin. She is devoted to him, by all accounts.'

So while she was proposing marriage, she was already married. Why had he not let the dead bury the dead? Why had he not been content with his secure life as a bachelor scholar? Fool! His own vanity had brought him to this pass.

'Where is she now?' Oakshott asked. 'Can nothing be done to stop her? I was entirely deceived, you know. She played upon my academic reputation to rob me of a small fortune, and even had the impudence to propose marriage to me—'

'And you fell for it all. I sympathize, Dr Oakshott, because I know you are not the first to have been misled in that particular direction. What specific enticement did she hold out to you?'

'She had excavated a hidden cache of ancient documents in the Levant,' said Oakshott. 'I was to have accompanied her out there to examine them. She actually showed me one of these documents, so I know that they did indeed exist.'

'Yes, they certainly existed, Dr Oakshott. Have you heard of Senator Otis Kennedy, the American collector? Well, on 27 September last, Mrs Lestrange was observed handing those documents to Senator Kennedy. In return, he gave her a cheque, drawn on the Bank of Philadelphia, for $5000.'

'Is this man heavily crippled? And was the handover of the documents made in Oxford?'

'It was. And the Senator is indeed badly deformed, which made following him easy for my agent.'

'Then I saw the exchange made! It was the day after my father's funeral. Luckily, Mrs Lestrange did not see me. What should I do now, Mr Lombardo? I am shocked beyond measure.'

'I should go back to Oxford, Dr Oakshott, and forget the whole business. You must realize that whatever money you handed over to this woman is irretrievably lost. The whole scandal will break within the week.'

'And she and her husband will be arrested?'

'No. Very late last night, they stepped on to a steamer at Harwich, bound for the Hook of Holland. Unknown to them, I had an agent on board, who will follow them to their destination. From information gathered from various confidential sources, we think that they will cross France by train to Marseilles, and take a boat there to Morocco, where they will effectively disappear. These things can be done, you know.'

'But what will they do? They are fugitives. All decent society will shun them.'

'Things are very different out there, Doctor. They intend to "go native", as the expression goes. They are both fluent in Arabic. They are also friends of the Sultan of Morocco. Go back to Oxford, Dr Oakshott. Reconcile yourself to your losses. Forget them.'

'What do *you* get from all this?' It was a rude question, he knew, but Guy Lombardo was clearly not offended.

'Me? I will proffer my bill for £120 to Mr Chantry, who, I am sure, will gladly accept it. You have been atrociously used, Dr Oakshott, and I am truly sorry for you. Ask at the reception, and they will call a cab to take you to Paddington Station.'

16

AN OXFORD ANOMALY

INSPECTOR JAMES ANTROBUS was feeling decidedly better. He was breathing more naturally, and without pain, and when he looked in the mirror he saw that the hectic spots had disappeared from his cheekbones. What had they called the process? Artificial pneumothorax. Well, collapsing his lung had worked wonders for him.

He was enjoying a leisurely afternoon tea with Dr Sophia Jex-Blake at the Clarendon Hotel in Cornmarket.

'It would seem, ma'am,' he said, 'that I owe my life to you for the second time this year. And after your exploits in Henning St Mary, I'm very tempted to make you a Special Constable.'

Sophia Jex-Blake laughed. How she esteemed this slight, badly consumptive man! Working with him was a welcome change from chairing committees, engaging with correspondents in the English and Scottish press, and working unceasingly to further the cause of women in medicine. And it was true, she *had* saved his life on two occasions, at the same time acting as his fellow-investigator in the uncovering of heinous crimes.

'I shall take up your offer of Special Constable if I can find the time to spare,' she said. 'As for my exploits in Henning St Mary – well, you would have achieved the same results had you not been prevented by illness from accompanying me. Now, I take it that you were convinced by Mrs Pepper's story?'

'I was. And so was Superintendent Fielding when I gave him a written account of your doings. That old lady has given a very convincing narration of what happened in the garden of Priory House, but her crowning achievement was to show you a living witness to Vivien West's murder.'

'Yes, George Potter, a little boy of ten, now grown to man's estate—'

'When I visited Henning St Mary, ma'am, all witnesses of every kind to anything were buried in the churchyard. I'd only to mention a name when the Rector would jerk his head in the direction of God's Acre.'

'Well, in the case of George Potter, Inspector, Providence was on our side. And it was young George who saw Jeremy Oakshott sneak into the arbour and cut that poor girl's throat. The boy said that he had the face of a demon. Well, perhaps he had. George suffered from brain fever as a result of what he had seen, poor little fellow.'

'We are ready to make our move within the next few days,' said Antrobus. 'George Potter is here in Oxford, staying with Sergeant Maxwell and his wife. He's more than willing now to tell what happened all those years ago, and cleanse his own memory, so to speak. You're staying with Miss Wordsworth at Lady Margaret Hall, I think? When we *do* make our move, will you accompany us? There's a certain lady who may be in need of your professional ministrations.'

'I shall be delighted.'

'Then that's settled. Besides Superintendent Fielding, myself and Sergeant Maxwell, we will be joined by Constable Roberts from Hadleigh. You remember him, perhaps? Oh, and Chief Inspector Hallett from Hereford.'

'And who, pray, is Chief Inspector Hallet?'

'Well, you see, ma'am, as the crime was committed in

Herefordshire, it needs a Herefordshire officer present to serve the warrant. As soon as we're ready to move against Oakshott, I will give you the word.'

'Good morning, Dr Oakshott,' said Tonson, the college porter. 'I hope you had a pleasant weekend in London, sir.'

Pleasant! This good man could have no conception of the weight of hopelessness that he had endured during his few days in London. Not only had he been duped by an unscrupulous harpy, but he had suffered a shattering loss of self-esteem. After his dramatic meeting with Guy Lombardo, he had secured a room in a small hotel near Paddington Station. On Saturday morning he had taken a cab to Jermyn Street, where he had bought a small present for Aunt Arabella. He had caught a late train for Oxford on Saturday night, arriving there at seven o'clock on Sunday morning. He had breakfasted in the King's Head, and then walked down to Jerusalem Hall.

She had fooled him out of £6000, a sum that he was bound to pay back to Hodge the banker. More, he owed £1000 to the vicious loan-shark in St Ebbe's. How could he have come to this pass? A widely-respected scholar with a European reputation, duped by the wiles of a clever, unscrupulous woman.

He had been too besotted to ask himself how that anomalous quotation from the Strasbourg Oath had found its way on to the back of an ancient Kufic parchment. Crude forgery, of course. The text of the Oath was readily available in any academic library. Perhaps Sultan Baibars's letter was a forgery, too. After all, he neither spoke nor wrote Arabic. Curse her! Was he ever to be free from her kind? Well, he knew what he had to do. What was Tonson saying?

'There's a gentleman called to see you, sir. He wouldn't give his name, but he said that you would know him. I told him that you wouldn't be in till ten, but he said that he'd wait for you. I took the liberty of showing him into your study.'

Oh God, what now? Tonson had called him a gentleman. Was this some shabby-genteel hanger-on of Michael Sanders, come to cadge a few pounds, and gossip about old times?

As Jeremy Oakshott walked along the path beside the college hall, he fancied that he heard someone walking with a staggering gait behind him. For a moment, the bright light of the morning was blacked out by the gloom of the gallery leading from his uncle's room to the main staircase of Hazelmere Castle.

He had almost fainted with terror on that fatal Friday when he had heard that clumsy footfall behind him, and turning, had seen his 'dead' uncle, eyes wide with a kind of mute questioning, staggering towards him. He had stabbed him with Aunt Arabella's scissors in his bedroom, and had left him for dead. Left the desiccated old miser where he had fallen. But Uncle had been able to walk out into the gallery, where he had finally collapsed into the great chair. He would remember that ghastly pursuit for the rest of his life.

He turned round on the path, but there was no one there.

'My dear Oakshott, I've finally tracked you down! I was going to write, but thought it would be much better if you and I could have a private chat together. How are you? You're looking rather peaky, if you don't mind my saying so.'

Who was this man? And what new terror did he bring? Did he detect a hint of mockery in his voice?

'I'm a little overtired,' said Oakshott, 'but otherwise in fine form. How can I be of service?'

His visitor shook his head in mock remonstrance, and smiled.

'You don't recognize me, do you, Oakshott? You should get out more! Being marooned here in Jerusalem Hall is very bad for you. If I were to mention All Souls' library—'

He almost cried aloud with relief. He had seen Alan Johnson at many university functions, but had never actually met him. He was the archivist of All Souls College, a man with a deep interest

in the many collections of ancient manuscripts held in the college library. He was a hearty man in his fifties, who had once played rugby in one of the Varsity fifteens.

'I expect you're quite content to remain here in Jerusalem Hall,' he said, 'especially as you are engaged on finishing the second volume of your great work on the Crusades. But I want to try and interest you in the Gilbertson Archive at All Souls. It hasn't been properly looked at since the 1750s. There's a mass of twelfth and thirteenth century material there, most of it in Latin and early French. The Warden would be very pleased if you would undertake to collate this material, and prepare an edition of the Archive suitable for publication.'

In God's name, why could this offer not have been made just one week earlier? To work on the Gilbertson Archive would be a delight, and to produce a critical edition for publication would be another crowning achievement in his already distinguished career. A week ago, the lure of the Archive would have made him view Mrs Celia Lestrange's overtures more warily.

'I expect you know what I'm going to say next,' Johnson continued. 'I can't speak officially for All Souls, of course, and that's why I wouldn't give my name to your man at the gate. But I'm quite certain that after the publication of your edition of the Gilbertson Archive, the Warden will offer you a Fellowship with us. But keep that under your hat!'

'My dear Johnson, I don't know what to say! This is a tremendous honour. I shall be delighted to undertake the task. I hope to have finished the second volume of my work on the Crusades by Christmas. I trust that I will be allowed to make a preliminary skirmish in All Souls' library before then!'

'Come to see us whenever you wish, Oakshott. Meanwhile, say nothing about the Fellowship until its award is publicly announced. I'm told that our Warden has already whispered in your Rector's ear. I'm due to see the Vice Chancellor at noon, so I'd better be on my way.'

Fame at last. He was still in his early forties, so he could real-istically hope for a professorship in a few years' time. What a fool he had been to fall for that woman's blandishments! How could such a tawdry relationship compare with reaching the pinnacle of academic success? It was all in the past. Let it stay there. Only the future had any validity now.

That fellow Antrobus had evidently fallen by the wayside, fooled by his having produced Uncle's letter at the reading of the Will. It had been delightful to watch him collapse in confusion, stammering out apologies which he had pointedly not stayed to hear. From the moment that he had received Uncle Ambrose's letter, deliberately excluding him from inheriting any part of his vast fortune, he had determined to put the old miser out of the way.

Uncle had known what he had done all those years ago. That letter from Tennyson had made that abundantly clear. And the great wordsmith had woven all the blood and horror of that time into his sonnet, 'The Dappled Partridge'. Uncle had been prag-matic enough to leave past transgressions undisturbed; but he had made sure that his nephew would not enjoy his fortune after his death.

Uncle's letter had come as a gift from the gods. He recalled his mock indignation against Antrobus with relish. 'Did you think I murdered him to inherit a sham castle that is worth only a few hundred pounds in real terms?' (Well, no; there had been more to it than that.) All carefully rehearsed, and secretly savoured.

The threat from the law had receded from that moment. Michael Sanders, the pathetic blackmailer, had been slaughtered by the brute John Smith. Good riddance! He had always hated him – hated him for winning Vivien's hand. When he turned up at Jerusalem Hall, begging for favours – begging allied to subtle threats – his fate was sealed. And John Smith had paid for the savage murder of Sanders with his own worthless life. There was a certain economy of justice about the whole thing.

Oakshott sat in his chair at the desk, lost in thought. The light in his study seemed to dim, and the morning sun faded from the sky. He was back in front of the garden gate at Priory House in Henning St Mary.

He could smell the scent of the box hedges, and felt the springy turf beneath his feet. He had armed himself with a sharp steak-knife from the drawer in the schoolhouse kitchen. He had brooded for days on the coming marriage of Michael Sanders and Vivien West. He was to be the 'best man', a kind of consolation prize for his rejection. They would both look upon him kindly and patronizingly, while secretly laughing at him.

He would never be able to harm her, of course; but he could frighten her, make her feel some of his despair. He was only twenty years old, passionate and resentful. He would frighten her by pretending to commit suicide only days before her wedding.

He had found her sitting in a basket chair in the arbour at the rear of the garden. She was wearing a white sprig muslin dress. Her straw boater lay on the grass, and her long auburn hair fell free behind her. She was reading the Prayer Book that he had bought for her. He had kept it secretly among his possessions, hoping that if she chose him, she would carry it with her down the aisle. When she had chosen Sanders, he had given it to her as a present.

She must have heard his laboured breathing, for she half turned round and smiled at him. How dare she smile so indulgently at the man whom she had rejected! Or was it mere indulgence? Was it not a smile of mockery and contempt for a weak, self-absorbed boy? He had known in his own heart that he would never be the man that Michael was.

And then her expression had changed to something between wonder and fear. It was then that the blood had rushed to his head, and he yielded to a wave of blind hatred for the girl who had rejected him. He had cupped his hand under her chin, pulled her head back, and then he had cut her throat.

Oh, Vivien, Vivien!

The light suddenly returned to the room as he was jolted out of his reverie. Time to move. There was work to be done. He took pen and paper, and wrote a letter to his friend Dr David McArthur.

'Your newly-acquired castle is looking quite mournful today,' observed Dr McArthur. 'I expect it knows that its days are numbered.'

'Once Aunt Arabella has left for France,' said Oakshott, 'I'll have it razed to the ground. It was never a happy place, you know. The reason I've asked you to come up here this morning is to talk to Aunt about what medicines she should take with her to Nice. I know nothing of medicine, but I've heard that one has to be vaccinated in order to live there. As her physician, you'll know what to advise.'

'That's very thoughtful of you, Jeremy. Yes, I think she could benefit from a review of her present medication, among other things. And you're going to give me lunch?'

'I am. The two of us will be alone in that monstrous dining room. It will probably be the last time that you will be obliged to eat there!'

They were shown up to Arabella Cathcart's suite of rooms by Albert, the young man who had been Uncle Ambrose's valet. He looked sombre and stern, and there was in his manner a hint of truculence surprising to detect in a well-trained servant. He had obviously been devoted to his late master. Such were the unfathomable ways of servants.

Aunt Arabella was looking particularly well. Much of the gauntness brought on by past suffering had disappeared. She had, Jeremy knew, opened an account with Festa & Co, the renowned couturiers in Carlos Place, Mayfair. She was wearing one of their creations now, a dress of grosgrain trimmed with tulle, sewn in panels of beige and mauve, complemented with a string of fine seed pearls.

Miss Arabella Cathcart was clearly on the verge of launching herself into society. She was sitting at her dressing table, where her maid Adèle had just finished arranging her hair.

'My dear Jeremy,' she cried, 'how nice to see you! And you, Dr McArthur. I gather that my nephew has prevailed upon you to come and talk medicine with me. I intend to leave for Nice at the end of the month.'

Jeremy produced the present that he had bought in London. It was a bottle of cologne from Penhaligon's, the prestigious perfumer in Jermyn Street. It was contained in a bottle of orange crystal, and crowned with a silver cap.

'My dear boy, how very kind! Look, Adèle, isn't that marvellous? I will try some of this later. Now, Doctor, when you and Jeremy have had luncheon, you and I can discuss medicines together.'

As they left the room, Oakshott picked up Aunt Arabella's blue glass bottle of cologne, and slipped it into his pocket.

'Really, Oakshott,' said Dr McArthur, 'I would hardly have recognized Miss Cathcart today as the poor, confused woman who came here to Hazelmere Castle just a couple of months ago.'

'Yes, it's by way of being a miracle. I have no doubt in my mind that she is entirely cured of her mental trouble. I'm afraid she'll always be slightly crippled, but it's a small price to pay for a whole new life.'

The two men sat at luncheon in the cavernous dining chamber. They were served by a competent young woman whom McArthur had not seen before.

'Aunt has retired Jevons with a small pension,' said Oakshott, 'and the other servants have found employment elsewhere. Albert, the valet, is staying on until the house is closed. The girl who's just served us is one of a number of agency staff hired for the month.'

'Is it true that you are to accompany Mrs Lestrange on her expedition to Syria next year? I've heard a rumour to that effect.'

'No,' said Jeremy shortly. 'I had considered it, but there are more enticing prospects in Oxford at the moment. Keep it to yourself, McArthur, but there's the prospect of a Fellowship of All Souls in the offing.'

'Indeed? Well, I'll save my congratulations until the prospect becomes a fact. Incidentally, your aunt's man of business here tells me that she has begun to take a personal interest in those charities your late uncle was keen to support. Having been herself a female in distress, she feels that she can identify personally with the unfortunate women helped by those charities.'

They ate in silence for a while. Jeremy's hand closed over the cologne bottle in his pocket. Aunt would assume that her maid Adèle had put it away somewhere, and would quite naturally turn to his present. With luck, she would not be able to resist trying the new cologne now, while he was at the table with a witness to that effect.

This was the solution to all his present problems. He would be able to repay old Hodge, the banker, and more importantly, he would be able to buy off 'Captain' McKerrow, the usurer of St Ebbe's.

An unearthly scream shattered the silence of the half-empty castle. McArthur half rose from the table with a cry of alarm, but Oakshott restrained him. The scream was succeeded by a deadly calm, and then, from the passage outside the dining chamber, they both heard hurried footsteps approaching the door. It had been a mad gamble, but it had paid off. His miser uncle's fortune was now his – all his, not a miserable pittance doled out to him by his aunt out of the goodness of her heart. He was now rich beyond his wildest dreams. He would pay that man Lombardo to seek out the Lestranges, and bring them back to England to face trial for forgery and deception. He would—

The door was pushed open, and Aunt Arabella, as pale as a ghost, staggered into the room. She was too shocked to speak in her normal tones, but the whisper that she managed to produce was all the more electrifying.

'Adèle is dead. You villain! *What did you put in that scent*?'

McArthur had sprung to her aid. They stood together by the door, looking at him.

Oakshott felt himself trembling. He was alone again, alone, and in crippling debt. But there was still time to bluff it out.

'Why, what do you mean, Aunt? Have you … have you taken leave of your senses?'

'Poor girl, she could not resist opening it. As soon as she had unscrewed the lid, she dropped down dead at my feet.'

'That is terrible news, Aunt, but it's most unkind of you to point the finger at me. Why on earth should I wish to kill a servant-girl? Adèle must have had a weak heart. Come now, Aunt Arabella, don't threaten your marvellous recovery by outrageous imaginings. If the girl is dead, then we must send for PC Roberts. Why on earth should I want to poison a bottle of scent? And if I had, would I be foolish enough to give it to you quite openly in front of witnesses?'

'You know perfectly well why you poisoned that scent, Jeremy,' said Vivien West. 'As surely as I know that you cut my throat.'

Yes, Vivien was there, standing at the great dining table. She was wearing the sprig muslin dress that she had worn on the day that he had killed her in his blind rage of hatred. How beautiful she was! Another figure emerged from the shadows, Michael Sanders, young again, handsome and vigorous. They joined hands, and melted away.

Jeremy Oakshott sat down at the table, overcome by a shuddering that he was quite unable to control. McArthur was talking to him, but he heard not a word. He was thinking of the day of Vivien's murder.

No one had seen him exact his revenge upon her, and he had returned in complete safety to the schoolhouse. He had washed the knife clean of Vivien's blood, and returned it to the kitchen drawer.

And then, his heart bursting with remorse, he had sought out an old friend from childhood, a simple-minded girl called Margaret Meadows, and had blurted out his frantic confession. He had told her every detail, and she had listened with quiet sympathy, at times repeating his words as though committing them to memory. He had never forgotten what she had said to him.

'You mustn't tell anyone else, Jeremy. I've always loved you, because you never called me names and never laughed at me for being daft when we were children. Vivien has been punished for rejecting you. *I* will take on your burden of guilt. Yes, it was *I* who cut Vivien's throat. Go your way, now, Jeremy. *I* did it, not you. They would never hang me, you see, because I'm feeble-minded.'

Poor, loyal Margaret. If I survive this latest impasse unscathed, I will seek her out, and make sure she lacks for nothing....

'Are you listening to me, Oakshott? What's the matter with you? You seem to be in a daze. Your aunt is naturally very upset, but I'm sure she'll regret her wild words when she has recovered from the shock of seeing that poor girl suddenly drop dead in front of her.'

Together they left the dining chamber, and entered the great hall of the castle. Albert Stead, the late Ambrose Littlemore's valet, was just opening the front door in response to a rather peremptory ring of the bell.

Jeremy Oakshott blenched with fear as he saw Inspector Antrobus, who was accompanied by Sergeant Maxwell and Sophia Jex-Blake. Albert Stead immediately took Maxwell aside, and after a brief conversation, the two men mounted the stairs to the first floor. On seeing Sophia, Aunt Arabella uttered a cry of glad surprise, and the two women retreated into the dining chamber. Dr McArthur remained by Jeremy's side.

Another man had come in with Antrobus, a silver-haired elderly police officer in the frogged uniform and pillbox hat of a chief inspector.

'This is Chief Inspector Hallett of the Herefordshire

Constabulary,' said Antrobus. 'He has a communication to make to you. Mr Hallett, this is Dr Jeremy Oakshott.'

Who was this man? What did he want? He shuddered as Hallett formally placed a hand upon his arm. Then the man reached into an inner pocket of his uniform frock coat and produced a folded document.

'You are Jeremy Oakshott,' he said. 'Now I show you this warrant of arrest, and say: Jeremy Oakshott, you are charged that, on 17 May, 1872, at Henning St Mary in the County of Hereford, you did cut the throat of one Vivien West, residing there, so that she died; and that you did murder her. You are not obliged to make answer to this charge now, but anything that you do say will be taken down in writing, and may be used as evidence against you.'

'Before you attempt to wriggle out of this charge, Oakshott,' said Inspector Antrobus, 'I will inform you that your murder of this woman was witnessed by a child called George Potter. That child, now grown to man's estate, is ready to testify against you in court.'

Sergeant Maxwell and Albert the valet joined them. Maxwell looked as though he was controlling a mounting anger with some difficulty.

'Dr Oakshott,' he said, 'I intend to search you. Raise your hands above your head.'

'This is an outrage!' Oakshott heard the hysteria in his voice as he spoke. 'Antrobus, can't you stop this fellow from treating me in this way?'

'Do as the officer says,' Antrobus replied. 'Raise your hands above your head.'

Jeremy complied. Sergeant Maxwell removed the blue cologne bottle from his pocket.

'Albert Stead here saw the accused remove this bottle from Miss Cathcart's dressing table,' Maxwell said. 'By doing so, he obliged her to use the bottle of cologne that he had bought for her as a present. Gentlemen, it's time for me to bring in our retained expert.'

For Jeremy Oakshott, it was as though he were living in a parallel but entirely different world from that inhabited by these people. Why had the past returned in this way to interfere with the even tenor of his way? Really, it would be as well to bid them all good day, and make his way back to Jerusalem Hall.

PC Roberts went out to the porte-cochère, and returned with Jonathan Grigg, lecturer in Chemistry at Jerusalem Hall. His usually genial face was grave and accusatory.

'I saw you take that phial of Dimethyl Mercury from my laboratory, Oakshott,' he said. 'I told you how lethal it was. You could only have taken it for some sinister purpose. A man has only to be exposed for one second to its fumes to die immediately.'

'I took every precaution,' said Jeremy. 'I cobbled together a hood of sorts, before emptying out a portion of the cologne that I had bought and pouring in a quantity of the Dimethyl Mercury. I am so sorry for the young maid-servant. But then, she shouldn't have interfered with her mistress's possessions. I meant it for Aunt Arabella, as you no doubt realize. It's no great crime, surely? You see, I was suddenly in urgent need of money, and couldn't wait for her to die.'

'Constable,' said Chief Inspector Hallett, 'manacle this man and take him out to the van. My work here is done. Whatever fresh enormities this man has committed, Antrobus, they're for you to deal with. Meanwhile, he will be lodged in Hereford Gaol, until he faces trial for the murder of Vivien West.'

He was manacled, and led out from the house to the police van waiting on the drive. There were five witnesses to his disgrace standing far off on the pasture. Uncle Ambrose, clad in his customary black, his face expressionless. John Smith, recidivist and murderer, was beside him, his shattered leg still crimson with his own blood.

Michael Sanders stood beside the man who had killed him,

his arms folded, and his throat cut. Adèle, bewildered and questioning, clung for support to a girl in a sprig muslin dress, a girl already surrounded by an aura of brilliant light.

As the rear door of the van was opened, the five witnesses turned their backs on him, and began to walk away. He could see the scissors protruding from his uncle's back. And then the girl in the aura of light turned and looked at him, with fear and disbelief in her bright eyes, but no pity, and no concern.

Oh, Vivien, Vivien!

The door of the van slammed shut, and the felon was driven away from the house that he had inherited from the uncle whom he had murdered.

It was a month later, on a chill, autumn day, that Detective Inspector James Antrobus came again to Lady Margaret Hall. Dr Sophia Jex-Blake had agreed to give the Lady Principal's protégées a lecture on medical jurisprudence. She and the Inspector sat on either side of the fireplace in Miss Wordsworth's study. Antrobus noted the neat pile of students' essays on the desk, and the carefully selected framed prints and portraits on the walls.

'Well?' said Sophia Jex-Blake.

'He was hanged this morning, ma'am, at Birmingham Gaol. And so the blood of his five victims is avenged.'

'You never thought that he might be mad?'

'No, I didn't. He was examined by an alienist while in custody in Hereford, and found to be sane. Fit to plead, you know. And so he had the grace – or sense – to plead guilty at his arraignment, so that the trial was soon over. He was as sane as you or me. And yet—'

'You think that you can vindicate him?'

'No, ma'am. I was going to say that, sane as he was, he was in reality a moral imbecile. He thought that everyone, and every thing, was created to do him service, to love and esteem him, and him alone. In that sense, I suppose, he was mad. But when brought to the bar of judgement in the real world, he was sane. Sane, and wicked.'

'An anomaly, would you say? A man justly renowned for his learning, an ornament of Oxford society, and yet a man who cut a girl's throat on the eve of her wedding, and a man who, decades later, had her fiancé butchered by that man – what was his name? John Smith. Scholar and murderer. An Oxford anomaly.'

They were silent for a while, listening to the ticking of a clock on the mantelpiece.

'We found a letter from Lord Tennyson among Miss Cathcart's papers,' said Antrobus. 'It appears that Oakshott had found it in his uncle's desk, and had concealed it in his aunt's sitting room. Tennyson had woven the story of Vivien's death into a sonnet, 'The Dappled Partridge', evidently at Mr Littlemore's request. Whether the Poet Laureate knew that the story was true is a moot point.

'Ambrose Littlemore knew that his nephew had murdered Vivien, but chose to keep the fact to himself, probably out of mis-placed family pride. Well, his reticence led to his own death. And today, his nephew suffered the supreme penalty.'

He half rose from his chair, then sat down again.

'What has happened to Miss Cathcart, ma'am, do you know? She is utterly alone in the world now, despite her great riches. She was much attached to that girl Adèle. I am so very sorry for her.'

'As a matter of fact, Mr Antrobus,' said Sophia, 'Miss Cathcart has made a second amazing recovery, thoroughly vindicating Dr Samuel Critchley's assertion that she is fully cured of her early insanity. I have for some time been trying to place an excellent girl, an impecunious clergyman's daughter, as nurse-companion to a suitable lady, and was able to effect an introduction. They liked each other immediately, and are now both settled in a villa in Nice. I have already received an invitation to visit Miss Cathcart after Christmas, and am very much inclined to do so.'

This time, they rose together. There was a world outside Miss Wordsworth's study, waiting for their attention.

'It's been a pleasure to work with you once again, Mr Antrobus,' said Sophia Jex-Blake, proffering her hand. 'You have my card, and know where to find me if ever you feel in need of my attentions as a physician, or my assistance as a Special Constable.'

James Antrobus laughed. Not many, he thought, could have forged such a friendship with this formidable and brave woman, who had kept him alive to see Jeremy Oakshott to the gallows.

'Goodbye, ma'am,' he said, shaking her hand. 'Or perhaps I should say *au revoir*.'

James Antrobus left the study, and made his way through the autumnal grounds of Lady Margaret Hall and out into Norham Gardens.

AUTHOR'S NOTE

SOPHIA JEX-BLAKE (1840–1912) was one of a group of remarkable women who laboured for the right of their sex to become doctors. Two of her fellow students at Queen's College, Harley Street in 1858 were Dorothea Beale, who became Head of Cheltenham Ladies' College, and Frances May Buss, founder of the North London Collegiate School for Girls. Sophia's elder brother, Thomas Jex-Blake, became Headmaster of Rugby in 1874. One of his daughters, Katharine, became Mistress of Girton College, Cambridge. Another, Henrietta, succeeded Elizabeth Wordsworth as principal of Lady Margaret Hall in 1909.